WARM FRONT

Seasons in a Small Town
What Are Friends For? (Spring)
The Right Brother (Summer)
Falling for Her (Autumn)
Warm Front (Winter)

More romance by Patricia McLinn

The Wedding Series
Prelude to a Wedding
Wedding Party
Grady's Wedding
The Runaway Bride
The Christmas Princess
Hoops (prequel to The Surprise Princess)
The Surprise Princess
Not a Family Man (prequel to The Forgotten Prince)
The Forgotten Prince

Marry Me Series
Wedding of the Century
The Unexpected Wedding Guest
A Most Unlikely Wedding
Baby Blues and Wedding Bells

Wyoming Wildflowers Series
Wyoming Wildflowers: The Beginning (prequel)
Almost a Bride
Match Made in Wyoming
My Heart Remembers
A New World (prequel to Jack's Heart)
Jack's Heart
Rodeo Nights (prequel to Where Love Lives)
Where Love Lives
A Cowboy Wedding

Bardville, Wyoming Series
A Stranger in the Family
A Stranger to Love
The Rancher Meets His Match

WARM FRONT

Seasons in a Small Town
Book 4 (Winter)

Patricia McLinn

Dear Readers: If you encounter typos or errors in this book, please send them to me at Patricia@patriciamclinn.com. Even with many layers of editing, mistakes can slip through, alas. But, together, we can eradicate the nasty nuisances. Thank you!
— Patricia McLinn

CHAPTER ONE

ANNE HOOPER IGNORED the implications of a grumbling rattle in the engine as she bumped her seventeen-year-old compact over the cattle guard, down a drive where gravel was merely a rumor, and into the farmyard.

Just as she'd been ignoring other implications since leaving another fruitless meeting and heading home this dreary late December afternoon.

She was too weary to deal with implications.

It wasn't at all like the muscle drained tiredness that lasted from planting through harvest. This was a blank-brained numbness.

Well, maybe not entirely blank, because her brain *had* spotted an unfamiliar car parked by the back porch.

She blinked at it.

It wasn't just *unfamiliar*. It was downright *strange*.

Not only was it not a pickup, van, or modest sedan—the common modes of transportation on the farms that surrounded Drago, Illinois—but it had lightly tinted windows, protrusions like curvy fins, and a glossy finish that had clearly never been besmirched by that haunting mixture of combining dust and cow dung.

Heck, this car didn't look as if it knew what dirt was, much less manure.

So what was it doing outside her farmhouse?

Well, *her* farmhouse was stretching it.

The two-story frame structure that was rapidly forgetting what paint felt like belonged to her late husband's great-uncle, Everett Hooper.

Still, it was her home, too. The home she was working her ass off to hold onto, despite days like this.

Nope, wasn't going to let those implications in to her head. Not until she had the energy to wrestle them to the ground.

Until then, she would put one foot in front of the other.

Which, at the moment, involved climbing three steps to the enclosed back porch that served as a mudroom, then into the kitchen beyond it.

" 'Bout time you got home, young lady," Everett groused the moment she walked in.

Maybe he'd been concerned about her. Maybe he'd been concerned he might have to get his own supper. Hard to tell with him.

She wouldn't have pursued the topic, but he also didn't give her a chance. "Got someone I want you to meet. This is Peter Quincy. Quince, this is Anne, the one I've been telling you about."

Before she could take in the strange man in her kitchen—even stranger than the car outside—he stepped forward and extended his hand.

She must have automatically raised hers—encased in a mitten since the car's heater wasn't worth spit and she reserved her warmest gloves for farm work—because there was her green knit-clad paw, wrapped in a large, bare male hand.

Her gaze dropped. Starting from clean, leather shoes planted incongruously on the faded linoleum, she panned up creased suit pants, a perfectly fitted jacket, past a crisp white shirt and richly colored tie, and up still more to a face as finely tailored as the suit.

Her stomach dropped, a sharp plunge that should have deposited it somewhere in the cellar.

"It's good to meet you, Anne—Ms. Hooper," the man said with a warm smile.

"Mr. Quincy," she responded, then found a reserve of energy to add, "I take it the car outside belongs to you?"

"You like it?" His smile turned less polished, converting to a grin. "The salesman promised it would make people think of a panther. And by extension, they'd think of me that way. Did it work?"

That salesman had been wrong.

The man didn't gain from the car's reflection; the man matched the car. Sleek, understated, and with the promise of power under the hood.

She pivoted away to hang her coat on its peg by the door, putting her back to the room's other occupants.

Power under the hood?

Where on earth had *that* thought come from?

Wherever it had come from, it needed to go back there. Right now.

She faced the room.

"In other words, it's built so low to the ground it's begging for farm roads to rip out its undercarriage," she said.

Peter Quincy's grin flickered, then surged to full wattage. "You're right. It wasn't built for farm roads."

Whatever satisfaction she might have gained from being acknowledged right—and, actually, she felt a little like someone who'd pricked a kid's balloon—evaporated when she stepped into the room far enough to make eye contact with Everett around Peter Quincy's broad shoulders.

Everett's look asked the question.

She shook her head.

No, this banker hadn't agreed to the loan they needed, either.

No, she didn't know what she was going to do next … except to keep putting one foot in front of the other. And refuse to contemplate that the next step might be over a cliff.

"Then it's a good thing I got Quince to come on out here," Everett said with a nod.

Peter Quincy looked from Everett to her and back, clearly knowing he'd missed something.

Belatedly, a possibility hit her.

Oh, God, what if this man was a buyer?

That would explain her stomach-dropping reaction—instinctive fear. Fear that the world had turned upside down in the past few hours and Everett Hooper had decided to sell this farm after all.

No, wait, her sluggish brain protested. That didn't make sense.

First, Everett would never sell. Second, this man didn't look like any buyer she'd ever seen.

"Yup," Everett continued in a self-congratulatory tone. "You don't think I have good ideas, Anne, but this was one. Sure was."

And then she got it.

The old man had gone stark raving mad.

As if she hadn't told him six dozen times—

"Everett." She forced her words to crisp certainty. "You can't be serious. What possible use could he be to me?"

"*Hey.*"

She ignored the stranger's combined protest and half laugh, focusing on her great uncle-in-law, who sputtered in a good imitation of innocence.

"This has got to stop, Everett. I am fed up, and this one has got to be the most desperate, bottom-of-the-barrel—"

"Hey. I *am* here, you know, Ms. Hooper."

Unlike the others, this stranger—this Peter Quincy—wasn't going to be ignored. So she'd deal with him first, then set things straight with Everett once and for all.

And *then* she'd collapse.

She turned to look him up and down, pausing on his hands. Large and apparently capable, but if they'd experienced manual labor any time lately, she was a super model.

She pronounced judgment. "You're no farmer."

"True."

"That's what I meant—you're not fit for farming. You might be fine for other things."

"Thank you," he said, solemnly. "I believe I am."

She looked up sharply. His eyes were alight with laughter.

It caught at something in her. Something buried deep. Something she didn't recognize. Or didn't want to.

"Then you should have better sense than to listen to his fool idea." She jerked her head at Everett.

"It didn't seem like a fool idea when Everett suggested it," Peter Quincy said mildly.

She propped her hands on her hips. "Oh, really? What could a man like you do on a farm like this?"

"Sleep."

She blinked. "What?"

"Sleep. Eat breakfast, perhaps occasionally another meal."

Before she could make sense of that, Everett erupted in wheezy laughter. "You thought I brought *him* in to *farm*? Oh, Lord, preserve me from nonsensical women."

She spun back to the old man. "Don't you start on me—not now."

Apparently he recognized a woman at the end of her rope—or the edge of her cliff—because, for once, he gave a succinct explanation rather than launching into a meandering account.

"I rented the man a room, Anne. You know," he added with a deliberation meant to warn her, "the large room at the end of the hall with its own bathroom."

Everett met her gaze. She read his concern—several concerns, actually. Starting with the fact that the large room at the end of the hall with its own bathroom had once been the room she'd shared with her husband.

But if she'd been inclined to fall apart over such things it would have happened when they'd rented the room once before.

They hadn't needed the money then nearly as much as they did now, and she'd been newly a widow, instead of a three-year veteran of that status.

She licked her lips.

"How much? Or—" Hope blazed. Maybe if they got enough rent, combined with her income from her part-time job at Stenner Autos…
"—did you leave it to me to settle the amount?"

"No," Peter Quincy said. "We agreed to a monthly rent."

With hope sputtering out, she repeated, "How much?"

He named an exorbitant figure. Even higher than she'd have held out for.

Not enough to get rid of the wolf entirely, but enough to keep him on the far side of the door awhile longer.

And since minutes ago it had seemed she had no time left until the wolf battered down the door and set up camp in the middle of the kitchen, *any* time seemed like boundless luxury.

"Excuse me."

She walked away from them at a reasonable pace and made it across the center hall. But when she hit the bottom of the stairs and her hand cupped over the familiar newel post, she picked up speed.

She pounded up the stairs, around the corner and into the hall bathroom, slamming the door behind her, and locking it before she burst into tears.

CHAPTER TWO

Peter Quincy had made a number of females cry in his lifetime, but never quite like this.

"What do you think you're about young man?" demanded Everett Hooper.

Quince slowly brought his gaze back from the patch of ceiling overhead, above which he figured Anne Hooper was huddled, crying like a banshee.

"Not a thing."

Everett squinted at him suspiciously. "You're slick, but don't start thinking I'm stupid. We agreed to a rent. Why'd you go and up it?"

"I hadn't seen the farm when we agreed. It's a much nicer situation than I expected."

Everett's suspicion showed no visible sign of dwindling.

Quince added, "With all the Zeke-Tech people trying to find places to stay, I knew that if someone else heard what I was paying, they'd offer more, you'd toss me out to bring them in, and I'd be right back where I started, with no place to sleep."

The other man's gaze eased at that self-interested explanation.

"As long as you're not thinking thoughts you shouldn't be thinking about Anne."

Good God, what did the old geezer think he was? A monster?

Anne Hooper looked like she'd shatter from one good puff of wind.

Oh, she seemed physically strong enough. But thin in a way that made him think of people who'd lost weight from overwork. Or grief. That gave her face a drawn quality. And her eyes appeared over-large and almost bruised.

Her mouth, though, now that was wide and generous, meant to curve up into an inviting smile. Or to open to release soft, desperate sounds.

And despite the thinness, when she'd taken off that shapeless old coat, static electricity had molded her sweater to curves of breasts, waist, and hips that left absolutely no doubt that she was a woman … and that he was a man enjoying looking at a woman.

Okay, maybe some part of him had been thinking along the lines Everett feared, but not with any intention of ever acting on it.

It was just the basic—or base—male reaction to a female.

But Anne Hooper's curves weren't the reason he'd upped the rent.

Her eyes were.

Those huge, haunted, stubborn eyes that were never going to quit.

EVERETT INVITED HIM to eat with them, but Quince figured Anne didn't need an unexpected mouth to feed.

She *did* need time to recover her equilibrium.

Time apart would make it easier for them both to pretend he had no idea she'd broken down in tears over the prospect of his rent.

Besides, he had things to attend to.

So he ate dinner at the café in Drago.

Then he went to Zeke and Darcie's house to stow his important belongings into a suitcase and laptop case, joined by a couple boxes with items accumulated in the past six months of being in Drago off and on.

Splitting his time between here and Zeke-Tech headquarters in Virginia had started after Zeke—born Anton Zeekowsky—returned to his hometown last spring.

Zeke had resisted visiting Drago, the town he'd been determined to put behind him forever. But once he arrived here, he rediscovered friends and feelings—especially about Darcie Barrett.

Before long, Zeke had decided to bring a division of his hugely successful company to Drago. Quince, who'd been in on the birth of Zeke-Tech and had worked with Zeke ever since, didn't begrudge commuting. Not considering how happy Zeke was.

With his minimal packing done, Quince went out the back door and climbed the stairs to the apartment over the garage where Zeke and Darcie were living during renovations to the main house.

This was the potentially tricky part.

Because they'd already discussed this and there'd been no consensus.

He'd said that with construction wrapping up, Darcie and Zeke would move back into the main house, and as newlyweds they needed their privacy.

Neither had argued that point.

But when he'd said he'd start looking for somewhere else, their solution was to swap, with him moving out of the guest room in the main house and into the apartment when they moved out.

"It's perfect," Zeke said. "You'll be right here whenever I need you."

As CEO of Zeke-Tech, Zeke used to feel he needed Quince—his COO and best friend—constantly, to run operations while he concocted endless ideas.

But since Zeke had reconnected with Darcie there had been less demand on Quince's time. Even with the company's new involvement with the community and moving a division, these past months had felt nearly like a vacation to Quince.

"Being so close is probably why he wants to get away," Darcie said dryly. "Give the man time off for good behavior."

And that's how they'd left it.

Quince had searched for a place over the past month, with no success because the influx of Zeke-Techers was straining Drago's housing seams to bursting.

He had also chewed over his reaction to their offer.

Camping out sporadically in the under-construction house had been one thing. But now that moving the division was picking up speed, he'd spend considerably more time in Drago.

Setting up a more permanent residence over Zeke and Darcie's garage—close, but not part of their happiness—grated.

That gut reaction had surprised the heck out of him.

He was genuinely happy for them.

But any doubts about the wisdom of gaining some distance ended three days ago with the celebration of Christmas.

He'd been welcomed warmly from Christmas Eve church services, through stockings and breakfast, into present-opening and a turkey dinner. He couldn't remember a better Christmas ... or one that made him feel more solitary.

As a swap-off for the upside, he'd happily live with that solitary feeling next December 25.

He just couldn't do it every day until then.

He didn't say any of that to Zeke and Darcie when they welcomed him into the apartment and he announced his move.

First, Darcie worried that construction in the main house had become too much of an imposition on him.

Since most of the time he'd spent in the guest room had been sleeping and the construction crew didn't work then, that hadn't been a problem.

Zeke started to get that stubborn look that meant he'd been pre-sented with a change he didn't like. So Quince launched into a long, involved recounting of how this came about to give his friend time to adjust.

Darcie eyed him a couple times in a way that made him wonder what she was thinking. Or if she saw more than he would have liked.

That wasn't an issue with Zeke.

When Zeke's stubbornness started to fade, Quince wrapped up his tale.

"...so striking up a conversation with Everett Hooper in the café at lunch when I got in from Chicago has turned out great all around."

"Everett's a good guy," Zeke said. "Don't know Anne well, but she's doing work for Jennifer at the dealership, isn't she, Darcie?"

"Yes. Jen says she's terrific with the books—always on time and never an error. But their farm's pretty far out."

"Not that far from the Zeke-Tech site," Quince pointed out.

"That's smart," Zeke said. "As long as you have what you need there."

"You mean water, heat, indoor plumbing?"

"Good connections for phone and Internet," Zeke clarified. "You can live without the rest."

"It's going to need to get out that way soon anyway. It's prime real estate, being between town and our site."

Darcie didn't look convinced. "A farm, Quince? I don't see you on a farm."

"I consider it educational."

Zeke frowned. When he spoke it was clear his concerns weren't about Quince being on a farm. "She's kind of pretty. Anne Hooper."

"She is."

Zeke's frown deepened. He seemed to be waiting for Quince to say more. Quince calmly met his look with silence.

"He's worried you'll lose your heart." Beneath Darcie's dryness rested a lot of fond amusement. "And then you might not be available whenever he wants you."

"He gave Vanessa a good shove in that direction. She's not working as much now that she's with Josh. Haven't heard him complaining about that."

"That," Darcie said before her husband could answer, "is because Vanessa made Zeke work more, always pestering him—his word, not mine—with annoying things like the company's bottom line and financial well-being. But you're an entirely different story, since you do work he might otherwise have to contend with."

"It's not only that," Zeke grumbled.

The other two laughed.

"Hey," he protested.

Darcie kissed him on the cheek. "We know. You're truly worried he might lose his heart."

"No need to worry. You know I don't lose my heart."

"You did." Zeke muttered. "Once."

Quince was aware of Darcie's laser attention. But he was an old hand at this.

"That's why it won't happen again," he said lightly.

CHAPTER THREE

Thinking about that conversation on his way back, he focused on the farm element.

Actually, the idea of a farm appealed to Quince the instant Everett mentioned it in the café.

Fields of corn—even in their current winter-stubble state—should provide plenty of mental elbow room. Plus, it was something completely new. Something he knew nothing about.

Maybe that combination would soothe the itch he'd been feeling for a while.

So when the casual conversation at the café's counter had turned into a specific offer from Everett, Quince said yes immediately—pending approval of Everett's great-nephew's widow and Quince's approval of the room.

Quince had approved the room—big windows flanking the headboard, showing sweeps of corn stubble that looked as if it went on forever—before Anne's return.

He wasn't at all sure, however, that he had her approval.

He breathed a little easier on that point when he returned with his stuff and she let him in. No warm words of greeting, but she did open the door.

"I suppose we'll have to get you a key," she said, stepping back for him to enter.

"That would be good," he said mildly.

With Everett downstairs watching television, Quince now was putting his clothes in the closet and drawers while Anne insisted on "seeing to" the bedroom and bathroom.

As far as he could tell, "seeing to" meant cleaning what looked to already be immaculate spaces.

He didn't begrudge the old man staying downstairs—he had a bad leg that clearly made climbing stairs uncomfortable. Plus, Quince guessed Everett came from a generation—and a mindset—that wouldn't have made him particularly successful at housework.

But Anne Hooper was clearly worn out.

Her eyes were slightly puffy. She blinked slow and often, as if fighting against the lids' longing to close. Each movement had a slice of hesitation before it, making him think she was exerting her will to activate her muscles.

He tried to talk her out of this cleaning.

She ignored him—he was being his most charming, too—and kept going.

At least now that she'd finished vacuuming the drapes, he could ask questions.

"How much help do you have here?"

"Help?" She gave no sign of being familiar with the concept.

"With the farm," he said, to narrow the discussion. "Everett says you run the place."

"Does he?" She sounded oddly pleased.

"Yeah, but you must have some help—hired hands? Or...?" He had no idea what else.

"Neighbors pitch in if they can at harvest. Everett helps where he can."

He waited, but she said no more. "That's it?"

She shrugged. "Most farmers don't have a whole lot more. Farming's the ultimate do-it-yourself project."

Quince's farm experience was of the Old-MacDonald-Had-A variety. Even so, this struck him as a tough situation.

One woman, with an elderly and partially disabled man trying to run a farm of—well, he had no idea what size.

"How long have you been running the farm?" He could have kicked himself as soon as the words were out.

Everett had said at the café that Anne took over when her husband died suddenly.

"Three and a half years."

Her flat response gave no hint of emotional turmoil. But it didn't welcome questions about the death that had necessitated her stepping in any more than Everett's tone had at lunch.

"Been on farms all your life?"

"No."

"Where'd you grow up?"

Silence followed that.

He knew this tactic. It was the Zeke defense. He hadn't let it defeat him as a freshman in college when they were randomly assigned as roommates. He sure wasn't going to let it stop him now, with her.

"Where did you grow up?" he repeated.

"All over."

"All over where."

She gave an exasperated huff. "All over the world. My folks are Foreign Service."

"Yeah? That must have been exciting."

"It was—" She clamped her mouth closed.

"It was what?"

"Interesting."

Yeah, like that was what she'd started to say.

"I bet it was. Glamorous, too, huh?"

With her back to him she set down the bedside lamp she'd lifted to dust under with a clank. "No. It was mostly feeling like you never fit. Anywhere. Always surrounded by strangers. What do you do for Zeke-Tech, Mr. Quincy?"

She clearly meant that to push back—*you ask me nosy questions, I'll ask you right back.* He chose not to take it that way.

"I'll tell you if you'll stop calling me Mr. Quincy."

She looked over her shoulder at him, a hint of wariness in her eyes. "You prefer Peter Quincy?"

"I prefer Quince."

"It says Peter Quincy III on your check."

"I prefer Quince."

The hint of wariness in her turned to something he liked even less. Like she'd spotted something.

"It's self-preservation," he said, deliberately deadpan. "I have this vision of there being a fire in the house and by the time you'd yelled, 'Fire, Mr. Quincy!' I'd be a cinder. Or a tornado's coming and you holler, 'Get in the storm cellar, Peter Quincy III!' but by then I'm swirling around in the sky with a cow. But 'Quince'—now that's short enough to get me out without being singed or sent to Oz."

She didn't smile, but her expression eased.

A little.

"Okay, Quince. What do you do for Zeke-Tech?"

"I'm COO—that's Chief Operations Off—"

"I know what a COO is. So you're the one who helped Zeke start the company. The one who's been his friend since college."

"Zeke and I roomed together, yeah, and I was around at the start."

She flicked him a look that seemed to doubt the sincerity of his modesty. But he meant it.

Zeke was the creator. Vanessa Irish, the second person to join the company after him, was the business brain. Each was brilliant. Him? He was the conduit between their brilliance and the outside world.

He put his empty suitcase in the center of the closet shelf. It took up a lot of room, but this way he could pull it out and be started packing in an instant.

"Did you farm before here?"

"No."

Anne had earlier pointed out a narrow closet in the bathroom with extra towels and supplies, now she took a set of sheets from it, and started to turn down the bedspread of the large bed.

"There are already sheets on it," he objected.

"These are fresh."

"How much fresher than the ones already here?"

"Enough to make a difference."

Oh, yeah, this woman was definitely stubborn.

He went to the opposite side of the bed and folded the spread in an echo of her movements. "You look tired. Let me do this."

She stripped the pillow on her side and bundled the sheets while he struggled with one pillowcase. "I am tired. But you will not do this."

That caught his interest.

Ninety-one out of a hundred women would have responded on the basis that his comment had been a criticism of their looks—whether a sarcastic "gee, thanks," or a needy "I know, I look just awful," or an incensed "you'd look tired too if you did everything I do."

Another eight women would have ignored his comment, either because they thought it was none of his business or they were too well-bred to respond.

Anne Hooper had answered with plain, flat fact.

"So you thought your uncle had brought me here as some sort of hired hand?"

"No on both counts." She snapped out the bottom sheet. He caught it and stretched one elasticized corner over the mattress and pad, drawing in a deep breath. It smelled like the last days of summer. A particularly nice smell as winter knocked at the house, trying to get in. "Everett is not my uncle. He is my late husband's great-uncle. And I didn't think he hired you as a hand. I thought he was presenting you as my potential husband."

Quince dropped his side of the sheet.

Without looking up, she continued tucking.

"Don't worry, Mr. Quin—Quince. You wouldn't have been the first and I'm very afraid you won't be the last. There is nothing Everett wants more than to keep this farm. He's lived here all his life. Generations of Hoopers have lived here. And he's convinced the way to keep it is to get me married to a farmer." She snapped open the top sheet, working efficiently. "In case you haven't noticed, Everett Hooper is a stubborn man."

She had a homemade blanket spread across the bed now and was reaching for a comforter.

Part of him wanted to comment that it seemed to run in the family, except she and Everett weren't related that way, and he had something more important to say.

"To be clear, I'm not interested in getting married."

He heard the grimness in his voice and wondered at it. Usually, he handled the issue with considerably more grace and charm.

Not that it came up every day, but over the years there'd been a few instances when he'd felt the need to be upfront with a woman on this topic.

None of the other women he'd informed he was never going to marry had reacted the way Anne Hooper did now.

She smiled.

As she tossed one side of the bedspread in his direction, a slow genuine smile spread those soft lips and curved that generous mouth.

He tugged the spread without looking at what he was doing.

The smile created a shifting around her eyes, added light to them. Even her voice smiled when she spoke.

"Even if you were interested in getting married, Quince, you'd be safe here. First, I'm not looking for any kind of relationship, much less marriage. And second, like I said before—you're no farmer."

THE FIRST MORNING, Peter Quincy returned to his room after breakfast, informing them he was going to work there using a mobile hotspot.

But he was downstairs when she came in from the barn shortly before noon, after a daunting inventory of necessary equipment repairs. He held the door open for her as she came in.

Then he resumed buttoning up a beautiful topcoat in apparent preparation to leave.

The coat was as well-tailored as the suit he'd worn last night. Its charcoal gray fabric made her want to reach out and touch it.

Not that she would with her work gloves on.

Or off.

"I was telling Everett that I'm going to need better connection," Quince said to her. "I'll take care of that—my expense and—"

"We can't—"

"Already said yes, missy," Everett interrupted triumphantly. "Man needs it for his business."

As if he knew all about it, despite refusing to have anything to do with computers, leaving all that to her.

"I'm going into town now—" Quince started.

"And I'm going with him."

Everett's announcement didn't surprise her. He had been eyeing that car out the window like it was the tastiest pastry in the bakery. Of course he was taking the first opportunity to ride in it.

"—and I'll get installation set up. You can always cancel it when I leave. But in the meantime it should help you, too. Need anything in town?"

She declined and they were gone, while she stood in the middle of the floor.

It made sense that he needed better connection. And it was generous for him to pay for it. Why did it make her feel uneasy?

Almost as uneasy as his presence did.

He hadn't done or said anything to warrant it.

He'd been a perfect gentleman last night. This morning he'd complimented the breakfast of bacon and eggs by word—"delicious"—and deed—eating seconds. He'd carried dishes to and from the table without being asked, loaded the dishwasher, and dried the bowl she'd hand-washed. Far, far more than Everett did.

Still the uneasiness was there.

Apparently, just because he was *here*.

But she'd take some uneasiness for the rent he was paying.

BY THE MORNING of New Years Eve day, Hooper Farm was in the process of getting vastly improved Internet connection.

Quince had known the hot spot wasn't going to carry the load for good, but it was worse than he'd thought. As for the Hoopers' setup, it felt like he should get out and hand-crank something or other to get it moving.

He'd thought Zeke was going to have a stroke these past couple days, but everything would be faster now that Larry was here.

Quince had only misled the Hoopers a little about how he was getting improved connection. Instead of using a tech from the local company, he'd called on one of Zeke-Tech's experts, who'd helped set up the newly complete computer lab Zeke-Tech built for the town and knew what was what in Drago.

When they drove into town the other day, Everett had made the mild deception easier by gruffly announcing he wanted to be dropped off near the library. So Quince hadn't needed to explain why he met with Larry.

Only after Quince finished his business and picked up Everett for the trip back to the farm did he wonder what the other man had been doing. Especially after he'd caught a reflection of Everett's face as he looked out the passenger window, and had seen the man smiling.

But he hadn't asked, because that might open the door to Everett asking questions, too.

"Are you all coming to the New Year's Eve party tonight at the computer lab?" Larry asked now, as he finished checking wiring in Quince's room.

"Sure," Quince said.

"No," Everett said simultaneously, but with considerably more emphasis from the doorway.

Quince looked past Larry, who gave a slight what-are-you-gonna-do roll of his eyes, to Everett. "Why not?"

"Foolishness. Staying up to all hours of the night, drinking things you wouldn't drink any other time, singing songs you wouldn't sing any other time, kissing folks in front of a lot of other people. It's—"

"That last one's a good reason to go." Larry chuckled.

"Bah," Everett said.

Apparently, he really meant it, because his lean, stubbled cheeks had picked up color.

"We'll I'm going," Quince said as his phone announced an incoming text. "Sounds like fun."

"It should be," Larry said. "Mrs. Richards and some of the other regulars at the computer lab have it all planned out. Including the food. Some of us might not have anybody to kiss at midnight, but nobody'll go home hungry. You want the primary here or downstairs?"

"Downstairs. Don't want it in a guest room," Quince said with divided attention as he responded to the text.

Vanessa Irish, Zeke-Tech's CFO and resident financial genius, was asking if she should bring a gift to the party tonight.

He'd been social tutor for her and Zeke from the start. It felt like role reversal to text back, "Ask Josh. He knows the local customs. Then tell me."

She'd truly blossomed since she'd met Josh Kincannon, the principal of Drago High School. Quince had to give the guy a lot of credit for breaking through her defenses.

"Guest room? This is the master, isn't it?" Larry's question didn't have much questioning in it.

That brought Quince's head up. Everett developed an abrupt interest in the view out the window.

They'd put him in the master bedroom.

Larry was going on. "But I guess downstairs makes sense if they're going to keep using it after you leave, Quince."

"We aren't. It goes when he goes," Everett said.

Quince recognized that abrupt defensiveness as an invitation to battle, but ignored it, because he also recognized it as an attempt at diversion. He stepped in front of the older man to prevent him from following Larry out. "This is the master bedroom?"

Everett met his eyes with a flat, level look. "Yeah."

"The room Anne shared with your nephew?"

"Great nephew."

"You could have told me," he said mildly.

"None of your business. It's the room we rent out. You agreed to rent it. Over and done."

The older man sidestepped Quince and limped past him, then started downstairs. The syncopated sound of his steps conveyed the difficulty he had with his leg.

Everett was right. It was a straightforward transaction. They'd offered it and he'd accepted. It wasn't like he'd requested this room.

The room where Anne Hooper had slept with another ma—with her husband.

Her husband.

He pivoted and started for the stairs, too.

None of his business.

CHAPTER FOUR

"**H**APPY NEW YEAR!"

It wasn't yet the new year for them, but the crowd at the brand new Drago Community Computer Lab cheered lustily along with video streams of the Eastern Time Zone's celebration.

The core group had been celebrating most of the day, with time zone after time zone reporting in as it stepped into the new year.

Mrs. Richards, in conjunction with friends she'd made in the past month around the globe while volunteering at the lab, had orchestrated the celebration. Zeke-Techers helped set up the communications, including web cameras, and the good people of Drago contributed food, spirits, and designated drivers.

Drago's turn to celebrate its New Year would come at the top of the next hour.

For now, Quince was enjoying watching conversations spill from Mrs. Richards to Wales, from Malaysia to young tech whiz Warren Wellton, and from Turkey to Malcolm Cottle, a high school counselor who coordinated classes at the lab. And then the conversations crossed and mingled.

Zeke and Darcie were part of a group near the heavily laden buffet table, along with their high school classmate and friend, Jennifer Truesdale, and her significant other, Trent Stenner.

High school aged kids also mixed in, a good percentage of them from the football team that Trent helped coach. Larry and a couple other Zeke-Techers were talking with Jorge O'Fallon from Stenner Autos and Ted Warinke, who owned the hardware store.

Quince spotted a flurry of activity at the front door, sending an eddy through the crowded room as three newcomers made their way inside.

"Ms. Irish! Ms. Irish!" called the first one in, a high school senior named Fay O'Hearn.

She was trailed by a man and woman, both beaming.

Years of habit as the designated people person among the three Zeke-Tech founders had Quince edging through the crowd to reach Vanessa Irish's side at the same time the girl did.

But Vanessa didn't look beleaguered, as she usually did in social situations.

Another way her relationship with Josh Kincannon had changed her.

Her relationship with Josh, *and* his three kids, Quince supposed.

He didn't know if she'd voluntarily opened up to the Kincannon family, or if it had been a coup, but either way, being drawn into their clan had relaxed her as never before in the years he'd known her.

The smile she gave Fay provided further evidence of that.

"It came in today's mail," Fay was saying. "Aunt Rose and Uncle Al brought it to me at work—I was helping serve at a party—and when I opened it, they said I could come to tell you—I got it! All the financial aid I need. My first-choice school. I wasn't even sure I'd get in—and then to get it *all*."

The girl flung herself on Vanessa.

Quince put a hand to Vanessa's back to keep her from staggering into the people behind them. She steadied herself quickly, and hugged the girl back.

"That's wonderful, Fay. You deserve it. You worked hard."

"If it hadn't been for you, it never would have happened. I know you don't like to talk about your past, and for you to be so generous—" The girl broke off on a sob and hugged Vanessa again, even tighter.

The man who had to be the uncle Fay mentioned reached them, grabbing Vanessa's hand from Fay's shoulder and pumping it. "All you've done, all you've done."

The aunt put an arm around Fay, then pressed Vanessa's hand, still caught in Uncle Al's grip. "Oh, Ms. Irish, we can't thank you enough."

"All you've done, all you've done for our Fay," the man kept saying, pumping Vanessa's hand.

"So wonderful!"

"An angel."

Quince saw two things then—the scene was about to overflow Vanessa's comfort level and Josh had nearly reached them, his gaze on Vanessa.

"Hey, Josh, did you hear Fay's great news?" Quince's question drew Josh's gaze—only for a second, but long enough to see they were on the same track. "I bet everybody here would like to know—maybe a general announcement?"

"Absolutely. C'mon, Fay, let's get to the front." Josh wrapped an arm around Fay, detaching her from Vanessa. He pressed his other hand to Vanessa's shoulder for an instant, before using it to corral the aunt and uncle.

Quince eased Vanessa toward a line of chairs at the edge of the room, where they sat, out of sight, as Vanessa generally preferred.

Josh hushed the crowd, got the computers muted, then made the announcement.

The room erupted into cheers and congratulations.

Vanessa smiled and put a hand to her heart, a gesture Quince had never seen from her before.

As the tumult eased, she faced him. "You always do that, Quince."

"Do what?"

"Step in like that, when things get … emotional, and I get uncomfortable."

He smiled. Vanessa noticing it was a major change. "Maybe I do."

"You do," she said.

On the other hand, she hadn't changed entirely. She remained blunt.

"Okay, I do. So where are the kids toni—?"

Before he could complete the sentence, she said, "Xena's at a sleepover. Topher and Livvy are with Josh's aunt. You step in and then you back off."

He stilled. Just for a breath, but he saw her recognize it.

"I always thought it was because *I* was uncomfortable and you were doing it for me. But *you're* uncomfortable, too," she said with something like wonder. "Peter Quincy uncomfortable? Mr. Smooth?"

"Mr. Smooth?" he murmured with most of his usual humor.

It didn't deflect her. "Some of the employees call you that. Why are you uncomfortable?"

Blunt could land a blow when you were on the receiving end. His chuckle wasn't quite right. He heard it. Hoped she didn't.

"We all have our moments, Vanessa. Even Mr. Smooth."

He saw sympathy and regret sweep across her face. "Oh, Quince. I'm sorry."

"What for?"

"I never noticed. You've been a good friend to me all these years, and I never—never noticed *you*. Not really."

His mouth quirked. "Don't apologize, Vanessa. You have no idea what a safe haven you've been."

"Oh. You mean because emotions never entered into the equation." She considered her own words, then frowned. "But, Quince, with the executive coaching and, uh, other things, I might not be a safe haven any more for you."

He laughed. It sounded and felt fine. "I'll muddle along, Vanessa." Then he sobered. "As long as *other things* make you happy."

She smiled slowly. "They scare me to death, but they do make me happy."

Josh reappeared, and Vanessa's expression proved the inadequacy of *happy*.

Quince felt a twist of concern. Vanessa was a special woman, not used to romantic entanglements. This man better treat her right or—

Quince saw Josh's expression and his protectiveness eased.

"Hey! Everybody listen up!" It was Darcie, using her cop voice. "There's another announcement."

As the crowd settled to whispers, the forest of shoulders and heads parted for an instant, and Quince saw Trent Stenner with his arm around Jennifer Truesdale and both wearing huge grins.

A teenage girl who could only be Jennifer's daughter stood to one side, until Trent gripped her shoulder and guided her in front of him. She wore that uniquely teenage expression of being simultaneously pissed to be ordered to join in and pleased to be included.

"Jennifer and Ashley have agreed that the three of us should be a family," Trent said. "We're getting married this summer."

Jennifer said something to him, and he added, "I'm told it will be a *small, casual* wedding."

It was almost lost in the surge of voices and bodies as it seemed everyone in the packed room tried to reach them simultaneously.

Quince, deciding he'd wait to add his congratulations, turned back to Vanessa in time to see her share a long look with Josh.

He'd worked a lot of years with Vanessa, and he'd wager he was pretty close in his interpretation: It was an acknowledgement that they weren't *there*—*there* being where Trent and Jennifer were. Not yet.

But it held another acknowledgement, too. They both hoped they would get there together. Soon.

"Okay with you if we head out right after the New Year?" Josh asked Vanessa in a tone that indicated there'd be private celebrating going on.

"Yes."

Quince turned away, stepping into the crowd with no particular destination in mind, but he still heard the amusement—and more—in Josh's voice as he said:

"Good. Because there definitely comes a time when being part of a community is too much of a good thing."

Quince's lack of a destination ended when he spotted Anne Hooper.

Interesting. When he'd left the farmhouse before dinner, neither she nor Everett planned to join the celebration.

As usual, she wore jeans, a shirt, and boots. But this combo was different. For starters, it wasn't built for durability. If any piece of this outfit had seen the inside of the barn it hadn't been often. The jeans fit well, the boots shone, and the cream shirt gave the impression that you could see through it if you looked hard enough.

He'd swear she was even wearing makeup and she definitely had fresh, dark red polish on her nails.

She was turning away from the throng still surrounding Jennifer and Trent, apparently deciding to wait until later to reach them.

Of course she'd want to congratulate them. As Darcie had told him, Anne did the books at the recently re-opened car dealership that Trent owned and Jennifer ran.

Tonight, he'd heard a number of other things about her.

None of it was hugely illuminating, but he'd found that understanding people was like a jigsaw puzzle. You had to gather a lot of pieces before you could hope to assemble them into any sort of order.

He'd heard what a hard worker she was. That the Hoopers had been in the county forever. She kept herself to herself—no surprise there. And a hint of something about the farm he couldn't pin down.

Chatting with Mrs. Richards' friend and Josh's babysitter Mrs. Mudge, he'd slipped in a statement about Anne taking over the farm when her husband died.

"Yes. That was a shame. She'd been good for him," she said.

That seemed promising, but before he could explore it, someone called to her, she patted his arm, and moved on.

Now, he plotted his route to intercept Anne.

The shifting crowd knocked him off course a time or two, but here she was—slipping between two backs, heading in the direction of the exit.

He stepped in front of her, plugging her escape route.

"Glad you decided to come, Anne."

She looked up and frowned slightly. "Wasn't my idea. Everett insisted the Hoopers be represented."

"After the unkind things he had to say about computers and New Years? I'm astonished."

He was half-distracted as he said that, having another matter on his mind.

That shirt lied.

It wasn't see-through. No matter how hard you looked.

"You seemed to have planted the idea in his head that he had to move with the times or be left behind," she said, accusingly. He raised his hands, declaring his innocence. She relented slightly. "It doesn't matter. I'm glad to have been here to hear Jennifer and Trent's news. I'd hoped to tell them how happy I am for them, but there's such a crowd, I gave up."

"Glad you did, since it brought you my way."

For a moment their eyes met and held.

He saw ... something. Gone too fast to grab hold of. And replaced in that instant by her intention to end the conversation, not to mention whatever he'd seen in those eyes.

Before she could, however, the man on her right, who'd had his back to them, turned, revealing a round, self-satisfied face topped by lank hair and a wide and unconvincing smile.

"Ah, Anne Hooper, how nice to see you. Happy New Year."

If the sound that came from Anne's throat was the man's name, it sounded remarkably like a growl. The man didn't seem to notice, already extending his hand to Quince.

"And you must be Peter Quincy of Zeke-Tech. I've been hoping to meet you. I'm Bob Chitmell of First Guaranty Security Trust of Drago."

Quince shook his hand and gave the normal responses, while most of his attention remained on the rumbling volcano of a woman at his side.

The guy's ruse of saying hello to her in order to introduce himself to a Zeke-Tech exec was blatant, but didn't seem volcano-worthy.

"In fact, I'm surprised we haven't met before now," the man was saying.

"I'm sure your focus is less on the newcomers and more on what's always sustained this area—farming."

"Farming," the man repeated with a snort. "You know how to

make a million farming? Start with two million and work real hard."

He laughed, not noticing or not caring that he laughed alone. Quince thought he heard a hiss from Anne.

Chitmell went on. "But a local outlook can fine-tune an enterprise like yours. Even such charitable efforts as this computer lab would benefit from an experienced local eye."

That caught Quince's attention on a couple levels.

This Bob thought pretty darned highly of himself to be talking of *fine-tuning*, Zeke-Tech.

Less amusing was the man's tone and manner in dismissing the computer lab.

That meant he was not the brightest bulb in the pack, since he was simultaneously putting down Zeke-Tech's charity and all the work put in by the citizens of his own town.

"They've done a damned fine job with the computer lab without you, Bob," Anne said. "If you wanted to lend your *experienced eye* to helping Drago, you could have done it any time these past five years."

"Ah, if only a banker had the choice of doing what he'd like to do instead of what he must."

Quince had no doubt about the effect that oily response had on the fire burning in Anne's eyes.

Unobtrusively, he started to put himself between the two of them. He needn't have bothered. Bob stepped in close to him, cutting Anne out.

"But I do hope we can talk—"

"You know, Bob, you should meet Zeke—Zeke Zeekowsky, the CEO of Zeke-Tech. If you'd like to, of course." With no doubt of the answer, he took the man by the arm to turn him away.

"Sure. I'd like to meet him," the banker said with would-be cool, though the self-satisfaction ruined the effort.

"I thought I saw him—yes, over there." Quince gestured Bob to go ahead of him, in the direction of the tallest man in the room.

He shot a look at Anne and said in a low voice, "Stay here," then followed the banker toward Zeke, who had no idea he was about to be sacrificed.

CHAPTER FIVE

For a good minute, Anne stood, aware of activity and movement around her, but not part of it.

Like a lone tree in a flooded field, potentially threatened by the force of all that surrounded her. Vulnerable to uprooting and floating away to nothingness.

She jerked her shoulders straight.

That might be the tree's fate. Not hers.

She didn't take orders from Peter Quincy. She didn't take orders from anybody … except maybe Everett sometimes, but that was different.

Just because Peter Quincy was the sort of man who could finagle things to get that upgraded internet service so fast—on New Year's Eve day, no less—did not affect the way the universe spun.

Stay here, my ass.

True, he and Everett handled everything with the installation while she was out in the barn trying to decide if they could salvage one useable combine out of the two pieces of junk they had, so she wasn't inconvenienced the least by it.

After that it would have seemed churlish not to include him in supper tonight. Besides, it wasn't like he could go around the corner to a restaurant to eat.

And somehow during supper it had come to be settled that Peter Quincy would be a regular at all their meals.

It had happened without her ever being able to say no without sounding like the meanest person since the Wicked Witch of the West—the "Wizard of Oz" version, not the reconstructionist musical version.

Especially after he insisted on increasing the rent he paid to cover meals.

She put her head down and made for the outside circle of the crowd, threading a path that minimized the jostling.

But as she reached the edge, a wave of people buffeted her. She braced herself against a wall. It was that or fall down.

She'd get her bearings, and then she'd leave.

"He does that a lot," a female voice said.

Anne swung her head around, and discovered Vanessa Irish sitting two chairs away.

The Zeke-Tech CFO, intimidating in her own right as well as being a close friend of Quince's, ranked in the 99.8 percentile of people Anne would have preferred not to deal with at this moment.

Before she could construct an exit strategy, Vanessa continued.

"Quince, I mean. That smoothing things over. Not leaving any awkward moments. Oh—" She frowned. "You don't like that I noticed he did that for you with the red-faced man. I'm sorry, I didn't mean to. It's because he's done it so many times for me, that's why I recognized it. But I shouldn't have said anything to you. I'm too blunt."

She paused, looked into the crowd, and then her face transformed. The movement of muscles was small—a curving of the corners of her mouth, a lifting of her brows, a faint fan of laugh lines at her eyes—but it transformed her.

"Some people like my bluntness," she added simply.

Anne followed the direction of Vanessa's look and saw Josh Kincannon some distance away, talking with a pair of older women Anne knew by sight from around town.

Apparently the rumor she'd heard about Vanessa and Josh was true.

"But a lot of people don't like it," Vanessa went on, "so I'm sorry."

Maybe it was the apology, or the transformation of a moment ago, or that the woman was sitting on the edge of the room by herself...

Rather to her own surprise Anne sat down, though she left a chair between them.

"No problem," she said.

Vanessa looked at her very directly, then seemed to relax. "Good. It's one of his duties for Zeke-Tech, you know—that smoothing-over—because neither Zeke nor I is a natural people-person."

"So it's a habit he's picked up from his job. Something he does all the time," Anne concluded. That might be irksome, but understandable. And impersonal. "Probably not even aware he's doing it."

Vanessa frowned in apparent serious contemplation. "I don't think it was from the job. He was like that from the start—from the start of Zeke-Tech, I mean. That's when we met, so I don't know about before that. And I can't imagine he's not aware of it, because he doesn't do it for everybody."

Anne's lips parted to dismiss any notion that his most recent smoothing-over service had been anything other than tenant-landlord courtesy.

But Vanessa grinned at that instant, and Anne realized the other woman's comment hadn't been directed at her. It was a statement of fact.

"I've seen him leave people, uh, twisting in the wind." Vanessa sounded like she was quoting, and when her gaze went to Josh again, Anne had a good idea of the source. "Sometimes I think he purposely adds to their discomfort. When he wants to make a point. Or he doesn't like someone." She gave Anne that direct look again. "But he likes you."

"Oh, no—it's nothing like that. He rents a room at my house— Everett's house. Hooper Farm. That's all."

She'd said too much. She'd denied too hard.

She saw that immediately, as speculation came into the other woman's eyes. Speculation that hadn't been there until Anne started running on at the mouth.

Vanessa looked from Anne into the crowd again—not in Josh's direction this time—then back to Anne.

"I see."

"What are you two talking about so seriously?"

Quince's voice coming from behind her didn't startle Anne, since she'd been forewarned by Vanessa's look.

But his taking the chair next to her, close enough to brush hips, did make her edge closer to Vanessa.

"The farm where Anne lives," Vanessa said. "Excuse me. It was nice talking to you, Anne. See you later, Quince."

With an expression that blended a frown and amusement, Quince watched her head toward Josh. "I think Vanessa's picking up new skills."

"Skills?"

She instantly regretted repeating his word, because it made him turn to her, examining her face.

"Not so long ago, I told Vanessa she was a lousy liar, but I'm not entirely sure about that anymore," he said slowly. "*Were* you two talking about the farm? Ah, I see—you wouldn't tell me if I pulled your red fingernails out one by one with tweezers. Because—yes, don't tell me, let me guess—it's none of my business what you were talking about."

"It isn't. And it wasn't any of your business to butt into my conversation with Chitmell."

"I thought of it less as butting in and more as saving you from yourself."

She wished with all her might that she'd had the forethought to be holding a drink at that moment so she could fling it in his face.

The glass, too.

Okay, she wouldn't have done that. But knowing she *could* have would have been so satisfying.

"I do *not* need saving. Not by you. Not by anybody."

"Fair enough," he said slowly, and with apparently unimpaired good humor. "But tell me this, do you really want to burn that bridge?"

"If he's standing on it—yes."

"Burning bridges—especially with bankers on them—isn't good business."

"Business? You have no idea what that man—" She clamped her mouth shut. This wasn't the place or the person for confidences, even if she were prone to them. "Never mind. I'm going to go congratulate Jennifer and Trent, now that the crush around them has eased. And then I'm leaving."

"Then I'll wish you a happy New Year now."

She stood.

He did, too.

It must have been her imagination that he leaned toward her slightly.

"Happy New Year," she said. "And good-night."

THE COUNTDOWN TO the New Year started, and the jumbled crowd turned into couples pairing off like filings finding their magnets.

"*Eight, seven, six.*"

Zeke and Darcie.

Vanessa and Josh.

Jennifer and Trent. And many more whose names he didn't know.

"*Five, four, three.*"

Quince stood beside the computer chair where Mrs. Richards sat, holding her anticipatory glass of champagne for her while she typed messages to people around the world.

"There! Finished."

"*Two. One! Happy New Year!*"

Quince lifted his plastic glass in a silent toast in the direction of the woman who'd exited shortly before the stroke of midnight.

His gaze might have lingered on the closed door.

"Your girl left, my guy's not here," Mrs. Richards said to him.

"She's not—" He broke it off.

No point in arguing when a nice old lady said the world was flat.

Instead, he handed over the glass he'd been safeguarding, then leaned down to give her a kiss on the cheek.

"Happy New Year, Mrs. R."

CHAPTER SIX

"LOOK OUT! GET back!"

The urgency in Anne's shout made Quince retreat two long strides, even before he looked around to see where she was and what the problem was.

That's what saved him from having a bale of hay fall on his head.

As it was, the dust raised by it splitting apart as it landed set him coughing and blinking.

He'd just driven in, returning from a meeting in town with Zeke, Vanessa, and the architects.

He'd say it was the first day back to work in the new year, except Anne had apparently spent yesterday—New Years Day—working while he'd lolled at Zeke and Darcie's house, watching football on TV, talking with other guests, and eating. Lots and lots of eating.

When he'd returned to Hooper Farm last night, he'd seen signs of how she'd spent the day—a pair of newly oil-stained coveralls in the mudroom, Everett grumbling over printouts of machinery parts, and new strain in those gray eyes looking at him over a mug of coffee held in both hands like she needed the warmth.

Like she needed the warmth...

Nope, not going down that road.

It had merely been curiosity that had made him start for the barn as soon as he got out of the car. He'd caught a glimpse of her up in the open doors on the second story of the old red barn, and he'd wondered what she was doing.

He didn't know about the cat, but curiosity had about done him in. Without her shout and his reaction, he would have been flattened.

He heard Anne coming while his streaming eyes refused to focus.

"You look okay," she said. It sounded half accusation.

And that made him want to grin. He would have, except it would let the still drifting grit in his mouth.

She must have caught the curmudgeonly bug from Everett. Why Quince liked it was anybody's guess, but considering Zeke and Vanessa had versions of it, too, and how he felt about them, it appeared to be a deeply ingrained flaw.

"I will be. What were you doing?"

"Getting hay out of the hayloft."

"Why?"

"Clearing it out. Leaving that old stuff up there's an invitation to every kind of critter. Not to mention mold."

"Why was it there in the first place?"

"Why are you asking all these questions?"

"It distracts me from wheezing."

His eyesight must have been cloudier than he thought, because he could almost convince himself that her mouth quirked into a brief smile.

"Fine. We used to have livestock. We used it for them."

"Why no longer any livestock?"

No smile now. "We're specializing."

She was better at lying than Vanessa was. But not good enough.

"Ah." He nodded, as if she'd explained everything. The motion dislodged dust and hay residue from his hair, so he kept doing it, assisting the brushing with his hands. "So that's why you're cleaning house—or cleaning barn, in this case."

She reached toward him, as if she might assist with removing debris from his hair.

Changed her mind.

Fast.

"You couldn't have dropped it inside?" he asked.

"Not unless I wanted this all over everything stored in there."

"No." He coughed. "Far better out here where it only got me."

"I didn't see you until the last second."

Mildly, he asked, "Is that how it's usually done, removing hay from a barn?"

"No, that's not how it's usually done," she said with a bit of snap. "A pulley and cable that let it be lowered slowly so it's all usable instead of—this." Her gesture took in the partially dispersed bale of hay, sitting within a settling dust cloud.

"Did a cable snap?"

"The pulley's—It's gone."

Nothing odd about the words, but her choppy delivery said there was a story behind them. Maybe a full novel. One she clearly wasn't about to share with him. Her voice would have told him that, even if his gradually clearing vision hadn't spotted muscles at her jaw jumping.

"What're you going to do with the hay?"

"I'll drag what I can. The rest I'll put in a wheelbarrow."

"I could help. That—"

"No. Thanks." She looked from his topcoat covering his business suit to his leather shoes, attire worn to remind the architects of Zeke-Tech's status. Zeke and Vanessa could wear whatever they wanted. They were geniuses. He wasn't. "You've got cleaning up of your own to do."

He pivoted to follow the path of her look.

His car.

It looked as if it had been caught in a sickly green dust storm.

Him, too, he realized, scanning down.

With a wry grimace, he turned back to Anne.

She was gone.

Only a movement in the dimness beyond the barn doors indicated her presence.

By the time he entered the back door of the house, he'd gotten the worst off his coat and recognized it was going to take more than his hand for the rest. The car was going to take a good washing in town.

Everett sat on the bench in the mudroom, grumbling and cursing as he awkwardly yanked at a boot half on and half off one foot—the foot at the end of his hobbled leg.

"Anything I can do to help?" Quince asked.

"Yeah. Long as you're still in your coat and all, you can put this box in the shed. Saves me having to get these gol'durned boots on. You'd think these things were bank vaults they make 'em so hard to get into these days."

Quince hefted the cardboard box labeled *Christmas—Outdoor.* "We'll give it a try anyway."

He hadn't seen any outdoor decorations when he'd arrived three days after Christmas, not much inside for that matter. Maybe the Hoopers were the kind who dismantled their decorations as soon as Christmas Day passed.

The box was less heavy than awkward. But he was glad to be carrying it, instead of Everett, with his bad leg.

Plus, Everett accepting his help made a nice change from his great-niece-in-law always saying no.

That great-niece-in-law hadn't wasted any time. A good percentage of the shattered bale of hay was piled up in an out of the way spot. He'd have thought she'd put it closer to other hay already in a fenced enclosure that wrapped around a lean-to shed attached to the side of the barn.

Another shimmer of movement indicated Anne was inside the barn. Possibly going after that wheelbarrow she'd mentioned.

Glimpses, that all he seemed destined to have of her, he mused.

By accident or design?

And did it nag at him for any reason other than curiosity?

Maybe.

If it did, it was because even with his dearth of agricultural background he suspected Hooper Farm—and the Hoopers—were struggling.

Maybe he could help.

Not with his non-existent farming skills, as Anne had pointed out. But what about skills and resources he did have—ingenuity, imagination, persuasiveness?

He considered that.

He'd used those skills and resources at maximum capacity for years to help Zeke-Tech get off the ground. Years that had drained and exhilarated. Sometimes simultaneously.

But Zeke-Tech had been flying on its own for a long time now. Heck, even his role as social shepherd for Zeke and Vanessa had just about disappeared lately.

I think I might have been getting a little bored.

He'd admitted that to Vanessa a couple months ago when they were talking about his enjoying the challenges of bringing a division of Zeke-Tech here to Drago.

Now that process, too, was well on its way, running remarkably well. And his enjoyment had faded.

He balanced the box against a fence post as he opened the gate of the enclosure he'd have to cross to reach the shed.

Was he getting bored again?

Maybe he'd have to look beyond Zeke-Tech. Maybe it was time to move on, to find a new challenge to absorb him, to consume his days—and nights—the way their start-up efforts had. Maybe he—

"Close the gate. *Close that gate!*"

This time Anne's shout didn't come from above him, but from behind. From the vicinity of the barn doors, he thought.

Quince put down the box on a patch of new hay, to keep it dry, and returned to the gate, closed it and reached over the top to latch it.

Yet Anne kept coming toward him, clearly still in full-scale alert. She seemed to be forcing herself to move slowly when she wanted to run.

"Get that box out of there. You can't leave it there." Her voice echoed her stride. Like she wanted to shout again and was forcing herself not to.

Quince dutifully picked up the box.

Any woman who got that wound up about a gate and box needed to take up yoga or drink buckets of chamomile tea or something.

"Now, come out of there." At least this order was spoken in a low, calm voice. Though why she was so wound up about this he couldn't imagine.

"First, I'm going to—"

"Right. Now." As she interrupted, she looked past him. He followed the look and saw a dark shape emerging from the shadowed shed doorway.

A big dog?

But he'd heard nothing about the Hoopers having a dog. And the shape seemed odd for a dog.

Behind him, he heard metal on metal as Anne worked the latch.

He didn't take his eyes off the figure by the shed, because now he could see a glowering face staring at him.

That was no dog.

The eyes, pale except for a dark bar instead of an ordinary iris, protruded from the sides of a head that was lighter colored than the rest of the body, except for thunderous eyebrow-like markings under a pair of curved horns.

Horns.

The eyebrow markings disappeared from his focus and the horns came into sharper focus—*sharp* being the uppermost impression—as the animal lowered his head. And opened its mouth emitting a tongue-wagging, guttural scream.

"Fast, Quince. *Now.*"

He followed Anne's order to the best of his ability, hampered by a flap of the box top catching on the gate post. He lifted it free, spun out of the opening, and Anne slammed the gate closed.

Just in time.

Denied his primary target, the animal butted the gate, setting it shuddering and shaking. The animal puffed out annoyed clouds of vapor through the wire of the fence, then, with a disgusted shake of its head, and a final braying scream, plodded back toward the shed.

"What on earth were you doing?" Anne demanded, dispelling her own annoyed clouds of vapor.

"Putting this box of Christmas decorations in the shed so Everett didn't have to wrestle with his boots."

"Christmas? We never decora—Oh." She turned and pointed to a wooden structure next to the garage. "The shed is over there."

He tipped his head toward the nearer structure. "That sure looks like a shed to me. Besides, you said you don't raise animals."

"We don't. Other than a few chickens and Grandy—who is Everett's pride and joy."

"Exactly what species is Everett's pride and joy?"

"You can't even recognize a goat?"

"My image of goats is that they're friendly and cuddly, beloved by kids at petting zoos the world over."

She didn't react to the tone that he was pretty sure even Zeke and Vanessa would have recognized as joking.

"Not this one. He's old, and the meanest creature in three counties. And you were this close—" She held her index finger and thumb an inch apart. "—to having a close relationship with that goat."

"Yeah. Closest thing I've had to a relationship since—in a while." He brushed down his coat. "To avoid any confusion, you are talking about the four-legged guy in the pen, aren't you?"

She gave him one of her heaven-preserve-me-from-fools glares.

"Of course I am. What else could I—? Oh." She gave herself away with a glance toward the house and a twitch of her lips, but she recovered fast. "Grandy—the goat—has been ill-tempered all his life, from what I hear. Most goats prefer company. Crave it even, because they're herd animals. Not Grandy. He doesn't like people or dogs or even other goats except females in season to breed. He tries to get loose every chance he gets, and if he succeeds he wreaks havoc everywhere he goes."

"Sounds like a lovely pet."

"He's no pet. Goats *can* make great pets—just not Grandy. But he sires great milk givers. People breed their does to him, even though he's a scrub—not a purebred."

"Providing another source of income for the farm?"

She nodded. "It's not huge, but we've been able to raise the fee some, and a number of people who make cheese and beauty products from goat milk love getting a bit of Grandy's blood into their herd." Her gaze returned to the shed. "Trouble is, he truly is an old goat. And he can't last forever. Someday he'll be gone, too…"

For those last few words, her voice roughened. She was worried about her great uncle-in-law.

He wondered if Anne Hooper knew how transparent she could be.

No, or she'd do something about it. So he wasn't about to tell her.

"You know what they say—old goats are tough. They can surprise you," he said. "Now, where is this shed? And while we're at it, you better tell me what you call all these buildings so I don't lose life or limb or more valuable parts by wandering into the wrong place again."

CHAPTER SEVEN

A MODERATE DAY in early January was a bonus not to be taken for granted.

No snow falling, no life-threatening wind-chill, no ice on the roads … yet not mild enough to demand that it be devoted to outdoor chores.

The perfect day to knock off a yard-long list of errands, which she hadn't done since…

Her mind went sideways at the thought.

Damn him.

Damn him and his quickly covered *since* and all the questions it left simmering in her head. *Since when? Since what? Since*—oh, and this was the one that bubbled and bubbled until it couldn't be contained under the lid any more—*who?*

None of her business. Her business now was an itinerary for her trip into town that jostled farm needs, her job, and everyday life, coalescing into a carefully plotted battle plan. No back-tracking, no wasted time or gas.

She'd already hit the farm supply center, post office, bank, and library. After stopping here at Stenner Autos, she'd go to the grocery store last.

Most of her work keeping Stenner Autos' books was done through a secure network, which was so much faster since Quince's upgrades that it seemed like a miracle.

But even at its pre-miraculous speeds it had allowed her to work from home, while it let Jennifer access information from the dealership or her apartment. Trent's financial consultant, who was out on the

West Coast, could also check in.

But Anne made a point of coming into the office in person period-ically.

She'd bring Jennifer backup thumb drives, make new ones to take home with her, pick up additional paperwork, get supplies, and touch base with the people.

"Anne, how wonderful to see you."

Even as Jennifer spoke the welcoming words, she stood, leaving her desk—and computer—to Anne. They'd developed that routine at the start.

It had been a necessity in Jennifer's original, minuscule office be-cause two people couldn't fit behind the desk.

But even after Trent insisted Jennifer take the big office with the window overlooking the showroom floor because she was here daily and he, though the owner, was not, they continued this routine.

What was different this time was that Vanessa Irish was sitting in one of the guest chairs across the desk.

Anne hesitated, but Jennifer gestured for her to take the chair behind the computer.

"I'm glad to see you, Anne, because I have a question," Vanessa said with her usual directness.

It was the directness that had Anne's shoulder's tightening.

"Mrs. Richards said you might be willing to give me a supply of your oatmeal. It would be for Josh's kids. We used up all of Mrs. R's. Are you? Willing, I mean. Topher loves it and since he forgets to eat sometimes—Why are you laughing, Jennifer?"

Anne had a feeling her abrupt shoulder-droop of relief had drawn Jennifer's chuckle. After New Year's Eve, she'd been braced for the Zeke-Tech CFO to ask something far more personal.

But Jennifer said, "Oh, uh, the idea of forgetting to eat. I wish."

Vanessa studied Jennifer a moment, turned that assessing look on Anne, then sighed.

Before Vanessa followed up her sigh with any possible observa-tions, Anne quickly said, "I'd be happy to give you oatmeal. You and

Josh and the kids and Mrs. Richards."

"Thank you. I can come out and pick it up."

"You don't need to come out, I'm in town most every week, so I can—"

"I'd like to see your farm."

Surprise held Anne still and silent a moment.

"Do you not want me to come to the farm?" Vanessa asked.

"I… It's not that. I don't want to inconvenience you or—"

"It's no inconvenience. Do you want to schedule a time?"

Before Anne could respond, Jennifer said, "Farms often don't run on schedules the way a business does, Vanessa. Farmers do what needs doing when it needs to be done."

Thoughtfully, Vanessa nodded. "Then I will call before I consider coming out to be sure it's a convenient time for you."

"Good idea," Jennifer approved. "If I can get away, I'd like to come along, if that's okay with both of you."

"Of course. You'd both be welcomed any time. You don't need to call. But it's nothing fancy, and I might be in work clothes, so—"

"I'll call," Vanessa said firmly. "I will go now."

After her to-the-point good-byes, Anne and Jennifer settled into a more routine business conversation until Jennifer came out with "How's it going with your boarder?"

That kind of question was *not* part of their routine.

"Fine." Anne realized she'd spoken abruptly when Jennifer stopped filing, and looked over her shoulder at her.

Anne kept her head down, watching files copy onto a fresh thumb drive she used as an added layer of back-up.

"Quince strikes me as fairly easy-going," the other woman ventured cautiously. "But I'm sure it means more work for you and it must be different having someone new in your home. Stopping the flow of your work when they ask for things. Needing to, uh, make accommodations for them and for their ways."

"If I couldn't accommodate other people's ways, Everett Hooper would have been murdered years ago."

Jennifer chuckled, and Anne felt the grim compression of her own lips ease.

They worked in silence for several minutes.

Anne was pleased—relieved—the topic had been dropped.

So it made no sense at all when she burst out with "It's not that he asks for things—he doesn't have to—it's just *there*. How different he is. It's like having an exotic animal around. Like a panther showing up when you're used to barn cats—and a panther needs a lot more tending than a barn cat."

"I can understand that," Jennifer said slowly.

"Do you know what he did? He went in Grandy's pen—not only in it, but he left the gate open. Wide open."

"Did Grandy get loose again?"

"No. I saw it in time. In time to save Quince from getting butted in the ass, too. In the ass or other places. If he'd gone down, that coat of his that must have cost the earth would have been ruined forever, if it's not already because of the hay bale that dropped right in front of him and covered him, his coat, and that car in a film of moldy hay dust."

"All that happened in one day?"

"In about five minutes."

Jennifer started chuckling. Slowly at first. Then it became a full-blown laugh.

"I'm sorry. I shouldn't laugh. I know Grandy's valuable, and it would have been awful if something had happened to him. Or Quince," she added hurriedly. "I mean, if Quince had been hurt... He's so pulled-together, and to think of him coated in moldy hay dust." She sucked in a breath, laughing between the words. "What I would have given to see him with that cranky old goat..."

Anne didn't exactly laugh, but tension in her jaw she hadn't realized was there released, and she smiled.

Jennifer quit laughing, then sucked in another long breath. "You've got to give Quince credit for not packing up and leaving."

That poked something sharp into Anne's solar plexus. Must be because she hadn't thought about the risk of losing his rent.

Jennifer turned thoughtful. "You know, it can't be all that easy on Quince—being a fish out of water like that on the farm."

Anne snorted. "That's the trouble right there. When you have a fish out of water living in your house, you have to keep pouring water over him or he'll die."

"Who'll die?" Darcie Barrett Zeekowsky asked, coming into the office.

"Nobody," Anne said quickly.

But at the same time, Darcie added, "I thought I heard Quince's name."

The unintentional duet had the effect of making Anne's *nobody* sound far worse than *nobody*.

"We were talking about the accommodations you make when someone else is in your house," Jennifer said.

Thank you, Jennifer. It was a far, far better answer than *nothing.* And had the added benefit of being the truth.

Darcie looked from Jennifer to her, then back.

Anne started to pick up her papers. "I'll get out of your hair now, Jenni—"

"You know, Anne," said Darcie, "if you ever want to talk to somebody, to find out more about Quince's past, the one to talk to is Zeke. They've known each other since the first day of college."

"Subtle as always, Darcie." Jennifer somehow combined rolling her eyes with a smile—and without looking like a gargoyle.

"I just thought, since his childhood sucked—"

"Zeke told you that?" Jennifer asked.

"Not directly. He's said how much more fortunate he was in his parents than Quince was, but then Zeke's parents were terrific. No, it was Brenda, Zeke's assistant, who told me about Quince's background. Zeke, Vanessa, and Quince are the official honchos, but Zeke-Tech couldn't run without Brenda. What she doesn't know doesn't exist. Anyway, according to her, Quince's father is a real piece of work. Sort of like Franklin Stenner, only on steroids." She looked at Anne. "That's Trent's father. Were Franklin and Ella still in town when you first came here?"

"I don't know." She *had* encountered them last summer, though not in the best of circumstances.

"Then they were gone, because you'd definitely have remembered Franklin Stenner. And do your best to avoid him. Sorry to say that about your once and future father-in-law, Jennifer, but—"

"It's the truth. The only downside to being with Trent is … well, maybe it's going to be better. Ella laid down the law. So we'll see."

Jennifer had previously been married to Trent's older brother. Anne had long heard rumbles that Eric Stenner had messed up the dealership before he walked out on it, his wife, and their child, leaving debts and employees without jobs. Last summer she'd seen how Franklin tried to bully Jennifer. And worse.

How had the woman gotten past all that to trust her ex's *brother*?

Trent Stenner certainly seemed like a good guy, but, still, talk about a hurdle…

"Ella's a major advantage Franklin has over Quince's father," Darcie said. "From what Brenda says, the man's divorced any woman strong enough to stand up to him. Except maybe Quince's mother, because apparently she left on her own. And left Quince behind."

Jennifer winced. "Ouch."

"Yup. To give her the benefit of the doubt, she might not have had a choice. It sounds like one of those situations where the man was determined to mold his son in his own image."

"But Quince—" Anne snapped her mouth closed.

Neither woman pounced on that, though Darcie nodded and said, "That's right. Quince remains unmolded. Resisting that could not have meant a fun childhood for Quince."

"Trent once told me he considers himself lucky that his parents ignored him rather than trying to make him over." Jennifer looked at her, then at Darcie. "That it was easier for him to find his own way because he didn't have to fight them off first."

Darcie nodded. "I can see that. Which means it was even worse for Quince. He's really a great guy, Anne. If you give—"

"Please," Anne interrupted firmly. "I'm sure you're well-intentioned, Darcie, but I want it absolutely clear that Peter Quincy is a boarder in Everett Hooper's house, and nothing more. The last thing Everett or I—or I would imagine Mr. Quincy—would want is for a rumor saying anything to the contrary."

A tinge of color showed in Darcie's cheeks. Anne's felt hot as well. She knew she'd been more emphatic than absolutely necessary, but rumors could start on far less around here.

"I never meant to imply anything improper, Anne. I guarantee if there's a rumor, it won't come from me." Her stiffness eased as she added, "I care about Quince and—"

"Thank you, Darcie. I appreciate your understanding," Anne interrupted again. The last of her things stowed away, she added a quick good-bye and walked out.

Aware the other two women watched her through the office's window to the showroom, she held her head high and kept her back straight.

Only on the drive to the grocery store did she start to wonder if there could be repercussions from ticking off her boss's best friend.

Not to mention her boarder's business partner's wife.

And a cop.

Sometimes this damned county was just too small.

CHAPTER EIGHT

THE TEMPERATURE WAS dropping right along with the sun. Anne automatically looked at the dashboard clock, even though it had been showing eleven-twenty-three for a decade, then checked her watch. Almost supper time.

The grocery shopping had taken longer than she'd expected. She was tired.

That's what had made her go blank so many times as she filled a bag with tomatoes, or looked at labels on canned peaches.

She would rush Everett and Quince through supper, then tackle the books for Jennifer as well as the farm accounts tonight.

Because if the weather forecaster was right, she'd be spending the next two—if she was lucky—days outdoors.

She hooked as many bags in each hand as she could carry, then struggled to bump through the unlocked back door.

Quince and Everett were sitting at the kitchen table.

Quince turned when he heard her, then stood and tried to take bags from her. She shook her head. She had her system.

"Supper's going to be fast and simple—soup and cheese and bread."

But the soup was homemade, the cheese a step up from their usual value brand cheddar, and the bread a partially baked kind that she would finish off with herbs and butter.

"No supper for me," Everett said. "Going to Ned's tonight for poker."

"Tonight? This isn't poker night."

"We missed last week because Ned had the flu and it's at his place.

Now Walt is sick, so Quince is filling in. So no supper for him, either."

"*You're* going?" She twisted around to where Quince stood in the doorway to the mudroom, holding a jacket. She turned back to Everett, trying to mask that surprise. "You're playing this early?"

"Nah," Everett said. "Regular time. We'll leave at the top of the hour," he added to Quince.

"Plenty of time to bring in the rest of the groceries," Quince said, pulling his jacket closed.

This one, unlike the beautiful gray coat, was designed for tough use.

"No need. I can—"

But he was gone.

"Why're you so sour with the boy?" Everett demanded, as if he were Mr. Welcome Wagon. And what was with calling Quince a *boy*? As if he were a decade or two younger than her. "He's trying to help, you know."

"I don't need help like letting Grandy loose."

"Done and past, woman. Let it go." Everett *tsk'd*, then stumped out of the room.

She had to admit that without the need for multiple trips to the car, it was nice to get out of her jacket and start putting away groceries.

Quince made three trips to bring in the rest of the bags—it would have taken her more—then pulled items out, set them on the counter so she could see them, and folded the bags.

"Thank you." She bypassed him to reach the packages of wide noodles for the next batch of soup.

"My pleasure, especially since you're feeding me." He folded the last bag, then turned and propped himself against the counter.

"Want something before you go?" she asked. "It's not much, but—"

"That'd be good."

She filled a bowl with soup and warmed it in the microwave— several minutes at a lower temperature to get it heated through, then a minute at the hottest, to add the steam that brought the aroma to life.

In the meantime, she cut bread and sliced cheese.

He'd used that time to stow a few items in the refrigerator and pantry. Leaving less familiar things on the island.

"Thanks again," she said as she set the bowl and plate before him.

"You're welcome and this smells great. Besides," he added, "it's nice to find something I can do around here—no hay bales, no gates, no goats."

He smiled, and she found herself smiling back.

She turned and stuck her head in the freezer, making room there for the roast that had been on sale.

When she emerged, he said, "Mmm, what is this?" indicating the soup.

"Corn chowder."

He gave a short chuckle. "That makes sense, with all the corn around you."

"Wrong kind of corn. We grow field corn. You need sweet corn for chowder. That corn came from Ned Benzil. He still plants as much sweet corn as when they had all six kids at home. Candy's forever trying to give it away."

"So you make soup when they give you the corn and freeze—"

"No way. No time for making soup then. That's harvest. Candy takes it off the cob and dehydrates it. I made the soup yesterday."

He ate another spoonful. "It's amazing. Thank you."

"You're welcome."

They'd been thank-you-ing and you're-welcome-ing each other ever since she got home.

She grabbed boxes of rice and went into the pantry.

It needed rearranging. So some time passed before she came out, and he was gone.

His place was cleared and there were no new dishes in the sink.

He didn't know the first thing about a farm, he wore impractical clothes, he thought all corn was the same, he made her uneasy, but she couldn't complain about his manners.

Everett was back, wearing his lucky gray sweater.

"I'd take a cup of soup," he said.

She ladled a cupful from the pot in the refrigerator and put it in the microwave. "Did you have lunch?"

"Got too busy."

"You know what the doctor said—"

"Fussy old woman," he muttered. She was at least eighty percent sure he meant the doctor. "I've been taking care of this body a lot longer than he has."

She sighed.

They'd followed the track of that ring-around-the-rosy discussion so many times a groove was dug into the ground. And it never succeeded in getting Everett to take better care of himself.

But there was something else that might be more useful to discuss.

"Everett, do you think it's wise to take Quince to your poker game?"

"Wise? Why? You heard something? The boy's a card shark?"

"No, of course not."

He cackled now, as if he'd meant it as a joke all along, but she wasn't so sure.

"Didn't think so. As long as he's no cheater, it's plenty wise. Remember, I played cards with him at Zeke's bachelor party. He'll do. And it's not like he won't be able to ante-up with the stakes we play for."

"It wasn't his card-playing ability I was thinking about."

"What then?"

"He's ... he's not ... from around here. He's not like the rest of them you play with."

"New blood can't hurt."

She shook her head, trying to pinpoint her uneasiness. "You won't have anything to talk about. He's ... an outsider. He won't have anything in common with the rest of them."

"He'll have fifty-two cards in common, that's plenty enough for poker. We aren't going to some hen party, sitting around yakking and yakking and yakking."

But they did yak. A lot. Next to Monday night bingo, this long-standing poker game was probably the most prolific rumor mill in the county.

Was that what made her uncomfortable? That Quince would hear things he shouldn't?

Things he shouldn't?

What did she even mean by that?

Yes, he was an outsider, but what did she think he could do with any information he picked up at the game?

Blackmail someone whose son got a girl pregnant? Deny them employment at Zeke-Tech because they'd slipped off the wagon? Hire them for cheap because their farm was in trouble?

No.

And yet ... something left her unsettled.

Everett brought his empty cup to the sink.

That was progress.

"Everett, I just think…"

She didn't finish. The thought drowned out by Quince's approaching footsteps.

"You're wearing jeans," she blurted out. Old jeans from their softness and fit.

"For poker? Absolutely." Once he had his jacket in hand, Quince looked back at her from the mudroom door. "You going to be okay alone? You know where we'll be if anything comes up?"

Surprise robbed Anne of speech, but Everett gave his characteristic sound of disapproval and disbelief.

"Course she'll be all right. She's a woman, but she ain't an idiot." Then he clomped out the back door. "C'mon! Or Ned'll grab my lucky chair, sure as shootin'."

Her lips twitched.

Almost as if that had been what Quince had been waiting for, his eyes crinkled into a smile, then he followed Everett out.

She leaned back against the sink, listening to the engine of that silly car.

Town was a bad enough trip for Quince's car, but Ned's farm-house sat down a stretch of dirt road before turning in to a drive possibly even worse than theirs.

That car was about as suited to these farm roads as stilettos were to walking a corn row. What if the weather forecasters were wrong? What if it snowed or iced? Or what if they went off the road without the aid of any bad weather? That little car could slide into a ditch and completely disappear from view.

Not that Everett was thinking of any of that.

The opportunity to show up in it in front of his poker buddies was too good to pass up. After all, they might have missed his trip to town. Wonder if Quince realized he'd been invited mostly for his car?

She hoped to heaven he had the sense not to let Everett drive.

Then the engine noise was gone, and she was listening only to the familiar sounds of the house.

She shook her head, pushed off from the sink, and turned around to the dirty dishes there.

Enough of this.

She had work to do.

ANNE DIDN'T LOOK up from the computer when they came in.

She didn't need to see him to know how Everett's card-playing had gone.

And Quince… She didn't need to see him at all. For any reason.

"I'm going to bed. Can't sleep the morning away like some folks," Everett declared the minute he walked in the door.

So he hadn't won.

If he had, he would have been expansive, wanting to sit around and talk—no matter that she had a long way to go tonight to finish updating the farm's accounts.

He also hadn't lost all his poker money.

If he had, he wouldn't have said a word.

She still hadn't decided if he felt bad for losing money—even though it came from his small "allowance" of personal spending money—or for losing to his cronies.

"Foolishness. Staying up all hours on that damned computer, as if it knows better than a *real* farmer," Everett muttered as he stumped toward the stairs.

She'd heard those words a hundred times from him, the sentiments a hundred times a hundred. It wasn't the words that gave her information, it was the attitude behind them at the time he spoke them. Sometimes they could be taken for affectionate teasing. Other times not.

She shot a look after him as he started up the stairwell.

His leg bothered him the most at night, making his gait more uneven.

Tonight was worse than usual—probably the weather. And they hadn't even hit the real cold for the season yet.

Quince moved around behind her, running water at the sink. She paid him no heed. Not until she heard him drawing a chair over to the desk.

She looked from him to where he'd placed the chair—with a view of the computer screen—and frowned.

He adjusted the chair, swinging it around to the side, where it didn't overlook the screen's contents. He did it smoothly, as if being able to reach the glass of water he'd set on the desk was the reason for the shift.

"Would you like some water, Anne? Happy to get it for you."

"No, thank you."

"Anything else?"

"No."

"Interesting group of men Everett plays poker with."

"Uh-huh."

"All long-time farmers."

"Uh-huh."

"You ever join them?"

"No."

"Why not?"

"I've never been asked."

"Ah."

Since he'd moved the chair she'd kept her focus on the screen, setting the program to adding and subtracting.

"Working on accounts for Stenner Autos?"

"No."

"But you do the accounts for them, right?"

"Yes."

"Working on them tonight?"

"Did them first."

"Uh-huh. So now you're working on the farm accounts."

She grunted. Would he ever go away?

"Fair amount of talk at the poker game about farming."

"They're farmers—what did you expect?"

"It was interesting."

She said nothing. She knew she was being ungracious, but she still had an hour's worth of work to do and planned an even earlier morning than usual.

"Last spring, Zeke had the guys at Zeke-Tech put together a program to help farmers figure out which crops to raise and the best ways to get them to the best markets. Turns out it was great for the produce farmers, doesn't help the crop farmers."

"I know."

From the corner of her eye she caught his nod, it didn't interrupt the flow of his words. "The crop farmers—and you're in the vast majority around here—are getting squeezed. Costs of seeds and fertilizer and other expenses have been climbing fast. That wasn't so bad when the prices that crops got were rising, too. But now crop prices have dropped and input costs haven't. Not telling you anything you don't know."

"No, you're not," she said.

That didn't deter him. "Add to that the pressure on farmers around Drago because of Zeke-Tech's arrival. Land has suddenly become more valuable for other things than farming. Land like the land Hooper Farm and a few others sit on."

Her typing paused, apparent in the sudden quiet.

"There was discussion about whether or not this land—your land and the farms around you—is prime farming land or not."

Prime?

No.

Decent, but their yield was unlikely to rate excellent even if she had unlimited resources and time.

But she didn't need prime land. She just needed more resources and time to farm *this* land.

To kill the quiet, she forced her fingers to move again, not sure what calculations they might be requesting.

Eventually, he started talking again.

"Quite the discussion. Including talk that land developers are—using Ned's image—circling around some county farms like wolves around a herd of sheep. Developers would pay the farmers the going rate, maybe a little more, for their land, and then turn around and sell it for multiples of that."

She kept her fingers going, showing no sign she'd heard.

But she had.

Not only what he'd said, but what others were saying.

Like Bob Chitmell, with his smarmy, want-to-be-your-friend snake-oil salesman approach.

We can't help you with another loan, but I sure can help you. A pretty young woman like you doesn't want to be farming, tied to the same place forevermore. You and Everett sell your acres and you'll be set up for life. You can travel and explore the world. Be real comfortable, the both of you. Now, I have contacts and I can make sure you make the right decision. You won't even have to pay me a fee, because the buyers do that. What are you—? You shouldn't walk out, Anne Hooper. This is the best offer you're going to get. You hear me?

She'd heard him and she'd heard the talk from others that Quince obviously had picked up tonight.

He said, "So far, those wolves haven't brought down any sheep.

But there's talk that some might be stumbling. Nobody'd be surprised to hear if first one then another got picked off soo—"

She swung around to him. "Do you want something, Quince?"

"I want to know if you and Everett—if the farm is in trouble."

"Why don't you ask Everett? It's his farm."

"Because you're running it and doing the work. Is it in trouble?"

She stared at him. She could tell him it was none of his business. She could tell him to go to hell—oh, that was tempting—but what was the point? It wasn't like it was a secret around the county. All he'd have to do was ask anyone in town.

She gave him a level look, willing it to be devoid of emotion.

"Please leave me alone so I can finish my work."

No secret, but that didn't mean she had to say the words. Why should she? Let him ask around town.

Slowly, he nodded twice. As if she had answered fully and he was both accepting and assessing the information.

Then he picked up the chair and the empty glass, returning the chair to its rightful place at the table and putting the glass in the dishwasher.

Heading toward the stairs, he said, "Good night, Anne."

And that was it.

Except it took her another twenty minutes of futilely re-playing the conversation in her head before she got back to work.

CHAPTER NINE

H ANDS KNIT BENEATH the pillow cradling his head, Quince heard her coming up the stairs more than an hour later.

How much would she hate that he was lying here thinking about her?

About as much as Everett would.

The old man had made that abundantly clear on their drive back to Hooper Farm.

The trip to the poker game had been mostly devoted to discussing his car and various vehicles Everett had owned over the decades, punctuated by directions to their destination and brief identifications of the farms they passed on the way.

He wondered if Everett realized how much he gave away with his laconic descriptions:

"Schmedlers sold off. City folks have the house, rent out the land."

"Todd and Tammy Van Winkle brought in her brother when he went bust. Small place to support so many."

Even the more optimistic "Will Larkin and his son're holding on" told a lot.

"You love farming, don't you, Everett?" he asked.

The older man snorted in derision. "You know why they use bought the farm as a synonym for died?"

"Something about a soldier's death benefit in World War I being enough to pay off the farm for the people at home."

"That's one theory. Never heard it proved. So mine's just a good. It's that some people see buying a farm as the first step toward working themselves into the grave. But I'll tell you this—How often do you need a car salesman or a lawyer or a banker—" Quince had the idea he would have spit if the car window had been open. "—or CEO or whatever it is you do? But you need a farmer three times a day, as long as you want to eat. Love farmin'? Sure I do. Love it because I love eatin'. Everybody should love farmin'."

There was more talk about the state of local farms—and farmers— at the poker game, most of it nearly telegraphic among men who clearly knew all the context so nothing needed any explaining.

That meant Quince missed details.

But not the gist.

He'd slipped in a few quiet questions. Adroitly, he'd thought, until he caught Everett's stare after he'd tried to tease out more information on two fronts by asking if the tale about a neighboring farmer selling off his equipment a few years back had happened around the time Chris Hooper had died.

"Oh, that was before," said Will Larkin.

"A full month after," disputed Ned Benzil.

While that debate raged, Quince had felt the weight of Everett's stare. Turning, he saw in the older man's eyes questions, concerns, and warnings.

He'd been careful to ask two more questions after that—neither related in any way to the Hoopers.

It hadn't saved him on the ride home.

"Don't get any ideas about Anne."

"What in the world makes you think I have ideas about her?"

"You were poking around in her business tonight. The rest of 'em might not've heard it, but I did."

"I'm curious about my surroundings—the farm. Including how Zeke-Tech's arrival might impact it. That's what I asked about."

Everett huffed in disgust. "Oh, you're clever enough, I'll give you that. Clever enough for the rest of 'em—bunch of old coots. Not me. I'm old, but I'm not blind. I see what I see. And what I see is you're not blind either. Anne's something special. Knew it from the minute Chris came home after the first time he met her, looking like he'd swallowed the sun and the moon and every star in the sky. Looked at her that way right up to his last day. Not sure it—but that don't matter now."

Quince would have given a handsome number of his shares in Zeke-Tech to know what Everett had started to say, while accepting that no number of shares would get the man to divulge it once he'd decided against that.

"What's done is done," the older man said. "And what she needs now is a man who can farm—really farm. That ain't you, Peter Quincy."

"No, it's not." That didn't mean he was done asking questions. "On the other hand, there might be things a non-farmer can see that—"

"Nope. This farm's got all the non-farmers it can handle. You're a good enough fella, but you're not the right one for this farm. Or Anne."

"You can relax about that, Everett. It's nowhere on the agenda."

Lying in bed now, listening to the soft sounds of Anne in the hallway heading from her bedroom to the bathroom she and Everett shared, he knew she would agree with Everett.

She would agree with the order of Everett's priorities, too—the farm first.

Quince could have told Everett he had nothing to worry about. That Anne wasn't the least bit interested. Not in him. And, if he wasn't too far off the mark, not in having any man in her life.

If he ever let her know how attracted to her he was, she'd shut him out so thoroughly, he'd think he'd been sent to Siberia.

…how attracted to her he was…

Yeah, Everett had gotten that part right. Quince was attracted to her.

What the older man didn't know—couldn't know—was that this attraction wouldn't lead to action.

Not in Peter Quincy's world. He was no saint, but he was careful that any women he wasn't a saint with matched him in not looking for long-term.

Attraction was not what a woman like Anne needed. A woman who could commit her soul to a patch of land would do the same with a man—clearly had done it with her husband.

Nope. Attraction wouldn't do for a woman like her.

So, just as Everett didn't need to worry about Anne being drawn to Quince, he also didn't need to worry about Quince making a play for her.

He had his faults, but trying to seduce a woman when he knew he couldn't give her what she wanted, what she deserved was not among them.

At the same time he was drawn to her exactly because she was that sort of woman.

More soft sounds told the story of Anne emerging from the bathroom, quietly walking down the hallway, and shutting her bedroom door behind her.

He grimaced at the ceiling, shutting off his mind to any soft sounds—or images they might stir—from her room.

When it came right down to it, Anne was a lot closer in her suspicions than Everett was. Because she thought he had his eyes on her farm. That's what made her as defensive as a porcupine.

In a way she was right.

Driving in with Everett, he'd wondered about the state of the farm. Then there'd been that exchange of looks between her and Everett, her reaction to the amount of his rent, and her eyes. Especially her eyes.

He didn't know the full dimensions of the problem, but there definitely was a problem here at Hooper Farm.

If he could wish it away for the Hoopers he would. But he couldn't. So he didn't feel any guilt that his restless discomfort of the past months had shifted slightly, starting to realign toward familiar focus.

Ah, he did love a challenge.

QUINCE WOKE EARLY, starting in on his computer for basic information.

He had the beginnings of a basic background portfolio on farming stashed on his laptop when he heard Anne, then Everett stirring.

He switched over and knocked out emails for Zeke-Tech, then got in the shower. When he came out, the house was as quiet as an old house getting battered by winter wind could be.

Anne and Everett were gone. He knew that even before he went downstairs.

There, on the kitchen island, a note instructed him how to microwave the homemade oatmeal she'd left in the refrigerator for him.

A P.S. informed him they were taking Grandy to perform his studly duties a couple of counties away.

So apparently their encounter hadn't put the goat off his game.

Oatmeal was a hell of a come down from the eggs and bacon or pancakes that had started most of his mornings on Hooper Farm. But Quince was hungry and she'd left interesting jars lined up beside the oatmeal.

When he finished, he had to admit the oatmeal was surprisingly good. The nuts and strawberry preserves he'd put on top, selected from options she'd left, were delicious, but the base was even better.

Chalk up another lesson from living on a farm.

He left a return note, reminding her—them—that he was staying overnight in Chicago for meetings and wouldn't be back until tomorrow afternoon.

WHAT QUINCE DIDN'T include in his note was that he had free time before he needed to leave for Chicago.

He decided to spend it at Stenner Autos.

Jennifer Truesdale looked up from her computer when he tapped on the open door to her office. She smiled, and gestured him in.

After hellos, she said, "Your coming must mean you've seen the error of your ways and decided to trade in that flashy city car for something more practical for Drago. You've come to the right place."

"I hope I have, though I haven't come here for that." He lifted one hand. "At least not yet. If I make that decision this will be my first and only stop."

"Thank you," she said simply.

"I'm hoping you can give me some information."

He sat still while she looked him over for a long moment. He knew that she knew what—or, more importantly, who—he was going to ask about.

"Why come to me and not Darcie?" she asked.

"You know Anne Hooper better," he said, getting the name on the table.

"True. It's also true that Darcie knows you better."

"Knowing me isn't the issue."

"Isn't it?" Jennifer was a very attractive and nice woman. That didn't mean she wasn't smart, too.

He ignored her point. "I'm not asking you for anything that isn't common knowledge, that I wouldn't hear by spending a few days at the café or perhaps a couple nights at bingo."

She nodded. "Or a few more rounds with that poker group. But I'm not going to gossip the way they do."

"Fair enough. You tell me what you're comfortable telling. It'll still save me a lot of time." He allowed himself a small grin. "And think how much less gossip I'll pick up."

She continued to look at him for a moment. Then tapped her fingers on the desk in decision. "That's fair. What do you want to know?"

"Am I right that she works all the time?"

"Pretty much. Except when something more important comes up."

He snorted. "She doesn't think anything's more important than Hooper Farm."

"Yes, she does."

He raised a questioning eyebrow.

"When my daughter was hurt in a car accident at the end of the summer, Anne was one of the people who spent hours at the hospital waiting with me, supporting me until we knew she'd be okay. She'd just come in to the dealership when we got the word. A five-minute stop. It ended up being hours and hours." She smiled slightly. "And that was on a good farming weather day."

"What about her family?"

"Never met them. They're out of the country."

"Siblings, too?"

"Yes. One in Thailand, one in Brussels. She has good relationships with them and her parents."

Had he imagined a slight weightiness to that last comment? Maybe.

"She seems to be well-regarded around the county."

"Yes. Though she's not well known. And having been here years and not generations she's considered the newest of newcomers. Well, until you Zeke-Tech folks showed up. It's going to be a real culture shock for Drago and the county."

"For Zeke-Tech folks, too. And good for all parties."

She grinned. "I agree. So, if that's all—"

"How'd she meet her husband?"

"Online. Not a dating site. It was something about farming."

"Had she farmed before she came here?"

Jennifer lifted her shoulder, signifying she didn't know.

"How was she viewed when she first arrived in town?" he asked.

"The people in town didn't really notice until after she married Chris. The farm community, though, was probably aware of her from the first date." She rested her hands on the desk. What she would tell him next would be the truth. But not all the truth. That was okay. He had no right to expect all the truth. "People were glad. Chris had a reputation for being quiet. Very quiet. From the first, Anne brought him out of his shell."

He could have sworn he gave no reaction, but she said, "Yes, Anne. She wasn't as quiet then. She even got him to a few of the high school sports events, the Lilac Festival parade, things like that. It's only been these past few years that she's been more withdrawn. Of course she's been busy. They had a hard time after Chris died." Jennifer gave him a questioning look. "You know…?"

"Yes, I know he died unexpectedly three and a half years ago."

"Oh. Yes. Unexpectedly." She seemed to be processing that he knew that.

"What kind of hard time?"

She paused a moment, then said, "Among other things, he'd been on a spending spree. Well, maybe that's not fair. He wasn't buying things for himself or anything frivolous, but he went out on a financial limb buying brand new equipment. New, fancy, and pricey."

"They couldn't afford it." It was no question.

She nodded a brief confirmation. "After he died, they had to sell all of it, not getting anywhere near the amount he'd spent. That left them—Anne, really—with old, beat-up equipment being held together with baling wire and duct tape. Sometimes literally. Anne brought in the harvest that year practically single-handedly, not to mention newly widowed. It wasn't a real good harvest, but still, it was a major job for one person."

"Not a real good harvest… How much financial trouble are the Hoopers in?"

Jennifer withdrew without moving. "I don't know that."

"And you wouldn't tell me if you did," he filled in. "Jennifer, there might be ways I can help them."

She frowned. "Anne's a very proud woman. And Everett is equally as proud and even more stiff-necked."

"I've noticed. I don't want to be immodest, but I've dealt with some of the most powerful executives in the world. I like to think my skills are up to tactfully drawing out Anne and Everett."

Though he did see a major obstacle.

Not the obvious one about his ignorance about farms.

It was the people involved.

He would never have predicted he'd view Zeke and Vanessa as easier to assist through the maze and obstacles of human interactions—which were a vital part of running a business—than a couple of farmers in the middle of Illinois. But that's how it shaped up.

Zeke and Vanessa respected his ability. Believed him when he told them something was necessary. Trusted he'd guide them in the right direction. So they eventually—after requisite grumbling and resistance—did most of what he said had to be done.

Anne and Everett didn't respect, believe, or trust him.

Yet.

That's why he couldn't come at this problem straight-on.

"I hope you succeed," Jennifer said.

He chuckled. "But you doubt it."

"Let's just say I'd rather face the toughest executive than get on Everett Hooper's bad side. Or Anne's."

CHAPTER TEN

ANNE FELT A jump of nervousness when she spotted the new pickup from Stenner Autos pulling to a stop near the back door Thursday afternoon.

Silly to be nervous about a couple women coming to pick up oatmeal for heavens sakes. It wasn't like this was really a social call. No matter what Everett had grumbled about hen parties and coffee-klatches when she told him at lunch that Vanessa and Jennifer were coming by this afternoon.

Yet, she couldn't shake off the knowledge that they were the first people she'd ever come close to entertaining at Hooper Farm.

Unless you counted Quince.

But of course he didn't count, because he was a boarder. Not a guest. Certainly no one to fuss over, as Everett had accused her of doing for these visitors, simply because she'd dusted and vacuumed the parlor and given the kitchen a once-over. At least Quince wasn't here to give her grief about it, since he'd been gone overnight.

Not that his absence was notable. Except that last night's dinner and today's breakfast were one-third easier. Even his help cleaning up wasn't missed because Everett had stepped up to the job—though she'd had to bite her tongue from commenting on wonders never ceasing.

If she'd said the words would Quince have given her grief? Or would he—?

No. Didn't matter.

Totally irrelevant.

Everett had made a quick phone call after lunch—if she let her imagination run wild she could say his manner had been surreptitious. Then he took the aging farm truck for an unspecified errand. She suspected it was all to avoid the company coming.

Before they could knock, she opened the door to the two women.

Except there were three.

"We come bearing baked goods," Jennifer announced.

"It's to make up for me inviting myself," Darcie said as she followed the other women in. "Hope you don't mind me horning in at the last second."

"No." Hearing the flatness of that, Anne added, "I mean you're not horning in."

Then she wished she'd left it at *No.*

If any of them recognized her awkwardness, they gave no indication of it.

Vanessa drew off gloves and slid them in her pockets before handing over her coat to be added to the collection on the hooks.

"They do this," she said. "At least they did it to me in the fall. The pastries are good."

Jennifer chuckled. "Are you saying that's the only compensation?"

"No. But it doesn't hurt."

Amid general laughter, they came into the kitchen.

"I have tea and coffee. If you'd like to come into the front room—the parlor—"

"Oh, this is so warm and comfortable, can we stay here in the kitchen?" Jennifer asked. "Do you mind?"

Anne looked around the room rather doubtfully. "If you really want to."

"Absolutely." Darcie went to the sink. "Now *this* is a true farmhouse sink. I encountered a few designers who'd kill to get their hands on this."

Busying herself with getting their orders for coffee or tea, Anne gestured the others toward the table. "I hear your renovations are terrific, especially the kitchen."

"The absolute best thing about the renovations is that they're nearly over. Don't get me wrong, I love everything we've done, but I was more of the big picture person. Taking down walls, reconfiguring a few things, that's what I liked."

"So Zeke is the detail person?"

"Not with the house," Darcie said. "And that's probably a good thing. It's a lot nicer than it would have been if Zeke and I had made all the decisions. To tell the truth, most of what the renovators call finishes were picked by Zeke's assistant Brenda, with input from our mothers. They didn't cut us out completely, but they narrowed it down and did a lot of the legwork, so we could point and say, 'I like that.' "

She grinned and, despite the disparity between what she had heard was now the nicest house in Drago and this worn and utilitarian farmhouse, Anne found herself smiling back.

Darcie helped her carry the coffee and tea to the table.

"Oh, I'll get a plate for the—" She gestured to the bakery box in the center of the table.

"Why? We can serve ourselves from the box and use our saucers," Darcie said.

Jennifer chuckled. "In other words, Darcie's hungry. But I second her."

"Third," Vanessa said. "Did you get any of the raspberry tarts?"

"Of course." Jennifer opened the box and held it out to each of them. "Now tells us about this oatmeal that Vanessa's so enthusiastic about."

They talked of how Anne grew the oats, then made the oatmeal. The conversation slid to Josh's kids, then to his and Vannesa's plans to take the kids to Virginia for a summer trip to soak up the history. From there it jumped to Jennifer and Trent's wedding plans. That segued to the progress in bringing a division of Zeke-Tech to Drago.

"This whole effort must have meant a lot more work for you," Anne said to Vannesa.

"A bit. But since Zeke became so adamant that I hand off duties—"

"It's called delegating," Darcie murmured around a bite into a pecan bar.

"—even with the move I'm working far fewer hours than I was."

"That," Darcie informed Anne, "means she's finally dropped below twenty-four hours a day."

Vanessa placidly continued, "Quince, however, carried much of the responsibility for getting the process started and keeping tabs on it now that it's in progress."

"He works too much," Darcie said flatly. "It's like he hides behind the work."

Anne happened to be refilling Vanessa's coffee cup and for an instant their eyes met. In the other woman's face, Anne saw concern.

But her voice was even, almost flat when she said, "Quince is excellent at what he does."

"Of course he is. That doesn't change—"

"Anne, would you consider taking us on a little tour when we finish our drinks?" Jennifer asked.

Anne turned in time to see that Jennifer accompanied the question with a quelling frown at Darcie.

"A tour? Of … of the house?"

"If you don't mind. It's a great old house. And I'd love to see a little bit outside, too. Especially the barn."

Anne wished she'd done a lot more cleaning. But she could have spent all month on the place and it would still be what it was.

Long before she was ready, the cups were empty and the tour began.

Frequently Anne had to plead ignorance to Jennifer's questions about the history and architectural details of the house.

Chris had never talked about that aspect of Hooper Farm. The one time she clearly remembered him and Everett touching on it had ended with Chris shouting, "You're living in the past, old man."

She'd steered well away from the topic after that.

As they bundled up for the outdoors, Anne said to Jennifer, "You definitely know more about the styles and history around here than I do."

"I find it all so fascinating. And you truly can't find buildings like this anymore."

"Most people won't put up with them," Anne said.

Darcie and Jennifer chuckled. Vanessa did not, possibly recognizing that Anne had been serious.

After a side stop for them to put the bags of oatmeal in the truck—large for Vanessa, plus small bags for Jennifer, Darcie, and Mrs. R—they headed across the yard toward the barn.

The sky was piling in, gray and voluminous. Snow clouds, backed by a lusty wind, seemed to push the sun out of the way.

It made even the dubious warmth of the barn very welcome. When they'd had more animals, that had helped hold some warmth here. But lamenting their absence was as much living in the past as Chris had said.

"Here's the barn," she said, pulling back one door, and revealing the combine corpses she'd been trying to Dr. Frankenstein into an operable machine. She'd welcome a monster-looking result with open arms if the thing would just work.

"Oh, my, look at this space." Jennifer's voice caught as she looked around, then up to the ceiling, sucking in a breath when Anne flipped on a few lights against the shadows.

A new round of questions started that Anne didn't have many answers to.

Ask her the average yield per acre by field and she could spout off stats. Invite her opinion on till or no-till and she could go all day. Request a rundown of Hooper Farm's finances and she'd probably say it was none of your damned business, but she'd know the answer.

This stuff she didn't know.

Jennifer's interest was genuine. Heck, she was downright smitten with the place.

But she was the only one.

Anne caught Vanessa and Darcie looking over the machinery with faint frowns. Other than that, they seemed distracted.

Possibly also cold.

The benefit of being in the barn's shelter had worn off and the cold penetrated every bit of exposed skin.

"Let's go back to the house and I'll get you more coffee and tea so you all can defrost before the trip back to town," Anne said.

"Sorry, we don't have time. I need to get back soon," Vanessa said.

Jennifer, instantly contrite, said, "I'm sorry I've kept everyone out here so long. But no need to ply us with hot drinks. The truck's heater is a beast."

"Why don't you and Vanessa go start it while I help Anne with the doors," Darcie said.

Anne was tempted to point out she handled these barn doors by herself many times a day, but Vanessa and Jennifer were already agreeing and heading out.

"You go ahead and get warm, too, Darcie. I'll be right there."

Not only did the other woman not follow those instructions, but she stopped, faced Anne, and said, "There's something in Quince's past."

"What?"

"I don't know."

Anne scrambled for the words to tell her she hadn't meant the question that way—she'd been startled into that "what," *not* asking for further information on something that wasn't any of her—

But Darcie was already going on. "At least... I *do* know he isn't close to his family—no, that's an understatement. He has some half-siblings he stays in touch with a little, but not with his parents. At all."

Anne had started toward the doors, but at that she looked around. "They're not... They're still living?" He'd said so little, she'd assumed they were dead.

"Oh, yes. His father's some big muckety-muck."

She recalled his tone when she'd called him Peter Quincy III, the same name as the father he didn't stay in touch with.

I far prefer Quince.

"And his mother's off somewhere—I don't know—I guess doing what used to be called jet-setting," Darcie said. "Anyway, they're divorced. Have been since Quince was a kid."

"That's rough." Her own family wasn't geographically close, but there was love, support, and interest there, despite the distance.

"Yeah, but that's not all. There's something else. Something… deeper. And that, I truly don't know anything about. Zeke's made some references, dropped hints, but he's never… I have a sense of something."

"If Zeke's trying to tell you something—?"

Darcie chuckled. "Oh, he's not trying to tell me. If anything, he's trying *not* to tell me. He's doing his very best to keep Quince's confidence, and mostly he does. But sometimes he slips, usually not even realizing it. Bits here and there. Enough to convince me there's something … major."

They were outside now and Anne slid the door closed. Without help.

"Speak of the devil," Darcie murmured.

Anne turned her head and saw Quince's car pulling in. In a second he was out, greeting Vanessa and Jennifer.

Darcie kept talking. "Even if I did know the details of whatever it is in his past, I wouldn't tell you. I wouldn't betray Quince's trust in Zeke or his in me."

"I understand. Because I feel the same way about honoring Quince's—anyone's—privacy."

Darcie showed no sign of feeling the prick of that pointed remark.

"That, of course, doesn't mean you can't do your own detective work," she continued. "Ask a few leading questions here and there. It would do him a lot of good to quit storing up whatever it is he's got locked away."

With the door now closed, Anne faced the other woman straight on. "I'm his landlady. Not his—Nothing else."

"You could be. If you want to be," Darcie added with dangerous softness.

DARCIE AND ANNE came up as Jennifer began to wind down from

telling him about the historical and architectural wonders of Hooper Farm.

Anne looked as if she'd been backed into a corner.

Darcie looked bland.

Not a good combo. He greeted them both, then said, "So you all came out to explore the history of the farm?"

"No, we came out to get more of Anne's oatmeal," Vanessa said.

"What do you mean, Anne's oatmeal?"

"She makes it."

"When she cooks it you mean?"

"No—well, yes, she must do that, too. But before that, she grows it, and harvests it, and separates the chaff from the oats."

He looked at Anne. "That's homegrown oatmeal?"

"Yup." Jennifer said.

"Huh."

"I see that brain of yours going," Jennifer said. "What are you thinking?"

"Nothing special." He tipped his head to the road. "Isn't that Everett coming in now? Say, Darcie, what time do you want people over Saturday night?"

She lifted one eyebrow, letting him know she hadn't missed the change of subject.

"After the game ends. So you have to attend the game to know," she said pointedly. Her tone changed when she turned and said, "Anne, we'd love to have you and Everett join us for food and conversation after the high school basketball game."

"That's very nice of you, but—"

"Think about it. And now we really should get Vanessa back to town."

As the women got in the truck, Quince found himself beside Vanessa, who said in a low tone, "You don't always change the subject to help other people. Sometimes you are trying to help yourself."

But possibly not low enough, because he was pretty sure Anne heard it.

"HAVE A NICE afternoon?" Quince asked her, once they and Everett were inside.

"Yes. Now I've got to catch up on work." She went directly to the desk, waking the computer.

"What are you working on this time?"

Had she caught an undercurrent to his tone?

Must be her imagination.

"Looking at ordering seed."

She'd done most of the order in December, but had held back some of the tiny budget, hoping to fill in with late-breaking deals.

With the right seed, a good—better yet, a great—growing season, and a lot of luck, it could be a first step toward getting back on track.

Without those elements, this might be the last seed-buying she did.

As if his thoughts had gone in the same general direction, Everett said, "Don't pounce on the cheapest just because they're cheapest."

She'd have to be six-ways from stupid to do that. She clamped her tongue between her teeth.

Quince, however, said easily, "Anne doesn't seem the kind to overlook quality or to jump to a bad decision."

Everett looked surprised.

"I suppose not," he conceded.

By way of praise, it wasn't much. But it was better than she'd gotten from him before. She suspected the surprise was mostly that Quince had levered the words out of him. As the surprise wore off he'd probably try to take it back.

Well, she wouldn't let him.

CHAPTER ELEVEN

PPARENTLY THE SEED-BUYING didn't go well, because Anne was
edgy as the afternoon waned.

It got worse when Everett started grumbling about if they were
ever going to have supper, that some people lolled around having tea
all afternoon so maybe they weren't hungry, but honest working men
were.

She glared at him, but said nothing, working on the computer a
few more minutes before closing up.

Something clearly was wrong when she took a container out of the
fridge that he'd seen defrosting in there. Spaghetti sauce, he'd thought.
When she put it into a saucepan, her face drew tight, and she muttered
something about runny as water.

She put butter in another pan and started the heat, then pulled out
a flour canister and a measuring cup. She also had a pot full of water
going.

Her hands moved around like a pianist playing at double-time.
Then she started stirring the contents of that second pan in triple-time.

"Can I help?" Quince asked.

"No."

Figuring that applied only to activity around the stove, he began
setting the table, staying well out of her way.

After a few minutes, she pulled the second pan off the heat and
put its contents in a bowl on the counter.

She pulled out salad makings and alternated between that and the
pan with the sauce and the pot with the water.

She tested the temperature of what was in the bowl, did more with the salad, put pasta in the tall pot, then added what was in the bowl to the saucepan, all in record time.

"You sure I can't help?"

"I said no. And why are you grinning?"

Ah. He'd thought she wasn't aware of him. "Enjoying the dance you're doing."

"It's no dance. And nothing to enjoy."

Everett tutted. "My daddy always said never corner something you know is meaner than you are."

She turned on her great uncle-in-law. "If you're saying I'm meaner than you, you better remember that and quit riding me about things."

He snorted. "Didn't say you're meaner than *me*. But you're meaner than *him*, and he shouldn't be trying to corner you with questions day and night, night and day."

She opened her mouth, clearly thought better of whatever she'd been about to say, shot Quince a suspicious glare, as if she knew he was fighting laughter, then settled in with a narrow-eyed stare rein-forced with one hand on her hip, while the other kept stirring.

"That part's true. You *have* been badgering me with questions and you better stop it, because I *am* meaner than you."

She had a dash of flour across the ridge of her cheek, another dab on her nose, and a smear of something that might have been butter in a lock of her hair.

He wanted to laugh.

Even more, he wanted *her* to laugh.

He *really* wanted her to laugh.

Damn, it was getting to feel like he *needed* her to laugh.

If so, that need clearly wasn't going to be answered any time soon.

"She sure is meaner," Everett corroborated. "Especially this time of year."

She turned back to the stove, adjusting the heat under the tall pot.

"Why especially this time of year?" Quince asked, partly to keep the older man talking, partly because it would keep her riled, partly to distract his own thoughts about Anne.

"I'll tell you why. Because there isn't much real farming to do this time of year."

Her head snapped around again, though her hands kept going.

"No, hardly anything at all," she said with full sarcasm, "because after straining every resource to haul the end of last year's crop to market, it's not *real* farming to start marketing next year's crop, to analyze yield results and use that to adjust seed and crop plans, to try to line up credit—" She pulled in a sharp breath then spoke quickly. "—and of course trying to fix everything that broke last year. Hardly anything to do at all."

Everett didn't back down. "Like I said, not much real farming. It's mostly that computer and Internet and email nonsense."

Before that provocation could cause Anne to fire back, Quince stepped in. "But you've got stuff growing now, right? Wheat—I hear a lot of farmers plant wheat in the fall, then it goes dormant for the winter, but has a head-start growing in the spring."

Anne slanted a look at him that had him wanting to pat his shoulders to be sure he hadn't grown two heads.

"You heard, huh?" she muttered.

Everett said, "Most years we do, not this year."

"Why not this year?"

"Because we were harvesting right up to Thanksgiving."

Quince felt as if he were listening to a foreign language. He understood the words, but they did not convey to him the nuance they clearly conveyed to the other two. For them those words appeared to pack a wallop of emotion.

"Uh-huh," he said, out-neutralizing Switzerland. "That's interesting."

Everett snort. "Interesting? I'll tell you what it is—it's late. Real late. Damned near criminal late."

"I can't do anything about the weather," Anne snapped.

"Never said you could. Said November was late for harvesting."

She swung around. "Like you never said doing anything other than conventional tilling was idiotic."

"What I said was only an idiot wouldn't see his new method was a disaster waiting to happen—equipment won't get through that thick residue and—"

"It would if the equipment wasn't from half a century ago. Modern planters—"

"—you get a slow spring and you're planting in August. And disease—it'll grab hold and never let go with this no-till. Not to mention—"

Anne extended the spoon in her hand like a sword. "*I* never said no-till, and you know it, Everett Hooper. Conservation tillage, that's what I'm trying. You just hate any change, so you stop listening."

"If it ain't broke, don't fix it. If Chris hadn't started messing around with—"

"But he did. It *is* broke—and there might not be any fixing that."

For a beat, they all froze.

Then Anne jerked back around to the stove.

Everett looked down at the table.

In minutes, she served plates of steaming spaghetti with salads on the side.

Except for Quince's fill-in conversation, dinner was silent. And even he wasn't interested in what he was saying.

Anne left the table first, carrying her not-yet-empty plate to the sink. She began to clean up.

Everett moved only after he'd cleaned his plate. He left the kitchen, went to the front parlor, and closed that door after him.

Quince heaved a sigh. So much for putting his skills to work to tactfully draw them out on the state of the farm.

He'd picked up a fair amount despite not speaking the language. Enough, he decided as he took his and Everett's plates to the sink, that he might benefit from a farm-speak translator.

But first it was time for some plain talk with Everett Hooper.

"YOU KNOW SHE'S not going to make a mistake like buying the

cheapest seed, so why say it?" he said to the older man.

"What I know and what I don't know are no concern of—"

"So why say it?" His repeated question cut through the bluster. "You insulted her."

"*Insulted?*" Everett sounded incensed, but also surprised.

"Insulted and disrespected all the work she does here."

"I did not—"

"She's holding together this place you love single-handed. You better appreciate her more."

"Appreciate? Seems to me you're appreciatin' her enough for two men."

Quince had pushed too far, and now he was caught in his own words. "That's none of your business."

"It is if you go taking her away."

"She'd never leave this place."

Damn.

As soon as he said the words, he knew he should have said something else. *I'm not trying to take her away.* Or even back to *It's none of your business.* Anything that didn't sound as if he were wishing she would.

"I'm watching my program," Everett said. "Go away."

It seemed like the best course of action at the moment.

SHE WAS HEARING voices.

First, she could have sworn she heard Everett and Quince from the front parlor. Though why Quince would have bearded the dragon in his den she had no idea.

And now, lying in bed when she should be snatching every second of sleep possible, the voices were in her head. In her memory.

There's something in Quince's past.

She didn't care.

It was in the past. If it existed at all. And who knew if it really did.

But that didn't matter. None of that mattered. Because he was their boarder. Paying his rent on time was all that mattered to her and so far, so good.

Just because he'd been prying into her life—past and present—didn't mean she should do the same. It might even encourage him to do more.

Far, far better to demonstrate to him how they could coexist in the same house without prying apart each others' pasts.

And besides that, it wasn't any of her business.

Hooper Farm. That was her business.

If it ain't broke, don't fix it. If Chris hadn't started messing around with—

But he did. It is broke—and there might not be any fixing that.

She and Everett had never even come close to saying those things before and there'd been good reason for that.

CHAPTER TWELVE

WHEN SHE CAME out to get in the farm truck Saturday, Quince was hunkered down, taking photos of it from a low angle.

"Sorry. I need to remove your model."

She sounded cheerful. No, amend that. She sounded determined to sound cheerful.

"Where are you going?"

"Need to check how the north field is draining."

"Can I come?"

She hesitated. "Suit yourself."

Then she watched—clearly impatient—while he brushed off the passenger seat.

"There's got to be more dirt in this truck than out in the fields," he said, wondering about her determination to sound cheerful.

"Possibly. First rule of farming is dirt's everywhere, you're living on a farm, so get used to it. Besides the truck has the advantage of four wheels. You want to ride or you want to stay?"

"Ride."

"Then get in. Have to get there before the light goes."

She treated these farm roads like the Autobahn.

Flat. That's what everyone said about the Midwestern prairie.

Pancakes, flounders, tables. Flat, flat, flat.

That's what he'd always thought about Illinois.

Not anymore.

Not after being driven across it in a pickup without great suspension. Or possibly any suspension.

He was pitching and rolling like he was on the deck of a boat in a squall.

Not Anne.

He wished he could say it was because she was clinging to the steering wheel. But her hands rested comfortably on the clunky thing. She wasn't using it for balance, just to steer the truck.

She adjusted to the dips and rolls with no apparent effort. Almost anticipating them, as if she could feel it through the soles of her feet.

Or through her soul.

She belonged here. She'd grown roots that were deep and strong.

No matter where she'd come from originally, she belonged here now.

"Hello? Are you awake over there?" Anne's voice jolted him.

"Yeah, yeah." They'd stopped. "Is this where we get out?"

"This is where *you* get out—temporarily. Second rule of farming—close every gate after yourself."

"Ah. The Grandy Rule."

"Yes, though Rule 2B should be don't go in Grandy's pen. Ever. Anyway, to close this gate, you first have to earn your keep by getting out and opening it."

When he got back in after the truck passed through and he closed the gate, he said, "Hey, if you're giving me farming lessons you must think I have potential as a farmer."

She gave him a where-did-*that*-come-from look.

"C'mon. You said your family's in Foreign Service, so you couldn't have grown up farming. You had to start somewhere, too. Unless you had a spare farm in the family to practice on."

She chuckled. Briefly.

"Not hardly. It's like Chitmell said about earning a million as a farmer by starting with two million. Anyone who has money in Foreign Service had it before they got in."

"And your parents didn't."

"No, they didn't. I'm not saying they're poor, but it's not the extravagant, non-stop party lifestyle people think of. There are a lot of social functions, but they're more likely to have the regional equivalent of pigs-in-a-blanket than caviar."

"What about your siblings? Older? Younger?"

"Younger sister and brother. You?"

"Half-brother and two half-sisters. All older. Didn't know them at all growing up." She shot him a look, but he was used to skirting this. He gave his usual shrug. "Never crossed paths much. Did your sister and brother go into the family business?"

"No, though both work overseas. They inherited the family wanderlust. I'm the odd duck who didn't."

"Would have been tough if you had. Wanderlust would be a definite drawback for a farmer or a farmer's wife. You sure you didn't suppress it when you fell in love wi—"

"Absolutely sure." She looked out the driver's window as she added, "His being a farmer was one of the initial attractions."

"You always wanted to live on a farm?"

"I always wanted to grow things."

He started to ask another question, then spotted her slight smile and shut up, letting the silence give her room.

"In second grade, when we were stationed stateside, the teacher had us put beans in three Styrofoam cups," she said, "each with a wet paper towel, and we put one in a window, one in the middle of the room, and one behind a screen. We watered them every day—that was my job—and each week we measured them. I was fascinated. I don't think I'd ever associated the plants and trees all around us with starting from a seed until then, much less our food. We had green beans that night and I remember taking them apart, finding the seed within the bean." She grinned briefly. "I was told not to play with my food. When I explained, they said, okay, but I still had to eat the beans.

"After the first couple weeks, I started more cups at home—a whole forest of them—experimenting with the amount of water and what kind of water. And then using soil. When the weather warmed up, I transplanted them to a little plot behind our townhouse in Maryland, outside of D.C."

He had a feeling he knew where this was going.

"We were transferred that summer. Of course I never saw them fully grown. I tried a few things in pots in the apartment we had next, but there was a drought and a foreigner's daughter using water for plants was frowned on. When we cycled back to D.C. and our townhouse, I planted the whole plot. Every inch. Not just beans, but tomatoes, carrots, onions, garlic, miniature apple trees, a miniature peach tree. The second year I started pumpkins and…"

Her enthusiasm fell off the cliff of memory.

"We were transferred, of course, and the house was rented. When we came back the renters had pulled out everything and paved it over to park another car. I never had the heart to find out if my parents knew or approved it. After that, I didn't plant anything personally until I came here."

"Personally?"

"I did projects in classes."

"Classes?"

She glanced at him. "I got my degree in agronomy with a minor in agribusiness management from the University of Wisconsin. I was working with a co-op when I met Chris."

"And after you married, you started growing things again."

"Mmm. Before."

She was going to stop. No way. "He drew you in to the farm from the start?"

"Oh, yes." She sounded as breathy over it as some women would be over jewels. "Our second date was riding the tractor with him. From the start the farm was part of our relationship. How could it not be? When something on the farm needs attention, it needs it right then. It's not like you can slide it in a folder and put it in your desk until Monday. It has to be dealt with. Especially at that time, when Hooper Farm still had livestock. So dating worked around that."

"A lot of women wouldn't have like that."

She shrugged. "Then they're not realistic. There's a saying that when you marry a farmer, you marry the farm, too."

"You liked that, didn't you?"

"Yeah, I did. I do."

"But now the farm's in trouble."

He knew it was a risk, and when she hesitated, he thought he'd need a way to regain ground.

But, finally, she said, "It's not a secret and it's not the only one in the county. We ran on cash last season, but it's going to be hard to do that this year as long as Everett remains so stubborn."

He frowned. "I thought farms used credit—took out a loan to buy seed and stuff in the spring, then paid it back when the crop came."

"That's how it usually works."

"You don't want to take out a loan?"

She made a harsh sound she might have intended for a laugh. "I have been all over this county and a half-dozen others looking for financing. We're caught in a Catch-22. They won't give Everett a loan, because he's not doing the farming. They won't give me a loan because they say I haven't built up sufficient credit history. Plus, I don't own the land, so I don't have collateral."

"But you've been farming alone more than three years, plus before that—"

"Chris was the farmer. Anything I did then didn't count."

"How does Chitmell figure in to this?"

She shot him a surprised look, then tried to make her face blank and her voice flat. "He declined to renew our loan a year ago."

She made it sound like a dispassionate business transaction. Having seen Chitmell and how she responded to him, there was more to it.

"The other banks you've been talking to?"

"Start off polite, but pretty soon it comes around to their wondering why I'd go to anybody other than Chitmell, since Hoopers have done business with First Security Guaranty since the dawn of time. They're skittish in general, even more skittish about a woman farming alone, and with that…"

He considered that as they bumped over the entrance to a field.

"You think Chitmell's said things to these other bankers?" he said.

"I don't have any proof."

"I didn't ask if you have proof. I asked what you think."

"Yeah, I do. But maybe I'm making excuses, looking for somebody to blame."

He doubted that. He also doubted Chitmell was operating strictly from chauvinism. He'd dealt with his kind before and profit was invariably their prime motivation, with power mixing in.

Hell, he'd been fathered by a man just like that.

"Maybe the most frustrating thing is I've got money," Anne said. "Chris's life insurance. I want to put it into the farm, have from the start, but Everett won't discuss it. Doesn't want a woman *keeping* him—that's what he says, the stubborn old coot."

"Maybe that's what he says, but I'd guess it's that he doesn't want you to be without any options because you've sunk every last penny into this farm."

"That's what he's done."

"All the more reason to listen to him when he doesn't want you to."

"I believe in this farm, I believe in *me*. I can make it work. If he'd only listen."

"He's not going to, though, is he? So what does that leave?"

He knew she'd shut off the conversation even before she said, "Here we are. It'll be muddy, so stay in the truck."

"I'll survive a little mud."

HE DID SURVIVE, though it wasn't a little mud. It was a *lot* of mud in a slippery, slimy tour of a field's drainage.

His shoes did not survive.

His assistant was shipping him another pair.

In the meantime, he'd just bought stop-gap tennis shoes and was leaving the discount store near the Interstate in the next town over from Drago when he heard his name called.

Vanessa, Josh, and his kids were entering the store.

"Oh, good. I want to talk to you, Quince." Vanessa looked at the kids. "If you shop for the other things first, I'll be there to help with the supplies for Groundhog Day, if that's acceptable."

"Sure thing, right, kids?" Josh said. "Let's go get the boring stuff out of the way while Vanessa talks to Quince."

Quince bought her a small coffee at the snack area and they took facing seats at a plastic table.

"Groundhog Day supplies?"

"For a project on the seasons. I want to talk to you."

"You said that. We talk every day."

"About Zeke-Tech. Not about other things. I said I wasn't going to be a respite for you."

"Vanessa—"

"We had a very nice afternoon at Hooper Farm the other day."

"Glad to hear it."

She looked at him directly.

He sat still under her regard, not letting her see that he'd braced for questions.

She didn't ask any.

"When I first came here—" She broke off and considered a moment, then started again. "When Zeke first made me come here, I thought of it as only space. In Drago and all around Drago."

"That's what appealed to me about a farm. Having elbow room."

She shook her head. "But it's not elbow room, because it not just space. It's ... I don't know how to say it. It's people and their homes and their work and their lives and their dreams. It's all there, just like anywhere else. Except maybe it's even more here because people don't have up as many walls, as many dividers between them and everyone else. Because they need each other and help each other.

"Josh fought me on putting the computers in the lab into cubicles, because he knew people here didn't want dividers. They didn't want to be that separate."

"Then he doesn't know Anne Hooper. And Everett Hooper," he added, fast enough that it shouldn't have been recognizable as an afterthought.

"Zeke knew Everett Hooper from when he was a boy."

"Yeah, he did. And Everett isn't a total loner, but—"

"Anne does not appear to be, either. She is friends with Jennifer."

"She works for her."

Vanessa turned up the power on her disconcerting directness. "You work for Zeke, technically. You're friends."

He grinned. "Okay, okay. You win."

She acknowledged his acquiescence with a nod. "We're becoming friends, too, I think."

"I'm sure Jennifer—"

"Not Jennifer. Anne. She and I are becoming friends."

That caught him. Not quite a surprise. Certainly not an unpleasant one. Yet, still out of left field.

"Good," he said, because she was still looking at him. "That's good. For both of you."

She declined her head then raised it in a measured, single nod. "I didn't finish telling you about when I first came to Drago."

Vanessa was becoming downright chatty. He might have preferred a topic that didn't pin him to the wall with those intelligent eyes, but he could only be happy for her.

"Tell away," he invited.

"It felt like something was closing in on me."

He felt his forehead crease as his brows rose. "What?"

"I didn't know. Not when I thought there was just space here. After a while, after Josh and the kids, and Mrs. R ... that's when I realized how wrong I was about just space and what I felt closing in around me. It was people. I was afraid of it. But I learned to like it. People needing me. People helping me. People wanting to be my friend. People—"

She looked at him so directly, so openly.

He felt a *ka-chunk* in his chest. A hard, rapid beat he usually only got when the craziest of the crazies in Beltway traffic tried their best to turn him into road kill.

But there wasn't anything Vanessa could say to him that should set off an alarm in his system the way traffic crazies could. They'd known each other so long and she'd never pried or prodded or—

"—not letting me hide out any more. Like you've been doing for a long, long time."

SOMEHOW IT HAD become routine for Quince to spend most of his time at Hooper Farm in the kitchen.

Mornings, when he didn't have calls to make or appointments to get to, he helped clear up after breakfast, then read or worked on his laptop.

Anne couldn't complain about it. He didn't talk or otherwise intrude. Except by being there.

Evenings when he stayed home—*here*, when he stayed *here*— he would work on his laptop at the kitchen table while she worked at the computer desk.

Though he wouldn't be in the kitchen working tomorrow night or the night after.

He'd told her that a few days ago. He'd be away two nights because of a big Zeke-Tech event. He, Zeke, and Vanessa were leaving early in the morning for Virginia. The event was the next day and they'd return the day after that.

So she'd have the kitchen to herself then. But not now.

"Isn't your room comfortable?" she burst out.

He looked up, a questioning lift of his eyebrows. "It's very comfortable."

"Then why do you spend so much time here?"

She shouldn't have asked that. Shouldn't have given him the opening. Or maybe it wasn't an opening. Maybe it was a needy way of trying to get him to say something—

"The novelty."

"*Novelty?*"

"I haven't spent much time in kitchens."

A jet-setting mother who left him with his big-hitter father. Not a childhood filled with baking brownies with Mom in the kitchen.

She was *not* going to ask him about that. None of her business.

"Even when you and Zeke and Vanessa were starting out? The legend says you lived on noodles."

"We did. Microwavable noodles. Everything was microwavable, except the coffee. We set the microwave and coffeemaker up on boxes in one corner. That was as close as we got to a kitchen."

"But your house in Virginia…?"

"Gourmet kitchen. At least that's what the real estate agent said. It does have a good microwave. And one hell of a coffeemaker. I like this kitchen better."

She looked around at the worn surfaces and outdated appliances. "Why?"

"It's seen life. And family."

There didn't seem to be anything to say to that except a grunt conveyeing she'd heard his words.

They settled back into work.

An hour later, as she went to refill her coffee mug, she caught a glimpse of his screen as she passed.

It was enough to stop her.

That was *not* for Zeke-Tech.

"What are you looking at that for?" she asked.

"Reading up on growing oats in Illinois. Ever considered expanding your repertoire?"

"We seed oats as a cover crop. *I* seed oats as a cover crop."

"But you grew the oats to make the oatmeal you fed me and gave to Vanessa and the others. It's delicious."

"Yeah, we have a small plot of oats for us. But you liked that oatmeal because of all the other stuff in it, not the oats."

"The extras were great, but the oatmeal itself was the best I've ever had. Why not grow more?"

Her mouth lifted slightly. "There's a reason farmers around here grow corn and soybeans. Oats don't pay us as well."

"I'm still going to learn about oat-growing."

Despite herself, she chuckled. "Knock yourself out, Mr. Smooth."

He groaned. "You've heard that already? Can't decide if it's better or worse than Everett calling me slick."

She waggled her hand. He groaned again.

Time for her to get back to work.

If he wanted to do his studying up on oats in the kitchen because he liked the novelty of a working kitchen, that was no skin off her nose.

She could concentrate on her work just fine.

Just fine.

EVERETT, THE ORIGINAL tech-hater, had the computer on when she came downstairs Wednesday morning.

That was why she stopped in her tracks. Shocked that he knew how to turn it on.

She was sure that was why.

Not because of the voice she heard coming from the speakers.

Quince.

Supper had been quiet last night. So had the kitchen after Everett went off to watch TV and she began her work.

Strictly because she'd gotten used to having another person in the house. Which also explained why she'd tossed and turned last night.

She'd been so restless overnight, she'd succumbed to temptation and hit the snooze button a couple times this morning.

Why was it that getting up before sunrise seemed so much darker and harder some mornings than others?

Thanks to her late start, she'd prepared breakfast wearing her bathrobe—drawing a few pointed comments from Everett—then went back up to get ready for her appointment two counties over, which would be followed by another round of errands.

"What's going on?" she asked him.

"Shh. I can't hear with you yammering."

That was why she stayed to listen. And watch. It was the only way to get an answer to her question.

Everett did contribute a few words during periods of sustained applause. "Release." "Streaming." And in a burst of loquacity, "Quince set it up. Showed me how to run this thing."

By then she'd figured out that this was the big event—the official announcement of a new release from Zeke-Tech.

What specifically it was, she had no idea. If she'd concentrated she could have handled the tech talk. But she was less interested in what they were presenting than how they went about it.

Quince and Zeke were on a full-blown stage, sitting in easy chairs angled so they could see each other and the audience could see them, against a simple backdrop of drapes. Flanking the chairs were huge screens that provided close-up viewing for the live audience and the— well, she had no idea how many people watched on computers and devices around the world.

Zeke was the star, of course.

But she found herself focusing on how Quince kept the metaphorical spotlight perfectly centered on Zeke. He fed him questions, he filled in non-tech speak when needed, he gave Zeke confidence and ease by preserving the illusion that it was just the two of them talking, at the same time he made each member of the audience feel as if she or he were a privileged third member in that conversation.

When the camera went to Vanessa, standing in the wings, Quince smoothed over her abrupt pull-back and drew her in with a few questions, until it seemed natural to shift back to Zeke, leaving the last impression of Vanessa as assured and comfortable.

Quince was good at this.

No, he was great at this.

If it were the only thing he did for Zeke-Tech, she could see that he must be hugely valuable.

But of course this wasn't the only thing he did.

She supposed at some level she'd understood that he must be good at what he did.

Understood, but hadn't felt it.

Not really.

From that first moment of seeing him, she'd focused on what he wasn't, what he couldn't do, what he didn't know. She hadn't seen what he did know, what he could do, who he was.

Because she needed to be so focused on the farm. Because she couldn't afford to be distracted by anything.

Anyone.

But now it was as if the computer screen had reached out and grabbed her shoulders, giving her a good shake and saying, "Look. *Look.* For these few moments, look at Peter Quincy III and see him."

And she did.

CHAPTER THIRTEEN

AT ZEKE'S INSTIGATION, the deluxe town car delivering them from O'Hare back to Drago became the site of an impromptu executive meeting of CEO, COO, and CFO.

It wasn't the first time the three of them had met on the go.

In the pre-Drago days it would have been because Zeke wanted to get these meetings out of the way so he had more time to invent more things Vanessa had to finance and Quince had to make and sell.

Now Zeke wanted to make use of this time so it freed him to spend more with Darcie.

Not that the man had stopped inventing. By Quince's reckoning, the next release event would come up by mid-summer if he couldn't slow the process.

He wanted to slow the pace partly because the public was hard to excite when these events came too close together. *New! Exciting! Revolutionary!* Started to feel humdrum when trumpeted daily.

Also partly because it took a whole lot of work to pull these off.

Not that he could complain much about this one. His assistant had done a fine job handling the onsite preparations.

Which probably meant she'd be moving on soon.

Well, he'd make sure hiring her replacement was among her duties.

"…don't you think so, Quince?"

"I know you've put a lot of thought into it, Vanessa. And I trust your judgment."

"You weren't listening."

Six months ago, he would have gotten away with that.

He opened his mouth but she raised a hand, as if to tell him not to bother. "I said recommended that, rather than bringing business cars in from Virginia, we arrange with Stenner Autos for a fleet here. Folding in a repair agreement it would make it more economical, as well as generate good will locally."

"Good thinking."

"Speaking of doing business locally," Zeke said, "What about using Chitmell's bank? What's the name of it? Trusted, Secure something or other."

He directed the question to Vanessa, but Quince spoke up before she could.

"He's not a good choice."

"You're the one who introduced us," Zeke objected with surprise. Quince was aware of Vanessa's questioning look.

"Introduced, not endorsed."

"But—"

"Have you heard something that makes you reluctant to do business with him?" Vanessa asked.

He met her gaze. She was getting the hang of reading people faster than he ever would have believed. Sometimes he missed the old, unaware Vanessa. Especially when he wasn't sure of his own motives.

"Not directly," he said.

She gave a slight nod.

"What about the benefit of generating good will by keeping things local and the insights someone local can give us?" Zeke asked.

"We benefit from local perspective and good will most if we're doing business with the right people," Vanessa said. "I'll get recommendations from Jennifer. She has broad experience with how local banks treat businesses. I'll see what she says, then we can decide."

"*You* can decide," Zeke amended. "I only brought the guy up because Quince introduced us New Year's Eve."

"And that's a good point, too, Zeke," Quince said. "You don't want to be seen as playing favorites in your hometown. Far better to let Vanessa and me take on the role of saying yes or no to the locals."

"Yeah." Zeke brightened visibly. "I like that."

ANNE SAT AT the café counter, nursing her mug of coffee.

Her appointment had been yet another bust. She'd knocked off her list of errands by rote. She should have gone home and worked. Instead, she'd come in here to indulge herself by paying for coffee that someone else made.

The chatter around her was mostly about yesterday's Zeke-Tech event.

A year ago maybe a handful of people in Drago would have known it had even happened.

Now, the café seasonal conversation standbys of the weather, the high school basketball team, and the Chicago Cubs' prospects when baseball started were jostled by commentary on technical advances, stock prices, and how Zeke-Tech was positioning itself in the market.

"Here he is!" called out Ted Warinke from down the counter.

Anne turned and saw a grinning Quince enter, wearing his beautiful coat that looked no worse for its hay dust shower. It must have cost the earth in dry cleaning to have it looking this good. Though dry cleaning had nothing to do with the fit of the shoulders or—

Tailoring. Really, really good tailoring.

Ted and Mrs. Richards got up to meet him by the door and shake his hand. Over Ted's shoulder, he met her eyes and she found herself smiling back at him.

Amid congratulations and general comments, he sat next to her, with the others moving down a spot.

Had that happened by accident? She couldn't be sure.

He ordered another round for everybody and while Loris behind the counter was carrying that out, she quietly said, "They're right. You were really good yesterday."

"You watched? You thought it went well?"

"It went great. I can't believe—Never mind."

"You can't leave something like that dangling. You can't believe what? That we used the blue background again? That we couldn't get

Vanessa to come on stage? That I stumbled over the name of darned thing twice—well, one and a half times."

"Twice."

He grimaced. "Fine. Twice. What can't you believe?"

"That you did it so well so fast."

"Fast? We've been working on this for more than a year."

"The software, yeah, but—"

"The release presentation, too."

"But you said last week you were working with Zeke on the release announcement."

"*A* release announcement. Not *this* release announcement. Was talking to him about the one after the next one. Pulling these together is a process, a long process. If I don't get with Zeke when he's in the throes of developing something new, by the time it's released he's lost all enthusiasm for it. Heck, he can barely remember what it is. So I get with him early to capture what excites him about it so I can toss that back to him and rekindle that excitement for the release. Being there early-on also lets me start the ball rolling on what we'll need for manufacturing, packaging, marketing. So when—What? What's that look for?"

"It's like farming. Each season is so different and demands your attention. Yet in each season you need to think about the others or you'll miss important indicators and be behind when the others roll around."

He pulled his head back, studying her. She refused to fidget under that examination.

Or under the beam of the slow, spreading smile that followed it.

"That's right." He sounded pleased. "I never would have thought of it being like farming, but you're absolutely right. The planting, growing, harvesting, preparing, then repeating. And rotating, balancing, so you don't deplete the soil."

She was smiling back at him.

She could feel it. In the muscles around her mouth, at the corners of her eyes. And somewhere deeper.

She slid off the stool, going off the side away from him, finding her feet barely in time.

He reached for her, as if she might fall, but she stepped back, proving she wouldn't.

"I have to go. Just saw the time. No, Loris, thanks, I can't stay for another coffee. Have to run." She'd pulled on her parka and mittens with the speed of practice. She waved down the line at the counter. "See you. Bye."

Quince had turned on his stool, watching her.

"See you at home."

She flashed a look at him at those words, then away. Already pivoting for the door.

QUINCE WATCHED HER go with his head saying don't make something out of nothing.

Outside the door she barreled into Darcie, in uniform.

Before his muscles did more than twitch, Darcie planted her feet wide and kept them both from going down.

They had an exchange, accompanied by smiles—Anne's a little tight—then she continued on her way, while Darcie came in.

Spotting the empty stool next to him she took it, unzipping her jacket, as she exchanged greetings with the group. "Loris, you are an angel in heaven, already having a coffee ready."

"Thank Quince. He bought a round for the place and Anne left before she drank hers. So you've got her leavings. Clean mug, though." She drifted toward the other end of the counter where the Drago Dragons' latest basketball game was being dissected.

Darcie picked up the mug, toasted it toward Quince and said, "I thank you. When it comes to enjoying an alternative to the coffee down at the station, I'm definitely not too proud to take Anne's leavings. She did seem in a hurry."

She glinted a speculative look at him over the rim of the mug.

"You're welcome. Still on duty? Zeke will be disappointed. He was after the driver all the way from O'Hare to make better time. He might have mentioned it to the pilot of the plane, too."

She *t'ched*. "I told him I wouldn't be home until after eight tonight."

"He forgot, if he heard you at all. In fact, he tried to finagle an early departure last night until Brenda reminded him he was committed to meetings this morning."

"If Brenda won't move here, Zeke-Tech's next invention better be a way to clone her. You all did great yesterday, by the way. I already told Zeke on the phone to tell you and Vanessa you both deserve raises. I know, I know, he forgot to tell you that, too. But I mean it. You're miracle workers. Vanessa in the financial bowels of Zeke-Tech and you in making my husband appear like an easy-going *bon vivant* instead of the dear curmudgeon genius he is. And, yes, I did notice how you changed the subject away from Anne Hooper."

Even as he admired her delivery of that last part—didn't draw a breath, didn't change tone—he faced the reality that either the women in this town were sharper than he was used to or he was really slipping. He'd have to work on that. Especially with them infecting Vanessa.

In the meantime, he had another approach to try.

In the same easy tone that wouldn't be easy to overhear yet gave no indication they might be trying to keep their conversation from the others, he said, "You want to talk about her? Then tell me what her husband was like."

Her eyebrows hiked.

She sipped her coffee.

Spaced-out, thoughtful, tormenting sips.

Finally, she said, "Seemed nice enough."

"Seemed?"

"Don't read anything into that. He was a few years ahead of me, from kindergarten through high school, but I never got to know him. He kept himself to himself, if you know what I mean."

"Even after he married?"

"Yeah. Pretty much. I never knew Anne to do more than say hello to in the grocery store until she started working for Jen at the dealership. Maybe it was different with her fellow farmers. They help each other at busy times or if something big comes up, that kind of thing. So, once she was accepted as part of that community, they'd get to know her real well. Although..."

He waited. But, c'mon. How long did she need to think this over? "Although, what?"

"I know a lot of the farm families better than I knew Anne until recently. Maybe that's because of the other families' kids—so they're in town a lot for school things. But, then I was thinking, too, that I've probably known Everett better all along than I ever knew Chris. He was just so quiet."

So, once she was accepted as part of that community, they'd get to know her real well.

But what if she hadn't been accepted? Farmers spent a lot of time alone by the demands of their job. Plus, she'd been an outsider. With a quiet husband. Who died unexpectedly. So she had to work like crazy. That had to have kept her apart. Add in her great-uncle's pride and he had to wonder how isolated she'd been.

And then there were the finances of Hooper Farm.

"Quiet, yet he went on a spending spree not long before he died that left the farm in a hole?" he asked.

She studied him a moment. "That's what I hear. But—"

"Darcie. C'mon down here. We need somebody to settle this," Mrs. Richards called. "These two can't agree if it was four years ago or five when the Dragons lost the game that would have sent them to the playoffs on that horrible foul call by Oren DeWitt from over in Lee County."

"Four," Loris said.

"Five," disputed Ted.

Darcie put down her empty mug. "Keeper of the peace, that's me."

She patted his arm as she passed him on her way to arbitrate the dispute.

It almost felt like compassion.

CHAPTER FOURTEEN

ANNE SAW QUINCE'S car slow when it crested the rise.

But then he covered the rest of the distance to where her car was nose-down into the ditch beside the road in record time.

She waved him past, emphatic movements telling him not to stop.

She did not want to talk to him—to anybody. She was on the brink. If she lost it, she didn't not want an audience.

Especially not him.

Especially since he had to know she'd burst into tears that first day, no matter how discreet he'd been about ignoring it.

He pulled over and parked.

Then he got out.

"What are you doing? Didn't you see me waving you on?"

"I saw," he said. "I'm stopping to see if you're okay, and if you need help."

"What I *need* is a tow. How are you going to help with *that?*"

"The more important question was the first one: Are you okay?"

"This piece of junk—"

"Forget the car. I've already—"

"I can't forget—"

"—called a tow truck. But are you—"

"A tow truck? I can't afford a tow truck. Not to mention afford to fix this damned thing."

"That'll work out." He gripped her shoulders. "Just tell me you're not hurt."

She shook off his hold without taking her glare from the car. "I'm fine. As long as you or some other miracle-worker can tell me how the hell it's going to work out."

"I'll pay—No, okay, don't say it. I see that expression. You won't accept a gift. Fine. Borrow the money. Enough for the tow and repairs. I'll charge you interest rates that would make a Wall Street banker blush. Okay?"

"And go in personal debt with no prospect of getting out of it?"

He stared at her an instant, then swung away, swearing.

Long and proficient—at least from what she could tell, since it was all under his breath. When he turned back, he crossed his arms over his chest, his eyes still hot, but his face under control.

"Tell me what happened?"

"The engine just stopped. Everything stopped. No steering. I braked, but with going downhill and the curve…"

"Thank God you weren't hurt. It could have been a lot worse."

"It's doesn't matter how bad it is, since I have no way to pay for repairs. No. Way."

She hadn't meant to say that. Hadn't meant to say any of what she'd been blurting out to him.

She couldn't do anything about that, but she wouldn't cry. She would *not* cry.

"Trade repairs for additional work for Stenner Autos. A sort of advance on pay," he said.

The swirl in her head stopped as if someone had flipped a switch. Shreds of worry and fragments of despair, no longer suspended by the swirl, began to settle, like flakes in a snow globe.

She licked her chapped lips. "That might work."

"It will work."

"Probably." That was as far as she was going. She looked at him then, to be sure he understood that, and saw him—really saw him— here for the first time.

He wore that charcoal gray top coat that had to be cashmere from the way it made her fingers itch to stroke it. A gray and deep blue paisley scarf—more cashmere—filled in the neckline. It could have looked feminine, but of course it didn't. And leather shoes that probably cost more than the tow and repairs combined.

The idiot.

"You shouldn't be let out on your own."

He blinked. "Where'd that come from?"

"Look at you." She amended that. For clarity's sake only. "Look at the way you're dressed."

He looked down. "So?"

"You might be fine to go from limo to boardroom in *Virginia*—and I'm not even so sure about that, since it's winter there, too. What happens if the limo breaks down? Huh? But no way is it okay for Illinois, with nothing to break the wind, nothing to stop the cold. No hat—are you nuts? Do you know how much heat you lose through your head? Not even your ears covered. It would serve you right if you got frostbite. And those shoes. It's bad enough you aren't wearing boots, but slick soles? That's insane."

She propped her mittened hands on hips well-padded by her parka. "Not even gloves. That's so basic—even kindergartners know to wear mittens. At least have the sense to put your hands in your coat pockets as long as you're standing out here."

His mouth quirked. "No pockets. Ruins the line."

"Oh, for—Then get back in your car. Better yet, drive to the house."

"Sure. We can do that."

"Not me." In that tiny space? Right next to—But that wasn't the issue. *She* wasn't the one inappropriately dressed. Parka over layers, mittens, ear warmer, scarf and hood. She was fine.

"Then I'm staying. Without gloves."

She sighed. "Take my mittens. I'll put my hands in my pockets."

She started tugging them off—he'd be lucky to get half a hand in each, his hands were that much bigger than hers, but it would be something.

"No."

She looked up at that tone. "Quince—"

"No."

"The sun's going to set fast and frostbite is nothing to fool with."

"So get in my car."

"No. But you go ahead and—"

"Both of us or neither of us. Put your mittens back on. End of debate. But I'll tell you what. I will put my hands in your pockets."

The whirl was back, not in her thoughts this time. It seemed to be centered in the pit of her stomach.

"Since frostbite isn't anything to fool with," he added.

Frostbite.

Not an issue with her right now.

"Fine. Last thing I need is to have to take care of a frost-bit male."

His mouth quirked again, but he had it straight when he took the first step toward her. After that she didn't look at his mouth.

She kept her hands at her side, her gaze averted as he slid his hands into the parka pockets. He had to reach over and back to get the right angle, since the pockets were slanted for her use. It brought him close.

Too close.

Far too close.

Through the layers she seemed to feel the firmness of his chest. She certainly felt his breath, warm across her forehead.

If she looked up, with him right *here*...

She crossed her arms at her waist as a buffer.

His hands spread inside the pockets, seeming to grip her hips. Was the angle really so awkward that he needed something to hold onto to keep his hands in the pockets? But even if it was...

"This isn't going to work. I can't—" She backed away, her parka riding up as she pulled free from his hands. "Uh, I can't see the tow truck coming this way."

"Do you need to?"

"Yes," she said curtly. "You didn't have a precise location, so we might have to flag them down."

He looked up and down the otherwise empty road, but said, "Okay. Then I'll stand behind you."

She hesitated.

He balled his hands against the cold.

She pivoted, arms once more crossed at her waist.

His hands slid into her pockets more easily from this angle. He was right behind her. That cashmere coat must be warmer than it looked, because it had just cut her chill factor.

She no longer had her nose practically in his paisley scarf, but he was flush up against her back. This was—

"No better," she muttered.

"They're still cold," he said, apparently interpreting her escaped words as referring to his hands. "Put your hands in the pockets, too. That should help."

Help what?

"Heat up my hands," he added, as if he'd heard her question.

It would help warm his hands. And keep her hands warmer, too. And since she might need to help the tow truck driver, that was practical.

"Damned coat," she muttered as she added her mitten-clad fists to the pockets.

"Don't be so hard on my coat. It's all part of the presentation."

She half turned on the instinct to look at him, then stopped. But she did welcome the topic. "Presentation? Like the one you guys gave yesterday."

"Sort of. A lot of business is a kind of presentation. What you show to the world, what this coat or a suit shows, that's part of the presentation." His fingertips had found the tops of her mittens, sliding inside, against the backs of her hands. "Who you are is inside. Protected."

She shivered.

"Sorry," he said. "Want me to—?"

"No." If his hands were that cold—cold enough to make her shiver—he needed every bit of warmth he could get.

"Because the last thing you need is a tenant with frostbit hands." His voice seemed to be right at her ear. She didn't turn her head to check.

"That's right."

They stood like that, not moving. Except she felt the rhythm of his breathing, felt as if she took it inside her.

"That's quite a sight," he said.

She turned her head to look, bringing her cheek against the warmth and softness of the cashmere.

"Looks like a field of icicles," he added.

She tried to snort. It came out breathy, vulnerable. She spoke fast. "If icicles were a cash crop, we'd be doing fine."

That was breathy, too, and said more than she wanted to.

But he let it pass. Let it drift away, just like the vapor of their breathing.

There. Together. Then gone.

They remained like that.

How long?

She didn't know.

The sun was setting. She should be thinking about the temperature dropping. About how much longer before she'd have to put common sense over some inarticulate disinclination to get in his car.

Instead, they stayed there, watching.

The red ball of the sun spread at the horizon, bleeding across the snow, blazing Quince's field of icicles into a field of flames.

"That's something," he said, low.

"It's everything."

She felt him shifting. He was turning her. Or she was turning. Inside the circle of his arms.

Turning to him—

A beep jerked her back.

The tow truck. The lights coming down the hill toward them.

Closer and closer.

He released her and drew his hands out of her pockets.

QUINCE SLOWED AT the turn in to the drive to Hooper Farm.

His car's heater poured out warmth but couldn't make a dent in the coolness that had descended on her.

She'd been friendly enough with the cheerful tow truck driver, who'd freed her little car with nonchalant expertise, then carried its bedraggled carcass away while she watched.

Only when it was out of sight did she get in his car.

And then she spotted his gloves on the console between the seats. She didn't say a word, but the glare she sent them should have incinerated them.

His gloves. His car. His coat. What did she have against his belongings?

Or was it him?

He slowed more.

Stopped.

He hadn't noticed before—not consciously—the way the Hoopers' house sat so far from the road, its back up to a sweeping curve of trees.

That's what drew the eye—the trees. The house appeared an afterthought. In the spring, when the trees and bushes leafed out, it would probably disappear. Even now, it appeared as no more than a demure white block against the intricate web of black-inked tree trunks and branches. The snow-tipped green of firs and evergreens stood out more clearly. Even the mass of the barn snagged more attention than the house.

From here—the public view of Hooper Farm—the dormant fields swept cultivator-wide lines of stubble into a mesmerizing pattern that faded the house to an out of focus background.

Could say, he thought with a twist of his mouth, that the fields came first, while the house—and its occupants—sat nearly invisible under the overhanging drama of nature and behind the stubborn demands of farming.

"Getting fanciful, Quincy," he muttered to himself.

"What?"

He caught the reflection of her frown in the side window.

She didn't seem to notice that he'd stopped.

"Nothing."

He eased the car forward again toward the house.

ANNE BURROWED DEEPER under the comforter, welcoming the warmth.

Not, however, welcoming the thoughts slipping in now that she'd released her guard in hopes of falling asleep fast.

She should have gotten in his car at the start.

Or she could have climbed down and gotten back in her own car, although the tow truck might not have seen—

It had nothing to do with the tow truck.

She'd seen that fancy, impractical car sitting there, offering warmth and comfort, and she hadn't been able to accept it.

It had felt … disloyal.

She skidded away from that thought and slammed right into another.

No. A memory more than a thought.

Of turning in Quince's arms. Of turning to him. Of being a moment, a breath away from kissing him.

Disloyal.

CHAPTER FIFTEEN

INSTEAD OF GOING to his usual position at the kitchen table, Quince came closer. Closer. Next to her desk.

He set a piece of paper beside her computer keyboard.

"What's this?"

"A website I'd like you to look at."

"Quince—"

"Please."

Anne sighed and typed in the url.

In the three days since he'd held her…

She stopped and reworded her thought.

In the three days since her car broke down, they'd regained normalcy. Complete normalcy.

Except her car was still in the shop, with Jorge O'Fallon working on it in spare moments to keep the cost—or in this case the exchange of her labor—down. So she was driving the farm truck.

And now this not-normal detour and odd request from Quince.

On the screen, an image came up of a kitchen island—*her* kitchen island she realized after a moment. Though something had been done to the picture that made it look a whole lot better than it usually did.

There was type across the image, but it wasn't coalescing into words for her.

It couldn't be because Peter Quincy had pulled up a chair right off her shoulder to look at the screen with her. Had to be because the island looked so completely different. Warm and sunny and homey and … lovely.

"What is this?"

"Just what it says."

The breath behind his words stirred the hair around her right ear. A warm shiver of reaction arced down her throat and across her shoulders.

She shifted, blinked to bring the type into focus.

"Anne's Kitchen?" Her reading added a question mark that wasn't on the screen. "I don't get it."

"It's a prototype."

"A prototype of what?"

"You said you know what a COO does, so you know I spot issues and provide solutions. More revenue could help Hooper Farm in a lot of ways. Diverse sources of revenue spread out risk beneficial. Oats could give you a new revenue stream."

"Oats? Your reading didn't mention that oats don't compete with corn or soybeans in gross income around here? Premium oats, the kind horse owners use for feed and that captures top dollar, come from Canada or other cold-weather spots. What we could grow here wouldn't get us the return we need."

"Not as a feed crop. But it might as a specialty crop. Others are doing similar things. Working with dehydrated foods. Soups and—"

"Where did this come from? This website and all this?" She pointed to a new photo showing an angled banner of sunlight coming to rest on a pair of the worn white coffee mugs. It gilded them, making them look almost alive.

"I took some photos. I'd line up a professional for the real thing. But what matters is…"

This was as real as a thing got.

He'd taken these photos.

The bumper of the farm truck, with the sky unending beyond it.

This must be one of the pictures he'd been taking when she came out to use the truck to check the field draining.

His position had stretched the denim of jeans that had looked like an entirely different species from her work clothes. She'd refused to consider where they stretched and where they cupped.

…Except somehow she had immediate recall now of where they stretched and where they cupped.

Photos. Look at the photos.

The angle of her elbow from beneath a dishtowel as she dried a dish. Everett's scarred, wise hand dipping a spoon into a bowl of oatmeal, the milk flowing in, the rich toppings spilling over.

It all seemed so rich and full and … sweet.

Quince had captured moments and angles and vignettes that she'd stopped seeing—if she'd ever seen them quite this way. It made her heart pound faster and swell.

"…with the goal to monetize Hooper Farm—"

Her head came up at his words. "Hooper Farm *is* monetized. We grow crops. We sell crops. That's what a farm does."

"But you don't grow enough. You don't sell enough." Despite his even tone, that delivered a blow.

He reached for the mouse, brushing her arm.

She pulled away.

He pretended not to notice.

Though how she knew he was pretending…

She concentrated on what he was showing her. Other sites. Not as beautiful, but still nice. Other farms. Other farmers. Selling dehydrated soups or special flour or goat milk products.

"You and Candy Benzil could team up to do the corn chowder, but I'd recommend not doing that until later. Get established with the oatmeal first. It differentiates you from the others."

"Others…?"

"Call them retail farmers. You can't sell produce the way the farmers we helped last year do, but you can still benefit from people's interest in food coming direct to them from farms. In fact, you fill in when they can't serve their customers—winter—with dehydrated foods. So you could share customers.

"This could take you in a totally new direction. A profitable direction. Maybe at first it could be a sideline that helped the bottom line, but I've tasted your food. You could reimagine Hooper Farm, shift the emphasis to your recipes, your cooking."

"They aren't my recipes. They're from friends and neighbors, so they're *their* recipes. And my cooking is nothing special."

"It is. And we can work out the rights to the recipes. Actually, that could be good, helping other people in the area when you start selling."

He clicked to another photo.

The barn, looking stalwart instead of worn, Grandy in profile almost achieving noble. Winter fields framed by a front porch post.

Her.

In the kitchen. Having just chopped an onion, reaching for a pot with one hand, scooping the onion with the other.

It looked … elegant, graceful. Nothing like her at all.

She pushed her chair to the side so she could see his eyes. Yes, there was the same light of enthusiasm she'd heard in his voice.

"Quince, these photos are … amazing and gorgeous."

"Thanks, but a pro could—"

"Not possibly do what you've done. You've caught the heart of Hooper Farm here. And I can see you've done a lot of work on this."

"But?" he said with a faint smile.

She shook her head, not finding words.

"What part of the idea don't you like?" he asked.

"All of it. Reimagining Hooper Farm into something else. Shifting the focus from farming."

She expected him to deflate at that. Instead, he looked interested.

"Really? But you like cooking and—"

"I don't. Not particularly. I'd rather be driving the tractor. But Everett needs good meals and I like eating, too, so I do it. It's a lot of work, a lot of preparation for a short time while people enjoy it and then it's straight into cleanup."

"Sounds like farming to me."

Her mouth twisted with a dry grin. He had a point.

"Maybe. But this—" She gestured toward the screen. "—isn't me."

"I had a feeling featuring you wouldn't go over big, but it needs the warmth of a person and Everett isn't going to make anyone want to buy oatmeal. You're perfect."

She shook her head again. "It isn't what I want to do. It isn't who I want to be. I'm a farmer. A crop farmer. I don't want to be a market farmer and I sure don't want to become a food manufacturer."

"Homemade food producer," he substituted. "I'm not saying give up corn or soybeans, but I know you give the oatmeal you grow to people in town. Why not grow more and sell it?"

"Sell it?"

"Yeah. You know, make a little profit. You should have charged Vanessa and the others."

She shook her head. "I don't want to charge my friends."

"You do for bookkeeping."

"That's different. Besides, I don't want to grow oats." Even if she did, the time to learn the trade and establish a business? Hooper Farm didn't have that kind of time. "More specifically, I don't want to market oats. I'm a corn and soybean farmer. But I *would* like copies of these photos if you don't mind."

"Sure."

He didn't sound crushed. Not at all.

"And, uh, thank you. For trying to help. I'm sorry—"

"Don't be. I don't want you doing something you don't want to do. But don't count me out."

FOR THE PAST few days Anne had been almost solicitous of him, as if she wanted to make up for turning down his oatmeal idea.

It was rather sweet.

Especially since he was used to Zeke's brusque "No" to the vast majority of his ideas.

He decided to take advantage of it.

"How about getting out of here and coming to the high school basketball game and then to Zeke and Darcie's tonight?"

She shook her head. "Taxes. Everett said he's going to town for dinner and if you're gone, too, that means the whole evening to work on them.”

“Thought you’d finished.”

“Ours. I’m doing taxes for several other farms.”

“Do you charge them?”

“Most of the people pay me something.”

“In other words, you don’t charge. Even as tight as your budget is—”

“None of them are flush, either.”

“—and you stay locked up here working all the time instead of getting out and seeing people.”

“That’s—” She snapped her mouth closed. Something came across her face then. Something that made him oddly uneasy. She looked directly at him and said, “And what about you?”

“What about me?”

“You’ve been hiding out here.”

Blindsided. Completely blindsided.

Still, he produced a grin “Have you been talking to Vanessa?”

“Vanessa? No. What—? No, you’re not going to detour this. You get everybody else to talk about themselves, but you hang back, in the shadows.”

He leaned away, letting his lids drop lower. “Do I?”

“Oh, yes, you do. I bet you got away with all sorts of things like that at Zeke-Tech, specifically with Zeke and Vanessa, who don’t— didn’t—”

His lids flickered at her change of tense.

“—pay attention to people issues. So you’ve been able to hide out all these years not dealing with people.”

“Not dealing with people? Do you have any idea how many people a day I—”

“Strangers.” She waved her hand, grandly negating every one of them. “Or people you supervise. Nobody who’d ask you questions, poke, prod, and hold up a mirror to you.”

“Like I’ve done to you?” he asked with mild wryness.

“*Exactly.*” Her momentary triumph faded as he watched her absorb that. But she rallied. "Exactly as you've done with me. Which has been annoying and painful and helpful, all of which—" She looked up at him, eyes narrowed. "Ah, yes, how convenient—has kept me on the defensive, putting up barriers, and not asking *you* questions. That stops now."

"So, what do you want to ask?"

"Who was she?"

CHAPTER SIXTEEN

"S HE? AT LEAST half of the people I encounter are females, so—"

Anne took the plunge. "The one you don't talk about."

"How can I talk about someone when I don't know who you mean?"

"You do know. You just don't want anyone else to know." She studied him. "But Zeke knows, doesn't he? That's why you're afraid of Darcie."

He shook his head in would-be bemusement. "Afraid of Darcie? She's the best thing that ever happened to my best friend. Not to mention that she keeps him otherwise occupied enough that he's not working me and the rest of his staff toward a very early grave."

"Oh, yeah, you're grateful, but you're also afraid of her. Don't try to deny it. I've seen how you react. It's—*Oh.* Of course, *that*'s why you wouldn't stay in the apartment they offered you. It would have been perfect from a practical standpoint. You would have been right there whenever Zeke needed you."

"Now you sound like him. And as I told him, being constantly available is not a selling point to me. That's why I declined their offer of the apartment."

"Like you can't handle Zeke," she scoffed. "But Darcie, Darcie's a different matter. Because she knows people. She pays attention to them. She figures out what makes them tick. And what they're hiding. And you're afraid she'd have you taken apart before you knew it. Especially if she has the head start of knowing about the woman you won't talk about."

He straightened, smiling his sophisticated smile. "I never knew farmers could have such vivid imaginations. Thought you were grounded in the realities of nature."

Why hadn't she noticed before how much sorrow there was behind that smile?

He kept talking, smooth and calm. "I'm going upstairs now to connect with some of those people you said I try to hide out from. If I can get in twenty or so emails before dinner, I'll only have half as many to deal with after dinner."

As if emails were the point.

He'd reached the door when she spoke again.

"Quince."

He paused. For a moment she thought that was all she'd get, but then he turned his head, still with that smile. His brows raised slightly.

"You've had it all your own way up to now. Asking all the questions. Not anymore."

THE SPARKLE IN Anne's eyes these past days warmed Quince's heart.

And made his blood run cold.

She was a woman on a mission.

Okay, she was always a woman on a mission—Hooper Farm.

But now some of the zeal had been turned on him.

Not that she flirted with him or in any way invited carnal thoughts. Those didn't need an invitation. They walked right in and took over on their own.

No denying he'd been attracted to her from the start.

Was it the bout of would-be stealth crying that had done it? Or had it started as soon as he saw that mouth meant to smile and the wearied eyes so far from a smile?

Either way, it was there.

He'd wanted to put his arms around her and tuck her head under his chin and hold her, letting nothing hurt her ever again.

Now she glinted looks at him filled with challenge and intelligence and he wanted…

Oh, hell, yes, he wanted. To be inside her. To make her gasp and tremble. To explore each other until their lungs and muscles demanded that pause when you melted against the other person, and breathing together was all you had left in you.

He was in trouble.

And he had no one but himself to blame.

He'd pushed Zeke to come back to Drago. He'd welcomed his relationship with Darcie. He'd encouraged the connections both Zeke and Vanessa had created between Zeke-Tech and the town. He'd set up the whole scenario that led to his spending so much time in Drago.

Then he'd rented a room in this farmhouse.

And when he'd recognized his attraction to her instead of leaving, he'd dug in deeper.

He'd told himself the farm was a problem he could solve and he liked to solve problems.

Since she was part of the farm, he'd needed to understand her to solve the problem.

Right. That's what he'd told himself.

Now, she'd turned around and was looking back at him, taking up the challenge he hadn't known he'd issued.

QUINCE HAD A strategy in arriving late at Darcie and Zeke's.

They'd started these get-togethers as buffet dinners after Drago High School's home football games in the fall. Since the change to basketball season with more frequent games, they weren't officially dinners (though the amount of food didn't change) and they were after every home game.

The guest list represented Zeke-Tech and various elements of Drago, and changed each time, except for a core group of Zeke and Darcie's friends.

That was why Quince came late. The core group of friends.

He'd seen growing curiosity in Jennifer and Vanessa. Worse, he'd seen it in Darcie.

He stepped in, pushed along by the wind at his back, and spotted Darcie to his right. He moved left.

He needn't have bothered.

Zeke grabbed him by the arm, leading him into a small room off the kitchen, closing the door after them. It was a good thing a light came on automatically because Zeke seemed too focused to be bothered with finding a switch.

"Is this… Did you just drag me into the pantry, Zeke?"

"I guess. I want to talk to you. Alone."

"I never would have guessed."

"Did you know Everett used to play chess with my father?"

"Chess? No. I know he plays poker."

Zeke waved that off. "Of course you know that, you're part of the poker game. But it was chess he played with Dad." He leaned back against shelves of canned goods. "You know, it's strange. I used to ride my bike out to that farm as a kid. When something was bothering me. Get up real early and ride and ride and ride. It seemed like it was the edge of forever. And I'd sit on top of a fence out by this field—you can't even really see the buildings from there. Just fields and trees. Space and sky."

Leaving his friend to his thoughts—and knowing that could last a while—Quince unfolded a step stool and sat.

"Wasn't until this spring when I went out there that I found out Everett had known about me showing up back then. It's his favorite spot, too, and we watched the sun come up together a couple times this spring…. But you know, he never once showed himself when I was kid. I wonder if he told Dad he saw me out there. Seventeen years they played chess, were friends—and I never knew."

He shook his head. His elbow connected with a can of peaches and he pushed off from the shelves.

He followed Quince's lead with another step stool before continuing. "You know Everett Hooper was the first one to help us get data for the optimum market program for truck farmers around here?"

Quince frowned. "But the Hoopers aren't truck farming."

"That's right. But he helped us anyhow. And he got other farmers around to cooperate." A smile flickered on Zeke's face. "Even though he doesn't trust computers."

"Yeah, I've heard that rant. He can be quite eloquent on the topic—and other topics—when he gets wound up."

Zeke looked at him. "What's the problem out there at Hooper Farm? Everett seems worried."

Quince wasn't going to air their business. Before he could form an answer that didn't tell that truth, Zeke added, "Something happening between you and Anne Hooper?"

It took him completely by surprise, so he was a beat late with his answer. But it was firm. "No."

Zeke studied him, and Quince held still under the look.

This was the price he paid for having his best friend be happy.

His two best friends.

Since Zeke had found Darcie again and Vanessa had connected with Josh, they paid entirely too much attention to his emotional life.

It wasn't comfortable—neither of them was subtle—and given a choice, he'd prefer they didn't.

But what kind of friend would he be if he griped about bearing a little discomfort when both had blossomed in the past year?

"Why not?" Zeke finally asked.

"Sometimes it just doesn't happen."

"Because you don't like her?"

Quince spread his hands. "Appreciate your faith in me, but something doesn't always *happen* with every woman I like."

"I suppose not, but why not this particular one?" Zeke had that going-to-pursue-this-question-until-I've-wrestled-it-to-the-ground tone.

Quince tried not to groan. "First, she's nearly as against the idea as Everett is."

"Really?"

"Really. Whatever Vanessa says about Mr. Smooth—"

"Who's Mr. Smooth?"

Right this moment, Mr. Smooth was an idiot. Why on earth had he let *that* slip?

Quince calculated that the odds were better than even that Zeke would forget the whole thing if he ignored the question. "Women don't fall for me the way some people think."

"I didn't mean her—I meant Everett. I can see why she might not be interested—"

"Thanks," he muttered, his mouth quirking.

"—but I could have sworn Everett viewed the whole thing as a joke when you first went there and Anne mistook you for another of his suggested suitors. So—"

"How do you know about that?"

"Welcome to Drago," Zeke said darkly, then continued as if there'd been no break in his words. "—what makes him take it seriously enough now to not like it?"

Quince looked focused on a container of rice.

"Doesn't matter," he lied. "Because I'm not in the market for anything *happening*, as you put it."

Zeke tapped his closed fist on the shelf next to him as he nodded, "That's exactly my point."

"You've lost me."

"Why not? That's what I asked before—why isn't something happening between the two of you. You thought I meant Anne, but what about you? She's a real nice woman. Pretty, too. And smart. So, why aren't you in the market?"

"Zeke, you've found Darcie, and that's terrific. But you've got to stop thinking everybody's going to pair up like—"

"Like Jennifer and Trent? Or Vanessa and Josh? *Especially* Vanessa and Josh." His smile was smug, definitely smug.

"You can't tell me you're taking credit for Vanessa and—"

Smug evaporated. "No. I just wanted her to—what's Warren say?—get a life. She was working *all* the time."

"Weren't we all," he murmured. "That's why we're grateful Darcie came into your life—so you had less time to keep *us* working."

"Except for Vanessa. She didn't like it. Not until I told her she had to come here and build the computer lab."

"*Who* told her?"

Zeke didn't like telling people what to do—unless it had to do with one of his innovations, then, watch out. But telling Vanessa he wanted her to be in Drago more than she'd planned? That he'd decided was Quince's job.

"Uh, okay. You told her. But I told you to tell her."

"Yeah, thanks for that."

"Hey, she's happy now, isn't she?"

"I guess she is."

"So she should thank us both. And—wait a minute. You're trying to change the subject. She said you do that."

"Right now the subject is what Darcie's going to think about you disappearing for this long."

"Oh, that's okay. She'll understand."

"And what's going on out there. Sounds like a riot."

That was an exaggeration, but the volume of voices had risen. Enough so that even Zeke wondered about it and followed him out when he opened the pantry door.

CHAPTER SEVENTEEN

TRENT STENNER, COMING in from the other room, called to the latest arrival at the back door, "Josh, how bad was it?"

"Not a total loss," the high school principal said to everyone, "but it's put a major dent in our lab facilities. Not to mention Pratt's and Duggan's hair and eyebrows."

"But they're okay?" Jennifer asked.

"Yeah. They were checked out at the hospital and sent home."

"What happened?" Quince asked.

"Tell it from the start, Josh," Darcie said. "Trent's not much of a story-teller. Gave us the bare bones and said you'd be late."

"I was wrapping up post-game duties, and was about to leave the building when I heard a sound like a car crash, coming from the south wing. I took off running. Trent came up from the locker room level—"

"Needed something from my office," the football coach filled in.

"—and I'm happy to say I kept up with him, former NFL player and all, stride for stride down the hallway."

"Better than you did when I sacked you senior year," Trent added.

"Hey, that was—" Josh started.

But Vanessa interrupted. "What happened when the two of you ended your race down the hallway?" Count on Vanessa to pull them back on subject.

"We saw smoke billowing out around the charred door to the Chem Lab."

Someone in back sucked in a breath. "Oh, dear."

"Josh was on his phone calling 911, reporting the explosion, even before we got past all that stinking smoke," Trent said.

"That's when we found Pratt and Duggan—a couple of sopho-mores—standing stock still under streaming sprinklers, glassy-eyed, and hair singed, but otherwise not hurt. Too bad the Chem Lab can't say the same."

"How much damage?" Vanessa asked Josh.

"Hard to tell. Tim—the chemistry teacher—and I will look it over tomorrow. Then get together Monday with our building services people and maybe a contractor or two to start on estimates."

"What is this? The third or fourth incident this year?" Darcie asked.

"Fourth. The others weren't anywhere near as bad."

"It's Zeke's fault," she said.

Zeke gave an inarticulate protest around a mouthful of potato salad.

"We *have* experienced an upsurge in the number of students who think they have a future following in Zeke's footsteps," Josh acknowl-edged with a grin.

"Hey, I never blew up the Chem Lab."

"No," Darcie said, "but you broke in to do unauthorized experi-ments."

He grinned. "Yeah, I did. And who was my lookout?"

"Whoever your lookout might have been," she said with careful dignity, "would certainly plead the Fifth Amendment on that score so as not to self-incriminate himself or herself. And besides," she added in her usual voice, "your lookout knew you were a genius."

"Maybe these kids are, too," Zeke said.

"These kids need to climb up to decent grades before they try claiming genius status," Josh said. "While they're doing that, let them blow up their parents' garages or something other than the Chem Lab. In the meantime, I'm starved."

That broke up the knot by the door. Vanessa led Josh to the food, and Quince gladly followed in his wake.

After eating, he circulated.

From the Zeke-Techers he gained a sense of the mood about the move to Drago. It remained good. Construction on permanent headquarters wasn't near starting, with designs still being mulled, not to mention the winter weather preventing construction, but an advance group had headquarters in former store-fronts near the computer lab in the center of Drago. They seemed satisfied with their progress, and, as one said, they were enjoying the fast pace of work and the slow pace of life in Drago.

From the Dragoites he gained a sense of welcome and a few grains of insight into the county and its residents. Including those who lived out of town.

Nothing drastic or—

"You didn't bring Anne."

Uh-oh. Darcie.

He'd let his guard down and here she was.

"Was I supposed to?" Wrong question—because he could see she was about to answer it. "I didn't know you'd invited her for tonight. I would have been happy to give her a ride."

"I didn't invite her specifically for tonight. I thought you would. As your date."

"Darcie." The warning in his tone didn't alter her steady regard. He expelled a short breath. "We're not dating."

"Why not? You can't tell me you're not interested."

"I'm not—in case you didn't notice—telling you anything."

"And I can't believe she's not interested in you," she continued unimpeded.

"Thanks for the vote of confidence, but you better start believing. Anne Hooper is not the least bit interested in me."

His last sentence fell into one of those inexplicable, unpredictable lulls in conversational buzz, so it floated out over the group and hung there.

He was aware of concentrated attention from Jennifer and Vanessa, confusion from Zeke, amused sympathy from Trent and Josh, and curiosity from the ring beyond them.

"Are you sure?" Darcie insisted.

"Darcie," Jennifer said quietly.

The two women exchanged a look Quince didn't like any better than he'd liked the questions.

But at least Darcie retired from the Spanish Inquisition.

Temporarily.

QUINCE HAD HEARD Anne drive in—hard not to in that old farm truck—while he'd been on a conference call shortly before noon Monday.

When it ended, he went to the kitchen.

For coffee. Not because Anne's presence exerted a gravitational pull on him that put the moon to shame.

Their faces and the silence that fell when he walked in told him everything.

"I'll get some coffee and get out of here," he said.

Anne, leaning back against the sink, looked down at the mug in her hands.

"Might as well stay," Everett said gruffly. "Heard about your idea about oats and such. Seems you know we're in a bind. Seems everybody this side of the Mississippi River knows. Including these damned moneylenders who won't lend money to the people who need it."

Anne looked up. "I've tried every last place on my list. From the reasonable through the not-so-reasonable and now the last of the far-fetched. Everett, you know that if we can't buy more seed—and fast—we won't have enough acreage planted to even have a chance to turn this around. But there is one more thing we can do. What I've wanted to do from the start."

"No," the older man said.

"It's what Chris would have wanted. You know it is. When the farm needs—"

"No."

"Everett, it's the—"

"*No.* End of discussion."

In the silence that followed, Anne refilled all the coffee cups, stirring hers even though she drank it black.

Quince cleared his throat.

"No," Anne and Everett said in unison.

"If you won't consider selling oatmeal, how about a possible infusion of cash from another source and one that doesn't require any change from being crop farmers—farm tourism."

"What the hell is that?" Everett asked.

"Hooper Farm becomes a tourist destination. People pay to come here."

Quickly, he explained about programs in agritourism he'd researched. Hooper Farm wouldn't take on the major versions where guests stayed on the farm and sometimes joined in on the work. Certainly not right away.

But they could try a modified event. Drawing visitors from the city to see a real family farm.

Everett was not sold—to say the least.

"Strangers all over? What do you want that for? How is being like an animal at the zoo getting gawked at by these city people going to help?"

Quince explained again, never letting his enthusiasm or patience flag. He could make this work.

But he was concerned about Anne's silence.

Everett, on the other hand, was not silent. "What kind of fool would pay good money to come look at a bunch of frozen ground? It's hard winter."

"Right. So we couldn't charge a lot. Not for our trial run. But for anyone who hasn't been to a farm there's lots to see. You can tell them how it's changed since you were a kid, and show the machinery, and what it takes to get an ear of corn on their plate at next summer's barbeque."

Everett grumbled more without mounting any true protest.

As if aware of both of them looking at her, Anne raised her gaze from her coffee to Everett.

"We've got to try something."

Quince wasted no time in saying, "Weather forecast's clear for this weekend, so—"

"This weekend—*this* weekend?"

"Sure, why wait? We'll get the trial under our belts and then we can really start planning."

THE NEXT FIVE days were spent in outdoor house-cleaning. They couldn't wash much because of the cold, but they moved machinery into orderly lines, organized equipment, swept and re-swept, outlined paths with fence posts laid end to end, and spiffed up Grandy's pen. At night, Anne baked dozens and dozens and dozens of brownies, Quince cut the cooled ones, Everett wrapped them individually.

Last night, Anne had suddenly recognized that visitors would likely need to use the bathroom inside, and had set to a frenzy of indoor cleaning.

This morning, they'd set out the brownies, sturdy paper cups, and the urn borrowed from the Congregational Church filled with hot apple cider on a cleared workbench in the barn. Quince and Everett were finishing up spreading fresh straw on the paths to protect the visitors' shoes as much as possible from a patch of not-entirely-frozen mud.

Part of Anne had thought this would not actually happen, because no one would come.

But somehow Quince had lined up fourteen people willing to pay to spend a few hours on a real farm in the middle of winter.

Didn't these people have socks to darn or something else more exciting?

Now, with the "tourists" about to arrive any minute, Anne straightened the fresh towel hanging from the oven door handle, smoothed the clean tablecloth covering the mars on the kitchen table, and swallowed hard as the clock ticked toward the top of the hour.

Quince entered on a burst of cold air and warm enthusiasm that simultaneously swept around her even before the back door's slam resonated.

"We're all finished. Zero Hour is just about here."

"Zero Hour. That sounds suitably ominous."

"Hey, you're not worried are you? Everything looks great."

"Worried? Who, me?"

He grinned. "You shouldn't be. Consider this: You viewed me as an uber city-slicker when I arrived—"

"Still do."

"—yet now I love the place. So, if you converted me, other city-slickers will be easy."

He leaned in and kissed her on the cheek—solely to boost her morale, she told herself.

It was a contradictory sensation, the cold of the outdoors carried on the surface of his skin striking her first, but followed immediately by the heat of his lips and the warmth of his breath.

The second kiss, the one that definitely wasn't a peck-on-the-cheek, she didn't explain away.

Because her reasoning abilities left the building even before his mouth covered hers.

An odd pressure in her chest morphed to a whirling ball of heat shooting off emissaries to unexpected outposts in her body.

Her fingers—the fingers now clutching the collar of his jacket—should have been ash for all the heat flowing into them. And why was she clutching his jacket collar? Drawing him closer? How much closer could they get? Holding herself up? He was taking care of that with his arms now around her and—

Whack!

Instinct kicked in long before reason. The familiar sound of the back door slapping closed had the effect of a cattle prod. Anne jumped back from him, spinning away at the same time.

"They're here," Everett announced in gloomy accents. He stomped across the kitchen to the sink, ran some water, then stomped out.

If he'd seen Quince kissing her—no, in fairness, they'd been kissing one another—that would mean Everett was displaying tact by not reacting.

Tact. Everett.

So he *couldn't* have seen them.

But how could he have missed seeing them?

"Okay, here we go," Quince said with enthusiasm. "This is going to be fun."

The first few minutes outside, Anne was too shaken by the kiss and the fact that she had been nowhere near ending it to think about what was going on around her.

She drifted through the gathering group of visitors with impunity.

Then a hand plucked at her sleeve.

"Can girls farm?"

She looked down into a child's face of indeterminate gender. The knit hat made to look like the head of the Chicago Bears mascot was no help because girls and boys wore them.

"They can start learning," she said cautiously. "Takes a long time to learn everything and some of the equipment is dangerous, so you have to take it one step at a time."

"Are you a farmer?"

As she drew breath, two more kids dressed very similarly joined the first and a trio of adults started heading her way.

"When did you start learning?"

"Do you drive a tractor?"

"Why are barns red?"

"Do you kill the animals?"

"What about rats? Do you have rats in your barn?"

"Are there cows to milk?"

"Why does everything sleep in the winter?

"What do you do when it rains?"

"Do you have a pony?"

"Did you have a barn raising to make this barn? We read a story about barn-raisings."

Oh, God, these people weren't going to be content with just gawking at fields and building and machinery.

They were going to insist on talking to one of the rare animals on Hooper Farm—her.

CHAPTER EIGHTEEN

Q UINCE EMERGED FROM the barn, where he'd refilled the apple cider urn again, and took a moment to watch and listen.

He hadn't had many such moments, because he was busy keeping the gears turning while Anne and Everett talked about farming.

Right now, Everett was answering a question about the history of the farm.

"Second-oldest in the county to still be in the same family."

"Has it been divided up among family members?" someone from the back asked.

"Was split in two back at the beginning of the 1900s, but one branch sold back to the other after a couple decades. Then, in my generation, my younger brother married a girl whose father farmed and inherited that place with her. They had two boys who both wanted to farm. Made sense that one stayed on his mother's family place and the other came here to farm."

So that was how Everett's great nephew had ended up here with him.

"You never married?"

"That ain't part of the history of Hooper Farm."

That drew a laugh from the group around the Hoopers.

"It's kind of bleak this time of year, isn't it?" a young teenager asked Anne.

"Bleak? It's cold, sure, and the days are short. But it's that way in the city, too."

"But with nothing growing—" He gestured toward the fields. "—all you see is dirt. Or frozen mud."

"You might just see dirt—or frozen mud—but a farmer sees the crops that will grow there. A farmer plans for them and prepares for them. Farming is a profession of hope," she said.

It was a great insight and the people directly around her nodded their appreciation, but anyone not right there hadn't heard her words, because she spoke so softly.

"Hope," Everett repeated loudly enough that everyone heard. "And enough obstacles to make an Olympic steeplechaser sit down and cry."

That drew more general laughter.

Everett was a hit, with the guests taking him as an amusing character and chuckling at his grumbling.

Other than feeding her great uncle-in-law straight lines, Anne was struggling.

She tried, but she clearly wasn't comfortable. At least that was clear to him.

What she'd said about growing up as a Foreign Service brat echoed in his head.

It was mostly feeling like you never fit. Anywhere. Always surrounded by strangers.

Great, and he'd invited a load of strangers to Hooper Farm.

Most were pleasant, interested people.

A few weren't.

Quince herded a red-jacketed boy of about seven back to his parents for the third time, while Everett kept the rest of the group entertained with stories of growing up on the farm.

The boys' parents looked more annoyed than thankful for the return of their offspring.

Even Quince couldn't describe this afternoon as going really well.

Rather than sticking to the straw paths, a number of visitors roamed—then complained about their shoes getting muddy.

Instead of sticking in a neat pack, they spread out, which made it difficult for the hosts to talk to more than a few at a time and impossible to keep up with others.

Especially this wandering boy.

Quince had plucked him off the fence and later found him at the back of the barn, preparing to scoot out to the fields beyond.

A few visitors were genuinely interested, but more showed evidence of boredom.

Everett could be viewed as local color. The curmudgeonly old farmer. But Anne ... Anne was stiff and treated too many questions like an invasion of privacy.

This had been a mistake.

The recognition came into his head fully formed and obvious.

His mistake.

How could he have been so wrong?

What on earth had he been thinking?

Bringing all these strangers to Hooper Farm.

Wanting Everett and Anne to be comfortable with taking money from people for an *experience.*

Expecting Anne, who warmed to people only slowly and cautiously, to suddenly become a gregarious tour guide.

He'd had a vision of how this would all be, but any idiot could see Anne Hooper didn't fit that vision. How had he—who prided himself on his people skills—overlooked that glaring fact?

And then it hit him.

Hit him hard enough to make him grunt and stop where he was.

It wasn't *what* he'd been thinking about—it was *who* he'd been thinking about.

Fiona.

Fiona, who would have waded into a situation like this with pure joy.

Who would have every one of the visitors hanging on her words. Who would have them viewing mud as delightful and charming. Who would barely seem to ask, yet would have turned every last one of them into walking, talking word-of-mouth promoters of Hooper Farm that would make any ad man drool.

Who would end the day with eyes shining, cheeks flushed, high on an extrovert's buzz.

Instead of the hunted, wary, shoulder-tightened figure that was Anne Hooper.

God, Anne. I'm sorry.

He'd never meant to make her miserable, but he had. His good intentions had sent her right down the road to what her expression clearly said was her personal hell.

He should have known.

Her reaction to the oatmeal business wasn't solely that crop farming was who she was. It was also about who she wasn't.

The face of a business. The front woman who would tell the world about what she had to offer.

She'd made it clear she had no interest in that.

Why hadn't she refused to do this? Why hadn't she told him she'd rather be stuck with pins and rolled across the floor?

We've got to do something.

Because she would do anything, try anything to save this farm.

So that explained her. But what about him?

How had he been so off about this?

Memories of Fiona had never before mingled with his relationships—brief as they usually were.

It sure wasn't that the two women were alike. There'd been no question whom he was holding and kissing in the kitchen earlier.

Yet that had been another mistake.

He'd meant to give her a boost.

At least with the first kiss.

The second one, the one when she'd cooperated and the two of them nearly turned it into far more than a kiss—

But they didn't.

Wouldn't.

For all the reasons he'd thought through before. She wasn't a woman to take what he could offer.

Though he had been wrong about her not being interested—

Nope. Not going there.

Okay, so this was a disaster. The only thing to do about a disaster was to get through it with as little damage as possible. To avoid anything like—

Oh, damn.

—the red-jacketed boy was on the loose again. With neither of his parents showing the least recognition that the kid existed, the boy must have skirted the group and, using a high wooden trough to mask his progress, was now making a beeline for Grandy's enclosure.

The boy reached up to the latch.

"Hey!" Quince yelled as he sprinted toward the kid.

Not a good move. The shout and motion drew the attention of all the visitors. Worse, Grandy went on alert. And worst, the kid—never looking around—worked the latch even faster.

He had it open and was inside with Quince still half a dozen yards away.

"Get out of there! Hey, you, get out of there!" shouted Everett.

Grandy lowered his head, his malevolent eyes shining.

If the kid would hold still—but no, he kept running toward Grandy, and now he was screeching "Here goat, here goat!"

Grandy charged.

Quince changed his angle, no longer hoping to peaceably remove the kid. At the last second, he went airborne—it was the only hope of getting there in time.

The goat, the kid, and Quince all reached the same square yard of space at the same moment. Quince's leap put him between Grandy and the red jacket, taking the full force of the charge on the right side of his rib cage.

"Hey! That's a valuable animal. Get out of there. *Quince,* get that kid out of there," Everett ordered.

"I'm trying," Quince said.

At least he thought he said it. His mouth might have been too full of red jacket for him to say much of anything. And for sure no one could hear him over the kid's howls of blighted ambition.

Quince raised himself to his knees—not an easy task in the half-frozen muck while holding onto a squirming kid with one arm and keeping an eye on an irritated goat.

"Quit fooling around!" Everett barked from the gate. "Get that kid out of there before he really riles Grandy."

If the throbbing ache in his ribs—which made standing a real treat—was Grandy un-riled, Quince would hate to see the creature riled.

"Destin? Are you all right dear?" Great. *Now* the parents noticed the kid.

Quince looked around to see the mother trying to follow Everett into the enclosure. Everett slapped her hands, and growled. "Get out of here, lady."

"Mommy!" screamed the kid, and Grandy moved restively.

"Shut up, Destin," Quince growled low enough that only the kid could hear. "Or you'll be that goat's dinner."

Destin looked up at Quince's face, then around him toward Grandy, and miracle of miracles, he not only shut up, he quit squirming.

Everett slowly passed them without a glance. In a rumbling tone of reassurance, he vividly opined on the stupidity of city folk and their demon spawn.

Seeing that Grandy's attention had shifted to Everett—still not friendly, but no longer quite so threatened—Quince used his hold on the red jacket's collar and grabbed the seat of the pants to frog-march the boy to the exit.

"Destin!" screeched the mother, clasping the boy yet at the same time carefully keeping her shoes out of the mud.

"Lady, back up, so we can close the gate."

"Oh, my boy, my boy!" she wailed, while the kid obligingly whimpered in harmony. "How could you have treated him so roughly? My poor baby."

"If you don't get out of the way so we can close the gate, I'll let Grandy treat the both of you as roughly as he'd like."

Everett arrived just then, and started freely expressing his opinion of the traffic jam at the gate.

Quince reached out, intending to take the woman by the shoulders and bodily dislodge her. But Anne was there first.

"Everyone move back, give them room," she ordered, as if the press of spectators had prevented the woman from showing a grain of sense.

The clog at the gate finally backed up, allowing Everett to close it behind him.

"Be a miracle if this doesn't put Grandy off breeding for the rest of season," grumbled the older man.

"Look at this jacket. Brand new and the filth of this pigsty ground into it," griped the mother.

"Pigs? Where are the pigs?" asked one of the three kids in Bears hats.

"I didn't get to pet the goat," Destin whined.

Anne looked into his eyes. "Are you okay, Quince?"

"I'll live." He'd nearly produced a grin for her until pain fired up and down from the middle of his shin bone. "*Hey*. That little brat *kicked* me."

"How dare you! Do not call my child names. Carlisle, tell these people we will not tolerate such abuse."

"Yes, dear. We will not tolerate such abuse."

"You want to talk about abuse? How about the kid kicking me? How about him going into the pen after being told not to. How about the two of you letting him—"

"Okay, everyone. We're wrapping up the day now." Anne faced the wider group gathered around the knot of combatants. "Help yourself to any of the brownies left, then head on out."

The spectators dispersed, their mumbling divided between concern and ill-disguised amusement. "Best entertainment all day," one man said, dropping a twenty on the refreshment table.

"We should sue you," Destin's mother huffed.

Anne froze. The lank-haired husband murmured "Now, dear." Destin kept whining. Everett snorted.

But for Quince the words were a tonic, washing away pain and irritation as his professional instincts kicked in.

His voice was deceptively smooth as he said, "You'll find that the release you signed not only prevents you from suing, but lists instructions that your son broke—repeatedly. As his parents, you totally failed to supervise him, as you agreed to with your signature. And the form expressly says that failure to adhere to the agreement allows us to sue *you*."

The husband got it first. "C'mon, dear. Destin's not hurt, that's the important thing. Let's go."

"I wanna pet the goat," Destin wailed.

"In the car—*now!*"

The father's shout had both son and wife gaping at him. He scurried to herd them to the car. But before the last door closed, Quince heard the renewed duet of complaints from boy and woman.

Most of the others had already left. A few stragglers came from the barn, munching brownies and headed toward them. Anne took one look at them and made for the house, her command presence evaporating.

He and Everett fielded the final questions and a number of compliments. The taillights of the last car shone bright against dusk when he sent Everett inside and made a quick inspection, sticking a stack of comment cards in one jacket pocket, the final two brownies in the other, and hoisting the urn.

Anne was putting dinner on the table when he came in. The sudden silence told him they'd been taking about him—or more likely the debacle.

"Go ahead and say it," he offered.

Anne said quietly, "Take your jacket off and sit down. We'll talk after supper."

Everett's abbreviated snort carried amusement. "Good idea on the jacket. It stinks like Grandy, and *it* ain't ever produced a good milker."

Only at the end of his second bowl of stew did Quince start flipping through the comment cards.

"Throw those things out," Anne said.

"They're surprisingly positive. You should read—"

"I am not going to read them, because we are not going to do this or anything like it ever again. You can't honestly think otherwise after this afternoon."

"No," he acknowledged. He met her eyes. "I never meant to make you so miserable."

The moment drew out, long enough to burn something in his throat.

Then she stood abruptly, stacking plates. "No need to worry about me. But this isn't the way to save this farm—not and have it be a real farm, anyway. We'd have to spend so much time tending to people I'd hardly be able to plant anything. We're not in the business of people. We're in the business of farming."

"Too bad there's not a way to separate the stinkers at the gate."

"Some of 'em weren't as bad as I expected," Everett said.

Quince sighed. "Some were a lot worse."

Surprisingly, Anne chuckled. "Not as much a people person as you thought you were, huh?"

"Even people people have limits." He tried to grin, but shifting in his chair produced sensations that gave his mouth muscles too much else to do.

"What's wrong?" Anne asked.

"Can't you see, woman? The boy's hurting—"

"I'm fine."

"—that's what's wrong. Should have—"

"Quince, come upstairs, let me take a look."

"—been tending to him—"

"Really, I'm fine."

But she had a hold on his arm and had started him toward the stairs.

"—instead of sitting here jawing at him."

"Everett. That is out of—"

Anne tugged on his arm to stop his words, and said low but vehement. "Don't."

"He shouldn't—"

She added in a voice only he could hear, "He's worried about you."

He let himself be led upstairs.

Everett's voice, filled with proud gloom trailed them up the stairs. "Grandy's got a powerful butt. Probably broke a rib or two."

CHAPTER NINETEEN

ONLY AFTER SHE directed him to the hall bathroom she and Everett used and where she had a set of first aid supplies, did she realize that treating his injuries could—would?—involve his removing at least some clothes.

"Where did he get you?" she asked as casually as she could.

He sat on the closed toilet seat while she pulled out supplies. "Everett was right about the ribs. I suppose because I was bent over to protect darling Destin, but—"

She said a little thank-you prayer that Grandy hadn't gotten Quince anywhere normally covered by pants.

"—he was wrong about any ribs breaking."

"How do you know?"

"Don't know a hundred percent. But once they make sure you haven't punctured a lung or your aorta, they treat broken or bruised pretty much the same way. Let 'em heal. This doesn't feel as bad as broken ribs anyway, so I'd say bruised."

"You've had broken ribs?" She sat on the edge of the tub.

"Yeah. Played some lacrosse. Another time a drunk driver T-boned my car. Want me to take off my shirt?"

Yes.

No.

"Guess you better."

He crossed his arms in front of him, for an instant she remembered doing that while they waited for the tow truck, but this was entirely different. Because he grabbed the hem of his t-shirt in each hand, and pulled up and up and up, revealing the flat expanse above his pants, his belly button, then the ripple of muscles over bone of a man who was fit without obsessing.

The good news was the shirt covered his face as she swallowed several times. Hard.

The rising shirt bared more, as his chest widened to his shoulders.

Okay, the tailors of those beautiful coats and suits didn't deserve as much credit as she'd thought. They had plenty to work with.

As his shirt cleared his chin, his nose, then neared his eyes, she dropped her gaze to the kit in her hand. "You, uh, turn around so I can see—*Quince.*"

"What?" He'd pivoted away on her command, but now tried to look back over his shoulder. "Ouch."

"Don't twist. That's got to hurt more. You're already developing a bruise back here." She barely touched her fingers the right side of his back. "Sorry, I didn't mean to hurt you."

"You didn't."

Yet a shiver had run through him.

She swallowed again, forcing herself to speak normally to his back. "I'll clean this up a bit, but there's not much to do for it, except give you ibuprofen and a cold pack to bring down the swelling. It's going to be a beaut."

"At least this one won't be on my face."

She busied herself opening the antiseptic wipes, glad to follow the lead of his distraction. "Your face? Are you accident prone?"

"Nah. The face bruise was as a kid. There was this very proper party for the very proper kids of very proper people. I decided to liven it up. I found an empty plastic bin and there was this great staircase. I got in and started sliding down. The staircase curved and I didn't. Planted my face in an antique wrought iron baluster."

"Wrought iron? You could have been seriously hurt."

"Good thing they were wrought iron. If I'd ruined antique balusters, I really would have heard about it," he said dryly. "As it was, I had striped bruises up and down my face. The school wanted to take my kindergarten picture in profile to minimize their visibility. My father declared that it would be frontal, so I would have the reminder evermore of my poor judgment."

"You were in *kindergarten.*" Indignation made her sit tall.

He didn't answer directly. "It's the only picture of me he'd ever had in his office."

She bypassed what she wanted to say and invited, "Tell me about him."

He shrugged, then winced. "You've met his type. Hard-driving executive. Been CEO of a few firms you've heard of. Been in magazines and on TV, especially business and financial news shows. He's kept his assistant—his work wife—and housekeeper for decades, but he's gone through three wives."

Beneath the coolness she heard pain.

Yet Darcie had talked about the difference between Zeke's and Quince's families and upbringings before she'd said there was something *more.* Something deeper. Something more hurtful.

And there'd been the way he'd reacted when Anne had asked "Who was she?"

Was *she* coming up in this story?

"His first wife and their kids were the originals. He left them in the dust, along with his parents and siblings. A shame. I met them—not through him. Wasn't until I was out of college and sought them out myself. First encounters I'd had with my half-siblings, cousins, grandparents. All nice people. Really good people. His first wife, too. A really nice woman. Same can't be said for my mother," he said.

Anne gently stroked antiseptic cream over the abused area of his back, just in case.

"But she was an asset to him," he said. "She was part of his campaign to reach the next level. She brought Roselle and me in to his life and when she left—loved the money, not the man—he kept us both. Roselle to make sure his life at home always ran smoothly, me as the requisite heir, since he didn't consider his other children worthy."

She was chilled by Quince—warm, smiling Quince—talking with such dispassionate distance about his father, his mother, his family.

She slid along the edge of the bathtub, getting a partial view of his face.

"That opened the door for Wife Number Three. Outsiders might see her as a trite trophy wife—younger and beautiful—but it's sadder than that. Georgina is a decent human being who made the mistake of her life by falling in love with Peter Quincy II. She is perpetually disappointed and heartbroken by the fact that he does not return that affection."

He smiled. Nothing at all like his usual smile. Drawn and tight and dry, it looked like it hurt his face.

What it did to her… "Quince—"

"Don't stop me now. Besides, we just got to the part where I started disappointing dear old dad. Oh, I'd been disappointing all along. I was a good student, decent athlete, so I wasn't a total loss. But I wasn't stellar. No top-notch achievements to burnish his image. And I wasn't particularly good with people."

"You weren't?" she blurted.

"Nope. Especially not his associates. I tended toward surly. Maybe that was being a teenager. Or maybe something was brewing inside me I wasn't astute enough to recognize. Not until the day Roselle brought me to college—my father, naturally, was otherwise engaged. After arranging my things according to her standards, she drove away and I could not stop grinning.

"I was in the process of undoing most of what Roselle had done— not neatly—when in walked Zeke. Any other roommate would have recoiled in horror at the devastation I'd created. He didn't notice. Hell, he barely noticed me. Just walked in, sat on his bed, and pulled out a laptop, apparently prepared to bury his nose in that for four straight years. But a girl I'd met when we first came in the building had invited me and my not-yet-roommate to a gathering in her room after dinner."

Was this the mystery girl?

Part of that deeper hurt Darcie had alluded to?

"No way was I going to Fiona's room without him. The invitation had been to bring my roommate and I wasn't sure I'd be let in solo. So he was coming."

His mouth quirked, forming something closer to his usual grin.

"From then on, it became a goal to get him out of the room as much as I could. If I'd had a normal roommate, somebody eager to be my friend, to go out and be social with me, I suspect I'd have stayed surly. But Zeke being Zeke gave me the perfect opportunity to be as contrary as I'd always wanted to be to my father. Contrary to my father was surly. Contrary to Zeke was social and friendly. So there I was, being social and friendly."

"Are you saying you became a people person because Zeke wasn't?"

"Partly. He got me out of my own head and in to the challenge of trying to get into his. Hell, I took psych classes specifically to figure out ways to motivate him to be more social."

"And the girl who invited you to bring your roommate to the party?

"Fiona was my co-conspirator and Zeke was our project. Now it's your turn."

"To what?"

"Tell me something you'd rather keep to yourself. That's how this confiding thing works."

"There's nothing to te—"

"Then I'll pick. Tell me the history that makes you loathe Bob Chitmell. Did it happen before or after he declined to renew credit for the farm?"

"He didn't just decline to renew our credit. He waited until the last possible moment to do it. Gave no warning at all. Kept stringing me along, until the end, when he said, oops, no credit for you. When it was too late for me to line up another source of credit for the season. I paid up front for the seed we had to have, which cut our cushion to something more like a thread. If we'd had a decent harvest… But we didn't. As soon as we finished harvest, I started trying to line up credit for this coming spring. But with them already jumpy because I'm a woman, and Chitmell pulling our credit after all these years—there's got to be a fire when he's blowing smoke, right?—and the rotten harvest we had providing them reason to say I'm a lousy farmer…"

"An excuse, not a reason."

Small and wry, her smile still made his heart ka-thump.

"It would be really ungrateful to say: Like you'd know, Mr. Not-A-Farmer-At-All, wouldn't it."

"Totally ungrateful," he agreed.

"Anyway. No credit."

"So what are you going to do?"

"Keep trying to get credit. No, don't say it. I already know—the definition of insanity is doing the same thing over and over and expecting a different outcome."

She raised her hands and dropped her head. He expected her to drive her fingers through her hair.

Instead, she stopped the motion, sat straight, and spoke. "If we don't get credit, we'll plant as much as we can. I'm talking to a few people about potentially leasing some of our land. We'd put aside that money for seed for next year. With fewer acres, there will be less demand on our equipment, so that would be good."

"Less cost-effective and less income," he murmured.

"Yes. But that's the way it goes. We'll work our way back bit by bit, being careful and frugal, but not scared. That's what we're going to do."

He didn't believe he'd ever been more impressed by someone's quiet determination. And he'd been with Zeke Zeekowsky from the start.

Why the hell couldn't these bankers see what he saw?

"I'll stake you. Whatever you need."

First, she gaped. Then she started shaking her head.

"You don't know what kind of money we're talking, Quince. There's a reason even few well-to-do farmers don't self-fund. It's a whole lot to have tied up."

"I have money," he said quietly.

"That kind of cash? It's—"

"Remember, I've been with Zeke-Tech from the start. The stock—"

"No. Absolutely not. You are not selling stock in Zeke-Tech to gamble on Hooper Farm."

"A lot of people considered Zeke-Tech a gamble, you know. Besides, it's no gamble. I'd be investing in you."

"I can't—Thank you so much, but no…"

"Anne—"

She touched his cheek. Lightly, briefly. "No."

They held like that an instant, looking at each other. Then he took her chin in one hand, as he leaned in for a quick, soft kiss.

She tipped her head. Just a bit. Perfect as their lips met again. Not as soft.

The third kiss, she met him.

He parted her lips, stroked his tongue inside, shifted the angle and stroked a second time, a third, a fourth, building a rhythm.

One of her hands wrapped around his wrist, the other went behind his head. He had his free hand in her hair, his fingers sliding through it to shape to the curve of her skull.

Other curves beckoned.

Her throat to her shoulder first. Then cupping the point of that shoulder, which carried so much.

More curves. More softness. So much…

She jerked sideways.

Away from him? Trying to get away—? No. She'd slid on the narrow edge of the bathtub. If he hadn't had a hold on her she might have fallen in or off. But he held her steady.

So he felt the change in her immediately.

Her eyes were still closed, but it was gone. That moment. That closeness.

He waited until her eyes fluttered open. Yes. Those bruised, stubborn eyes had everything shut back behind her defenses.

Something had hit her. Hit her hard.

If he pushed now—to know what it was, to batter down those defenses—he might never get through.

"Just a few kisses, Anne," he lied. "Nothing for you to worry about."

She stood, the first aid kit falling to the floor. "I'm not worried. It just won't happen again."

She walked out. Straight-backed and determined.

"I'M SORRY, EVERETT."

She hadn't slept much the night before. She'd like to think it was because of disappointment that the farm tourism was not going to be even a partial solution to their financial needs.

But she wasn't completely self-deluded.

Quince had had the tact to retire to his room with an ice pack last night and was gone when she got up.

So she and Everett were having breakfast alone.

"What for?" He didn't look up from his coffee.

He was going to make her spell it out. Part of her penance, she supposed.

"I'm sorry you saw Quince and me kissing yesterday."

"Why're you sorry?"

"I know how much you loved Chris, and I never meant to upset you or—"

"Upset me? You think I don't know the boy's been dead these three years and more, and you've been living like a nun? You think I don't know that's not natural for a young one like you? Or'd you think I'm jealous? An old man—"

"Jeal—?"

"—who isn't gettin' any himself and don't want anybody else to get any 'cause of it. Well, I'll tell you, missy, I'm not so old as you might think. Now I'm gettin' into town regular, I've got more of a social life myself. You might just be surprised."

"You ... you're seeing someone?"

"Yup."

"Who? You haven't said a word to me."

"That's because once you've let the cat out of the bag, it's darned near impossible to get it back in. But it's time to let 'er out now. I've got a gal."

"SURPRISED? I WAS astonished," Anne told Jennifer the next day.

They were about to take a lunch break during an all-day working-on-the-books session at Stenner Autos in preparation for taxes.

Anne had carefully edited the conversation to remove any reference to how the topic had arisen, so there was no mention of her and Quince. Certainly nothing about kissing.

Although she caught Jennifer giving her a look that made her a little uneasy.

"Are you sure you should be telling me? Everett might not like it."

"Are you kidding? Not only was he positively boasting to me, but he also said that tonight, they're—and I quote—going public at bingo."

"So, who's the woman?"

"Mrs. Richards."

"*Mrs. Richards?*"

"What about Mrs. R?" asked Darcie, stepping into the office, followed by Vanessa Irish. "Oh, good. You haven't started eating yet. Rewrap those sandwiches, and prepare for a feast. Heard you were prepping taxes, so you deserve it."

She set a loaded shopping bag on the conference table at the other side of the room and started pulling out dishes, silverware, and tin-wrapped packages.

"She's taken to kidnapping, again," Vanessa said, setting an insulated bag on the table and pulling up a chair. "I was her first victim today."

"Sometimes it's the only solution with you workaholics. If I didn't kidnap Vanessa from the Zeke-Tech offices and show up uninvited to interrupt you two, you'd all work non-stop." Darcie unzipped the insulated bag and drew out a steaming pan. "Voila! Molly Harkin's famous lasagna."

"Ohhhh, that smells fabulous."

Jennifer followed the aroma, with Anne right behind her.

Only when they'd filled their plates, did Vanessa ask, "What were you saying about Mrs. Richards?"

The Zeke-Tech CFO rented Mrs. Richards' attic room, and Anne heard a note of protectiveness in her question.

So, for a second time, she told the carefully edited version of her conversation with Everett.

For a second time, the ending was greeted with gratifying surprise, as well as a level of delight expressed in Darcie's enthusiastic "Way to go, Mrs. R."

Less gratifying for Anne was their reaction after she'd answered their questions about the farm tourism fiasco.

For no reason she could see, her recap of the never-to-be-repeated day drew looks from each of the women that left her rather uneasy.

She put her head down and ate her lasagna.

She'd been talking too much anyway.

WITH EVERETT ACCOMPANYING Mrs. Richards to bingo, it was just her and Quince for dinner.

The first time they'd seen each other since … uh, since yesterday evening.

Cooking was done, eating was done. Soon the busyness of cleaning up would be done, too.

Anne could hear herself talking too fast as she told Everett's story for the third time today.

Quince wasn't giving her any of the looks she'd thought she'd seen from Jennifer, Darcie, and Vanessa—at least he didn't in the few times she looked toward him—yet she found herself talking a mile a minute.

"And you will never guess who it is." She squeezed out the sponge and set it in the holder to dry.

"I know who it is." He smiled.

"You know? Already? But it can't be on the grapevine yet. We all swore to keep quiet so they could have their drama at bingo tonight."

"It wasn't the grapevine. Everett mentioned it to me a while back."

She gaped at him. "I don't believe it. I mean, I'm not saying you're lying, I just… He *told* you? Why didn't you say anything to me?"

"Because I can keep a secret."

Something about the way he said that made her instantly wary. He seemed in a strange mood tonight. Not as even and relaxed as usual. She licked her lips but said nothing.

"Not as well as you can. Holding everything in, keeping it all heaped on your shoulders."

"All?"

What did he know? What had he heard?

"The present and future well-being of Hooper Farm, as well as Everett Hooper. Your own, too, but you ignore that."

"It's just the way farming is."

"You're too smart not to know you can't keep going on this way."

"Yes, I can." She had to.

"Do you know the segment of the population with the highest suicide rate?"

That startled a "What?" out of her.

"Farmers. Because they're isolated to start with, they deal with so many unpredictable factors they can't control yet they take on all the responsibility, and—here's one that will shock you—they think they have to do it all alone. In other words they suck at accepting, much less asking for, help. When was the last time you took a day off? When was the last time you actually relaxed?"

In her relief at the slight turn in the topic, she tried, "Relaxation's overrated."

It fell completely flat. Not even a flicker of a smile from him.

"Okay. Forget you for now. What about Hooper Farm? How long can it keep going on the way it's been going?"

Irritation came to her rescue. She welcomed it. "Quit interrogating me."

"Quit being evasive."

"I don't have to tell you anything. I'm *not* some rescue project for you to take on. Me or the farm. Even if I wanted you to, even if you took over, you can't magically fix everything. Quit thinking you can."

"I know I can't."

"You come riding in here on your white charger thinking all you have to do is learn a little about a situation and put your mind to it, and voila! Everything will be fixed from your magic touch. Well, let me tell you, Peter Quincy, these are problems that other people have wrestled with for a long time, and no matter how much smarter you think you are than anyone else—"

"I don't think that." Belatedly, something in his tone on the *I know I can't* tugged at her. But her irritation had carried them past that point. "However, a fresh view can see things that—"

"Seeing things that have already been seen a hundred times. It's like somebody has a car stuck in a snowbank and you drive up and say, *Have you ever thought of not driving into the snowbank?*"

"Okay, my ideas have failed so far. But you aren't going to solve anything by refusing to acknowledge what's happening. Ah. I see by that arrested look that as much as you'd like to tell me to go to hell, your innate honesty recognizes the truth of that. Why do you fight the truth so hard, Anne?"

"Because it stinks, that's why."

The short, sharp words stopped them both.

After a pause, he said slowly, "I suppose it does. But someone I admired a lot once told me that no matter how bad a truth or a reality is, facing it gives you more strength to make it work for you. Your way, you're just pushing against what is. This other way, you can make the most of what can be."

"Easy for you to say. The man with the gorgeous coat." She tried to make it light, to turn the mood, to gain space.

Tried and failed.

"I didn't say it."

"Fine. Your friend, this somebody you admired a lot. He probably had beautiful coats, too, and knew nothing about trying to hold onto a farm that's been in a family for generations when there's not enough money, land, time, people, or anything else."

"She. The person who said it was a woman."

She.

The one he'd thought of when she asked "Who was she?"

And then she knew. Absolutely. No question. Had to be.

Fiona.

The one who'd had the party he was determined to take Zeke to. The one who'd been his co-conspirator in drawing out Zeke. The one he loved.

The woman he didn't talk about.

"She did have beautiful coats," he continued. "She didn't know anything about trying to hold onto a farm. But she knew a lot about living. Living her very best. Until she died."

CHAPTER TWENTY

ANNE SUCKED IN sharply as if she'd had the wind knocked out of her by a blow and needed to resupply her oxygen in a hurry.

Truth to tell, she *had* had the wind knocked out of her.

Until she died.

The dark past Darcie had talked about. The pain. The loss.

The Girl.

Fiona.

The one who'd been his co-conspirator in bringing Zeke out into the world.

The one he loved.

Until she died.

"Quince." But without air it had no sound.

"Okay, I'm done interrogating. If you want to talk…"

But she couldn't. The breath was still not there to let her ask all the questions piled up in her throat.

He turned and left.

She could go after him—

No.

She'd complained about him asking her questions. She couldn't do it to him.

Could she?

Funny. From this side—the would-be question asker—she could see that the questions weren't to poke and pry. They weren't even plain old curiosity. They were concern. And wondering if, hidden in the answers somewhere was a key that might let her lift some of that sadness she caught deep in his eyes at unexpected times.

Still, it was none of her business. Just as she was none of his business.

Until she died.

Of what?

When?

Who was she?

Who was she to him…?

None of her business.

Especially that last question.

QUINCE WALKED IN to Zeke-Tech's temporary offices two doors down from the computer lab Wednesday morning and experienced a dim appreciation that every person between him and the conference room where he was to meet with Zeke and Vanessa was occupied. That meant nods and waves were plenty. He didn't have to talk or be pleasant.

Zeke was already in the conference room, tapping and typing, typing and tapping.

"Got an idea," he said without looking up.

"Great."

Zeke wrung the sarcasm out of that and responded literally. "It *will* be great. After I work out some kinks."

"I can hardly wait."

Zeke grunted in apparent acknowledgment that Quince had answered, though with no indication that he'd taken in the import of the answer. But then he added cheerfully, "Guess you're in a rotten mood because that farm tourism stuff was a disaster."

Quince had to give Zeke credit for recognizing his mood, if not for tact.

"Yeah."

After a few more moments of typing and tapping, Zeke frowned. "But the farm tourism experiment was over the weekend and you were normal Monday. What happened in between?"

"Nothing."

Zeke ignored that. His eyes narrowed. "It's Anne Hooper, isn't it?"

"What makes you say that?" Quince asked listlessly. Zeke would get bored with this fast.

"If it were something with the company, I'd know about it already. If it were your family—well, you don't have much to do with them, so I don't know why they'd make you this way. You were kind of this way when you had that really bad assistant for a while, but you fixed that and I thought the one you have now is good."

"She is."

"Ah-hah. So that leaves Anne, especially since Darcie said … uh, never mind."

"You're a tech marvel, Zeekowsky, but has anyone ever told you your people skills are lousy?"

"You. All the time. Does that mean you don't want to talk about it?"

"That's what it means."

Zeke continued looking at him for two, three, five breaths, then he slowly shook his head and said simply, "Not this time."

This wasn't the way things worked between them.

Quince didn't usually have moods, Zeke rarely noticed when he did, and if he did notice, Quince easily waved him off.

There had been only two other times in their friendship when Zeke hadn't complied when Quince indicated he didn't want to talk.

The day after Fiona told Quince about her terminal illness. And four months after her death.

"Tell me what's going on?"

Quince stared at nothing.

After a long moment, Zeke repeated, "What's going on, Quince?"

"I think Hooper Farm is going under."

Zeke closed his device and asked probing questions that pulled out what had made Quince suspect the farm was in financial trouble, his research, his unsuccessful attempts to improve the bottom line.

"You can't say Anne doesn't recognize the problem," Zeke said at the end.

"No, she sees it and her solution is to work herself into the ground."

That was dismissed with a hitch of one shoulder by the man who'd been doing the same to himself and those around him until Darcie came back in his life. "She let you try that farm tourism thing, so she's not closed to all ideas. But now you feel you can't offer any more ideas. Why?"

Figured Zeke would break it down that way. It wasn't nearly that simple. "Anne says I treat her like a rescue project. She seems to think I'm trying to fix the farm so I'd have something to pat myself on the back for."

"*Are* you treating her like a rescue project?"

"How the hell would I know," he snapped.

Zeke pulled in a breath, but the door opened at that moment and Vanessa walked in.

"Sorry for the delay. I have the top three options for local financial institutions. We must decide which to approach first. But we can't run over because the kids and I are making brownies for tonight."

"Tonight?" Zeke repeated.

"The Valentine's Day party at the computer lab. And don't forget you promised to give Warren a ride, since he's bringing the frame for the world map we're putting up."

"Oh. Yeah."

She shook her head, but once on the other side of the table, she stopped—walking and shaking her head. She looked from Quince to Zeke and back. "What?"

Before he could respond, Zeke said, "Anne says Quince likes her just because—"

"That is not what I said—"

"—he needs another rescue project—like Zeke-Tech or um…"

"Fiona?" Vanessa said.

"I, uh… You could—"

Quince covered Zeke's fumbling. "She doesn't know that Fiona was no rescue project. No lost cause."

"Huh." Vanessa came the rest of the way into the room, putting her briefcase on the table and starting to unload it.

"Huh what?" he demanded of her.

She didn't reply immediately. She finished straightening the files, folded her hands on the tabletop, and only then looked at him.

"You've met other women who needed rescuing since Fiona."

He side-stepped that. "I respect Anne—how hard she's working, how hard she's fighting."

"Uh-huh," she said this time. Zeke had the gall to nod in agreement.

"Uh-huh *what?*" He could have throttled both of them.

"In all these years there hasn't been another woman who could use your help—who needed rescuing to use your phrase—"

"Not mine—Anne's."

"—and who you respected because they were working hard and fighting hard?"

He twisted away tapping a pen against the table. "I'm sure I've met women like that."

From the corner of his eye, he saw her small smile, as if he'd just successfully learned to add two plus two. "But you haven't become involved—emotionally involved. Not with any of them. Not with any other woman at all. Not until Anne Hooper."

He stopped tapping.

"Good point, Vanessa." Zeke nodded sagaciously.

"Thank you, Zeke," she said, but she was looking across the table at him, her face and posture calm, her eyes warm. "The question you need to answer, Quince, is why Anne Hooper. That's what Anne really wants to know, too, even if she's not saying that. Why her?"

IF MONDAY NIGHT bingo was the big reveal for Everett and Peggy Richards being an item, then Wednesday night's party at the computer lab was their first official outing as a couple.

The place was packed, and the opportunity to witness the latest Drago news flash in person certainly contributed to it.

With wry appreciation for a job well-done, Quince had watched Anne skillfully weaving through the attendees while completely avoiding his vicinity.

What ease and comfort they'd built up in the weeks he'd lived at the farm were gone.

Lost in kisses and a dispute.

He was honest enough to realize that dispute had not been one-sided. Neither had the kisses.

The crowd was starting to thin out.

Anne was in a group with Everett, Mrs. R, Josh, Vanessa, Jorge O'Fallon from Stenner Autos, and Darcie.

As Quince prepared to skirt the group, Darcie reached across the flow of people, snagged his arm before he realized what she was up to, and said, "Come join us, Quince."

O'Fallon was saying something to Anne, but she flicked a look toward him that wasn't happy.

Wasn't my idea to join this group. Take it up with Darcie.

"…really keep the cost down. I could give you a list of what you need and possible sites to check."

"I don't know when I could get to it, Jorge. With needing to work off the car repairs, taxes, and all the regular work I need to pack into a short winter—"

"I'll do it," Quince said. He almost looked around to see if somebody behind him had blurted out that offer. Nope. It was him.

"Thanks, but with your job and everything else I couldn't impose on you that way. Not to mention you wouldn't know what to look for."

"I know enough about car parts."

"Oh, this is for the combine," O'Fallon said.

For half a breath, Quince saw O'Fallon as an opportunistic, preda-tory player trying to take advantage of Anne's mechanical needs to put the moves on her. Sure, he'd suggested the deal for the car, but that didn't mean the guy had to glom onto her, dragging out the contact by now fixing the combine.

The combine.

The piece of equipment that brought a worried frown to her eyes with every mention.

In Quince's next half a breath, O'Fallon regained his usual nice-guy status.

Everett said, "Quince doesn't know what to look for, but I sure do. Been running that machinery for longer than some of you've been alive."

"That's the problem," O'Fallon said with a grin.

"All the parts lists are computerized now, Everett," Anne objected. "The searching and ordering and—"

"Yeah, I know. Said I'd do it and I will."

"But—"

"I know how to do computer searches and find things. Can write emails and do more on there, too. Peggy has been teaching me. Private lessons."

They grinned at each other.

Anne gawked at them.

Filling the surprised silence, Quince asked, "You've been coming here for lessons and I somehow missed hearing about it?"

"The computer lab? Nah. Told you. Private lessons."

"How'd that come about?"

"Ask this forward woman," Everett said.

Mrs. R appeared to take that as a compliment. "I heard him telling his friends at the café how Anne was working all day on the farm and all night on the computer—"

Anne's gawk widened. Not quite a full jaw-dropped, eyes-bugged expression, but for her a definite gawk.

It was kind of cute.

And it twisted his heart that Everett's concern came as a surprise to her.

He's worried about you.

She'd recognized her great uncle-in-law's curmudgeonly ways as they applied to him, but not to herself.

"—and complaining that he was useless. So I marched up to him and said there was no reason he had to be useless. That he could help Anne with the computer work. He said he couldn't. I said I could teach him. He said no. So I just kept saying he could and he should. He said no, no, no, no. Until he said yes."

"But…" That was all Anne got out for a moment. They all waited to see if she'd gather more. "But you'd never learn, never even try…"

"Well, sorry to say this to you, Anne, but you're not the best teacher. You get all bossy and you don't explain it the way it'll get into my head and then you get all impatient with me."

Quince had a fair idea of who got impatient. But no sense bringing that up, not while Everett was on a roll.

"Come to think of it," he added, "Mrs. R gets bossy now and then, too, but I like it."

Another pair of grins.

Anne looked like she might fall over.

Everett turned more serious. "I'm not much in the fields, but I can do this for the farm—Hooper Farm." Clearly a thought hit him then—not a pleasant one. He held his hands up, as if in defense from an attack. "Not that I'll be doing bookkeeping or any of that, mind you. Hated it when I was running the place and not going to do it now. So don't be thinking it. None of that accounting stuff or what do they call them? Spreadsheets. None of that."

"That's okay, Everett." Anne swallowed. "I'll keep doing the books. Having you track down parts would be a tremendous help."

Everett Hooper's face contorted, and Quince guessed he was doing his best to prevent a beaming smile from erupting.

Mrs. R patted her beau's arm, then leaned close to Anne and said, "Don't worry, dear, we'll start working on the spreadsheets. He'll catch on to that, too. He's really very good with computers, no matter how much he grumbles."

Mrs. Mudge came up with her husband then and the two well-aged couples moved off.

Anne looked in the opposite direction from Quince and mumbled something about needing to get going.

"Was just about to say the same thing," he said easily. "Need to get with one of our Zeke-Tech people."

"Who?" Vanessa asked.

Quince fixed her with a look and said, "John."

"There are lots of Johns."

"I know. See you all later."

As he moved away, Quince heard Darcie ask, "What's up with Quince?"

But Josh spoke over her. "Mrs. R barely lets me cross the threshold, but she's carrying on with Everett Hooper? I'd never have believed it."

CHAPTER TWENTY-ONE

A T THE LAST four-way-stop sign before town, Quince was brought to a stop Friday morning by a Drago police car in the intersection and a stream of traffic coming the other way and turning in front of his lane.

A young man he didn't recognize but wearing the Drago Police Department uniform was directing the oncoming traffic to make that turn with a wide, sweeping motion of his arm, interrupted only by occasional waves in response to greetings from drivers.

He never even glanced toward Quince.

After a couple minutes, another officer got out of the police car and strolled toward Quince.

He lowered the window, letting in a gush of stinging cold.

"Hey, Quince," Darcie said.

"Hi, Darcie. What's going on?"

"What's going on? That's my question for you. Oh," she continued, as if she'd just made a discovery. "You mean here? Trainee directing traffic under my expert supervision. For the auction, of course."

Ignoring all subtext, he asked, "What auction?"

"You're as bad as Zeke, with your heads buried all the time. Sometimes in tech, sometimes just not seeing what's in front of you. I expect it of him. Not of you. Especially not when you're living at Hooper Farm."

He grinned at her. A better grin than he was really in the mood for. So that was a kind of triumph. "*Mea culpa.* Now, tell me what auction."

"It's the annual farm equipment consignment auction at the county fairgrounds. Today's the preview for county residents. Tomorrow's the auction. And you'll have a hard time getting between the interstate and the fairgrounds for all the traffic from all over the state."

"I'll remember that. How about today? When can you let me across the intersection so I can get in to town? Zeke said he has an idea he wants to talk to me about."

A craftiness came across her eyes. "Don't know that I can let you across. Stopping folks intent on getting their preview could be worth life or limb. You'd be better off just swimming with the current and going to the fairgrounds—"

"Why would I want to—?"

"—like Anne and Everett did a while ago.

Was her goal to deprive Zeke of an audience for his latest idea in hopes that would slow him down? Or to send Quince after Anne? Both? Impossible to tell.

Also impossible to tell if he wanted to go after Anne or not, especially not after the coolness these past days.

"Next to weekly bingo," Darcie continued, "this gathering is one of the best ways to get your fingers on the pulse of Drago. Heck, for the farming community it might be even better, especially if you're interested in the broader picture. Like you have a responsibility to be for Zeke-Tech."

"Are you saying it's my duty to go to this consignment sale preview?"

"Yes," she said flatly. "Also for the sake of traffic flow and safety. As a sworn officer of the law—"

"Fine." He didn't want to listen to Zeke's latest brainstorm right now anyway. "Think you can open a gap for me to slide in to that stream?"

"Now, that I can do."

HE SPOTTED EVERETT first. He was in deep discussion with Ned Benzil, one of the other poker regulars, and three more men of the same vintage.

Quince didn't approach him, instead continuing along the main aisle of a huge tent. Heaters blowing into the center didn't dent the chill.

On either side of the main aisle, huge machinery lined up like a beauty show for behemoths. Attachments gathered around like attendants at their skirts. Each grouping had a cadre of courtiers, almost exclusively men.

He received greetings from Drago residents. He also got a few puzzled looks from strangers, mostly focused on his coat.

And then there was Anne.

Standing out like a sunflower in a field of weeds.

The men here were mostly grizzled. They wore layers of shirts, hoodies, jackets, and pants that would never be new again. The theme of their attire was sturdy and warm.

So was hers, but it looked totally different on her. Maybe he'd gotten used to seeing her in those shapeless coveralls. So, just a few layers—and these actually meant for women—allowing even hints at her figure, seemed particularly appealing.

Her jacket stopped not long after her waist, allowing a view of her derriere and the long line of her legs.

Knowing he'd lose that view if he went up to her wasn't the only reason he stayed back.

There also was that coolness between them.

But right now the biggest factor was her expression.

She examined each of the behemoths with absorption, with acumen, with naked longing.

If he went up to her she'd put a guard on her reactions. He didn't like that she did that, but facts were facts.

So, keeping his distance, he followed her. A few times other viewers greeted her and there'd be animated discussion clearly devoted to the points of the closest mechanical giant.

Having finished examining the last one, she squared her shoulders and walked through the opening to a smaller, dingier tent with a worn sign over the entrance that read, "Parts."

"She should've gone right there first. Shouldn't've tortured herself with what she can't have."

He turned his head and saw Ned Benzil perched on the extension of one of the farm machines that looked like a giant set of teeth attached to a cockpit.

He hadn't been aware of the other man at all. That wasn't good.

Potentially worse, he had the feeling Ned had been watching him watch Anne for a while. It was worse, because from poker night he knew Ned loved to gossip.

"Small tent," Ned added. "You go back there and she'll spot you right off."

Ignoring that aspect, Quince asked, "Is that what she was doing? Torturing herself with what she can't have?"

"Yup." Ned slanted a look at him. "Lusting after machinery. Curse of a farmer."

…you haven't met any woman in those years who could use your help… who you respected because they were working hard and fighting hard? … why Anne Hooper?

He wished he'd had this answer to give Vanessa: Because she lusted after farm equipment and never, ever gave up.

"So you accept her as a farmer?"

The older man looked at him like he was nuts. "She's farming, ain't she?"

Quince squelched a grin. He should get Anne a bumper sticker saying that.

Its prosaic good sense would soothe frustration instilled by jackasses like Chitmell.

On second thought, not a bumper sticker. Mud on the back of her truck would hide it six days out of seven.

Just then she moved into the view between tent flaps.

She might have been lusting after the machinery in the main tent, but now she was completely focused on what was in front of her. She ran her hand over the base of a part that even from this distance looked more grimy than sleek.

That touch was as possessive and caressing as a lover's—

He cleared his throat. "How does this sale compare to other years, Ned?"

"Worse."

That brought Quince's head around. It didn't hurt that Anne had moved out of sight again.

"Worse?"

"Yup. A lot more for sale this year."

"How's that worse? Isn't it good for the buyers?"

He snorted. "Maybe for the few who can buy. There's more for sale because of folks selling out."

There was such sorrow beneath the unemotional acceptance that Quince didn't know what to say.

"Macklins over the other side of the county—that'll be one that hits hard if they go the way the rumors're saying. That family's farmed that land longest of anybody. Built it up to a real good-sized place. Real good-sized. But the next generation doesn't want to pick it up. Can't blame them. They're younger than me and I watched them growing up. Not a one of 'em has the touch. Not them and not their kids, either."

"The touch?"

He nodded, as if confirming what Quince had said, instead of leaving him in the dark. "Some have the touch. Some don't. Some that don't have it can still make it with the right situation—meaning the land and money and weather don't all turn against them at the same time several years in a row. But even those that have the touch have a real uphill battle if the land and money and weather aren't right."

"So land and money and weather's more important than the touch."

Ned stared off for a moment. Then he spit on the ground. "Hate to say it, but that's probably a true statement. Those with the touch can get the most out of the land, but money and weather can still swamp 'em."

"What about you, Ned?"

"Me? I've got enough to get by on. My dad, now he was one with the touch. Everett was probably closest to him when Everett was in his prime and Dad was starting to fail."

"What about Chris' father?"

"Not so's you'd notice, though he was a hard worker. Same with Chris. Difference was Chris thought he was better than he was. Took chances he shouldn't have. A lot of chances. No, in this generation … well, my older boy, Ned Junior, never wanted farming. Works in an office in the city. My younger boy, Kevin, is good. Definitely has the touch. Thought he was the best until—" His gaze slid toward the parts tent. "—Anne. My Kevin was the best of the young'uns, until she stepped in and took on the mess Chris left."

"Mess?"

"Yeah, he started in to no-till, then got caught in a wet spring and tilled and lost whatever he'd gained, along with being way behind."

Quince had no idea what that meant. Until he did, he'd follow the thread of something he *did* know.

"When you say money, you mean loans?"

"The loans, sure, but money in farmin's a lot more than that. It's how it all comes together. The prices you can get, the cost of seed, equipment breaking down and needing to be replaced or repaired, rents if you're working acres you don't own, taxes, hired help, crop insurance, storage, trucking … all of it. And it's all gone against her these past years. Worst of all last harvest." He sighed. "Her and the rest of us. Which is why my Kevin is gettin' the front end loader attachment for the tractor he's fixin' instead of a brand new tractor we could really use."

And why Anne wasn't even looking at attachments, but instead was eyeing old parts like a sugar addict in front of a candy counter.

He needed to find out exactly how much trouble Hooper Farm was in.

But Ned was not the one to tell him, not with that tendency to gossip.

Contemplating the best way to gather information, Quince started out.

But he stopped at the sight of Bob Chitmell smirking down the main aisle with an expression like a cat not only toying with a mouse, but finding a way to make a profit at it.

Quince looked back over his shoulder to see what Chitmell was looking at.

Not what.

Who.

Ned.

And Anne.

He fought down the urge to pummel the guy.

Use his skills. Do what he did best.

JOSH KINCANNON SUGGESTED they meet for lunch at the café when Quince called. "Topher and I are on our own. All the girls went to shop at some outlets up I-88."

When Quince joined their table, Topher looked up from his book with a shy smile and a quiet hello then resumed reading.

Josh shrugged, while his expression blended pride and love. "Vanessa says he's brilliant."

"*Da-ad*," Topher protested without looking up.

"She would know," Quince said.

While they waited for their meals, they chatted about the cold, Zeke-Tech, the basketball team, and Josh's concern about funding the Chem Lab repairs.

"Zeke—" Quince started.

"Offered. I think Darcie guilted him into it, saying he set the bad example. But we can't rely on him for everything. It won't be the same place—or the same people—if we do that." After they'd started on their food, he added, "So, what can I help you with, Quince?"

"Tell me about farming around here."

The other man's eyebrows went up. "History or current?"

Quince considered. "History first."

When Josh finished telling how a very colorful start had calmed under the influence of farming, he added, "Drago wouldn't exist as it is now without farming. Possibly as the Las Vegas of the prairies, but I doubt it. Those early crooks, con men, and counterfeiters were too far ahead of their time."

"What about farming and Drago more recently?"

"Before Zeke returned to town last spring, the town and surrounding farms were experiencing different but equal difficulties. Since then, the town has seen improvement with the prospect for a lot more. The farms haven't shared in that."

"The software Zeke—"

"Yeah, that's helped farmers growing direct-to-consumer crops. But most of our farmers are crop farmers, corn and soybeans, Large part of the corn goes to livestock feed. Companies also use corn and soybeans to produce medicine, paint, clothing, soap, wax, furniture, and more. And of course there's ethanol and biodiesel."

"You know that off the top of your head?"

"Do you have any idea how many class projects I've seen on what corn and soybeans can be turned into?"

Quince chuckled. "Point taken."

"Farming has a big impact on our students. Not only the ones living on farms. Most businesses in town have their fortunes tied to how the farmers are doing. Though that might change with Zeke-Tech here."

"Is that good or bad?"

Josh lifted a shoulder. "Probably some of both. Though I suspect more good for Drago and more bad for farmers. Especially—" He gave Quince a significant look. "—those between town and where Zeke-Tech is building. You know the housing situation. That's the logical spot to build houses. The value of that land's going up. So taxes will, too. Everybody in that swath is worried. And wait until construction starts. Don't get me wrong—Zeke-Tech is saving Drago. Pure and simple. Saving it. It's just not saving the farmers in its path."

Like Ned and others he'd met at Everett's poker games.

Like Hooper Farm.

As they paid, Josh said, "The person you need next is Darcie."

Quince stifled a groan. Josh patted him on the back.

"I know. But she keeps her fingers on the pulse of the county, and the county wouldn't have a pulse without farming."

AFTER SUPPER SATURDAY, Everett disappeared, destination unknown, though now guessable.

Quince headed directly to the high school gymnasium through snow squalls. Since Drago High was playing a home game, that's where just about everyone in the county would be.

Except Anne. Who was home. Working.

Quince found Darcie near the doors to the parking lot. She was in uniform, which was why there'd be no gathering tonight, and talking to two boys.

She waved them off and they scooted past like they'd been reprieved from prison.

"Friends from birth and they were going to go out—in this cold— to fight over a girl who's ga-ga for another boy who doesn't know she's alive. Thank God I'm not in high school anymore. What's up, Quince?"

"Have any time to talk—when you're off-duty?"

"About?"

"Farming around here."

"Huh. Come by the house tomorrow afternoon, stay for dinner."

SUNDAY'S SUNRISE WAS slow and cold as Anne turned the farm truck off the highway.

She'd gotten up in the deepest dark to check the fairgrounds.

Sometimes the sellers left parts or even complete equipment behind that they hadn't managed to sell. Never much. But Chris had picked up a gem one year...

Not this year. There'd been nothing left.

In the low light she almost missed a figure leaning against the snow-limned fence, looking toward the east.

Her heart stuttered, then resumed its normal rhythm when recognition hit.

What on earth was Zeke Zeekowsky doing out here at this hour?

She stopped, reached across the seat to roll down the passenger window.

"Zeke? Everything okay?"

He raised a hand, called hello, and started toward her. At the truck, he leaned down to look in the open window. "What a surprise to see you here."

"I live here," she said with a small smile.

"But you're driving toward the house, not away from it."

Okay, Zeke wasn't as absentminded as she might have thought. "Ran an errand. What are you doing here, Zeke? Are you okay?"

"Sure, I'm just thinking. Darcie goes running, I go thinking."

She smiled again. "What are you thinking about?"

"Quince."

She looked toward the house, automatically assuring herself it still stood intact, a shelter, not a place of danger for their boarder.

"He's okay." Then she added, "Isn't he?"

"No, he's not. He's worried."

"Abou—"

She didn't bite it off quite fast enough.

"You," he said.

His dark, intelligent eyes were fixed on her, making it impossible to follow her instinct to deny, deny, deny.

"I know he means well." She should leave it at that. The End. Not another word. Instead, she burst out. "He's just so damned irritating. He thinks he can solve everything. That all he has to do is put his mind to it, and everything will turn out okay."

"No he doesn't."

She opened her mouth to dispute that, then closed it in face of the absolute certainty in his voice and his eyes.

"What do you mean?"

Zeke looked away, down the track ahead of her truck. "I'm not much good at this sort of thing."

"What sort of thing."

He gestured vaguely. "People things. Love."

"This has absolutely nothing to do with—It has nothing to do with that sort of thing. It's—"

"Yes, it does. Quince loved her."

A hot poker slammed into Anne's chest. "What? No. Forget I said that. It's none of my business. This is all—" She gestured as if trying to shoo away flies. "—irrelevant."

"Is it?"

Zeke's question had no probing intonation. He was simply asking.

"Yes," she said firmly. "I have to go now. Sun's up and it's past time to start my work."

CHAPTER TWENTY-TWO

ANNE LOOKED TIRED at Sunday breakfast.

It didn't stop her from cooking a meal fit for a stevedore.

Breaking a silence as they ate, Quince told her he wouldn't be in for dinner because he was going in to town in the late afternoon and staying for dinner at Zeke and Darcie's.

"Thank you for letting me know," she said, distant and polite.

"Hey, I'll ride with you in and back if you'll drop me at Peggy's," Everett said. "She's been wanting me to come to supper, but I don't like taking the farm truck and leaving Anne with no vehicle while her car's still being worked on."

That might have been some of it, but Quince had also been aware that the man had been bent over and hobbling more the past two days. Perhaps he'd overdone it at the auction. Whatever the cause, it couldn't make driving the truck's stick shift any more comfortable.

"Sure, but that will leave Anne alone for dinner."

"I don't need anyone here to hold my hand." The instant the words were out, faint color rose in her cheeks, as if she'd belatedly recognized hand-holding could have a romantic application. "I'll get a lot more work done on the taxes not needing to stop to feed you two."

"Or stopping to eat?"

"Not your worry," Everett growled.

So much for breakfast conversation.

THAT AFTERNOON, THOUGH, Everett began talking up a storm as they put on their outerwear in the mudroom.

As if reverting to the previous week, he told stories about the farm's history.

When he ran out of steam as they neared town, Quince nudged. "You said your brother's son came to farm with you. Because you never had kids of your own?"

"Never did that I know of." He cackled a bit, which turned into a cough. "So Chris' daddy and his wife came here. We farmed here and another place that had a house on it. That's where they lived and raised Chris. Up until he was seventeen. That's when his folks died in a highway accident. It was hard on the boy, real hard."

"Must not have been easy on you, either."

"Whaddya mean, has somebody said I couldn't pull my weight, because I could. He moved in with me to finish out high school and I ran the place by myself, with help from him. Leg or no leg. And then we had the worst fight we ever had, that boy and me. He said he wasn't going to college and I said he was. Told him he needed to get some polish, a taste of living off the farm. When he came back to farm, it was his own doing. His decision. Because this place was in his blood just like all the Hoopers."

Like Anne, even though she hadn't been born a Hooper?

"We'd had a patch of bad years and with just me working alone, we'd had to let go of some of the leased land. But Chris worked hard. And the couple years after he met Anne and they married, those were good years. Real good years."

So had those couple *real good* years been followed by not good years? How many?

Asking would end the conversation right here.

"Did you have help with Chris at the end?"

"Help?"

"Hospice can—"

"*Hospice?*" Everett eyes went blank. "No. I'm not talking about this."

So the conversation ended anyway.

Quince let it go. Though he couldn't help but speculate about how much of the burden—time, energy, and emotion—of easing Chris Hooper's last days had rested on Everett's shoulders, and how much on Anne's.

They'd reached Mrs. Richard's house.

"Thanks," Everett said. "Call me when you're leaving, like we said."

"Wait a minute, there's something I want to say…"

"Spit it out, boy. I'm not sittin' here all day jawin' with you."

"I think you saw me kissing Anne the other day."

"You kissing her," the older man repeated without inflection.

"A week ago, the day the visitors—"

"I know what day was a week ago."

"Well, I owe you an apology, Everett. I told you at the start that anything between Anne and me was nowhere on the agenda. So you might be wondering—"

"Not wondering. Knew you were lying at the time." He pushed open the car door.

A rush of something went through Quince. Not anger. But he couldn't pin it down more than that.

"I wasn't lying," he said to Everett's back as the man maneuvered to exit the car. The first time Everett had ridden with him, Quince had tried to help him out of the car. Not a mistake he'd repeat. "I meant it. And there's really not anyth—"

"Don't get in a lather. I wasn't roughing you up for lying to me." Everett looked over his shoulder at him. "You were lying to yourself."

Zeke seemed distracted when Quince arrived at their house, not even trying to talk about his latest idea. Once he accepted that Quince and Darcie truly were going to talk about farming, he wandered off, apparently to the solace of his computer.

Darcie wasted no time. "What do you want to know?" She raised one eyebrow and added, "That you're afraid to ask Anne or Everett."

"It's not so much afraid as wanting to know what land mines I'm facing. So feel free to tell Jennifer she was right."

"Jennifer?" she repeated with unconvincing innocence. She quickly added, "First question?"

"What's no-till?"

"Ah, caught in the Anne-Everett crossfire, huh?"

"A few bullets whizzed past."

"Conventional farming is—as you might have guessed—how it's been done for centuries, by plowing up the soil. No-till doesn't. That's it in its simplest form. Proponents of no-till have studies showing that over the long term no-till is better for the soil and will produce a better yield. Conventional proponents dispute that and say no-till is a gamble."

"Everett wants conventional, Anne follows no-till?"

"Not that clear-cut. Everett's not totally conservative and Anne's more cautious. On the other hand, Chris was all for no-till. I mean *all* for it. Dove in completely. Not just no-till, either. He had all sorts of things he wanted to change and tried to do it all at once. Nothing gradual or measured. You've got to be an optimist to farm, but you've got to be realistic, too. Realistic and frugal and keep a good reserve on hand and keep your credit in good repair."

Not that different from how Vanessa made sure Zeke-Tech operated, with backups and cushions and contingency funds to weather tough times.

"How much of a mess did he leave Anne?" he asked.

"A major mess. On top of everything else, the spring before he died, it was wet. He tilled to try to dry the soil, get seeds planted. Short-term solution that undid whatever he'd accomplished over the previous years."

That explained what Ned had told him at the auction.

"Has Anne made it work since he died?"

"Better, but hanging on by the skin of her teeth. And that was before this past harvest."

"Okay, I know they were harvesting in November. That's late, right? Were they the only ones?"

"November is late, especially the end of the month, and most farmers around here were in the same boat. But it hit Hooper Farm harder." She held up a hand. "I'll come back to that. Harvest was late because the whole year was a mess. Not the sort you'd hear about on national news—not a dust bowl or major floods—just the kind that can drive a farmer out of business. A wet spring—always raining at the wrong time—seed couldn't get in the ground until late. The summer was cool. A few hot spells, but not what we normally get, so everything grew slow. With me?"

He nodded. "Late planting, short growing season."

"And then a double whammy. Wet fall and a really early freeze." She nodded, answering the question he hadn't asked. "Hit Hooper Farm hard. Killed half their beans—soybeans—because they weren't mature. The good thing is they plant more corn than beans."

"I hear a *but* in there."

"We'll get to that. The fields not hit by frost were just coming ready for harvest. Soybeans stay pretty well if they don't have to stand in the fields too long. Everybody went hot and heavy, because more rain was coming. The Hoopers' old equipment broke down. Anne tried fixing it, then improvised with even older equipment, but… Eventually a couple folks finished their fields and headed over to help. Just as the rain came. Hard."

"No harvesting in rain?"

"Not soybeans. They take the whole plant, and when beans get wet, the stems get ropey and tough. Like a wet mop in the combine. Can't get through them. Plus, there was flooding."

He rubbed the back of his neck with one hand. "Why didn't I know this? All that should have made an impression on me. I was here. I was right here in Drago and I don't remember people talking about what was happening."

"You weren't here the whole time." She shrugged. "But would you have cared? Sorry, Quince. I don't mean to be harsh, but are you sure people weren't talking about it? Or was it a matter of it not registering? Isn't that the way it is with most things? I mean, people in Drago focus on farming because it's all around us, but would we care if the price of, uh, microchips went up? At least before Zeke-Tech mattered here. Can't be aware of everything. There's just too much."

He knew she was right. So why couldn't he shake the feeling he'd failed somehow by not being aware?

Hell. Not just failed for not being aware, but for not being out there hand-picking soybeans in the rain … as if he knew the first thing about soybeans.

"Okay. Let's leave that. What's the rest of the bad news?"

She sighed. "The corn crop. You can harvest—"

"Hey," Zeke said from the doorway. "Aren't we going to eat?"

"In a bit. I'll finish telling Quince about corn harvesting and then we'll eat."

Zeke turned away, then back. "Oh, yeah, I came down to tell you because I could smell it in my office, something's burning."

"Burning?" Darcie jolted up and ran.

"It's smelled that way for a while," Zeke called after her. To Quince he said, "We need to talk about construction. And Vanessa's after me to get after you about the next five-year plan. So, no talking about corn harvesting at dinner."

ZEKE STUCK TO his edict.

There was conversation beyond construction and the next five-year plan, but none on farming.

With dinner—only slightly charred—and cleanup over, Quince said he needed to get back to Hooper Farm.

He was partly thinking of the early risers there, but he'd also picked up undercurrents that Darcie and Zeke favored an early-to-bed night … though sleep did not seem high on their agenda.

At the door, Darcie said, "You need to talk to Jennifer for the rest of the story."

"I could come back tomorrow and—"

"On duty," she said. "Suck it up and admit you were wrong and she was right. She won't make you grovel nearly as much as I would."

"Do you have time to talk?" Quince asked from Jennifer's office doorway.

She gestured him to a chair. "Some. Though Anne will be here soon."

"Why would you assume…?" He let it die at the light in her eyes. He shook the snow off his coat, dropped it onto one chair, and sat in the one closer to her desk. "Josh, Zeke, or Darcie?"

"All of them. Mostly Darcie. She mentioned groveling."

He grinned. "Consider me prostrated at your feet. You were right. I have stumbled and bumbled and screwed up."

"My, you don't hold back on the groveling, do you?"

"Not when it's well earned."

She generously let him off the hook. "Darcie said you were asking about the harvest."

"Corn, in particular. Darcie told me about the soybeans and was starting on corn when dinner intervened."

"You can harvest corn in wetter field conditions than soybeans, because you don't take the whole plant. The issue is the position of the ear. An ear of corn starts upright. As it matures, it drops—droops actually, and the shucks shed rainwater, protecting the ear. If the ear doesn't drop, rain runs in, and the ear rots. Or they can drop off the stalk prematurely in some weather."

"Good God, how does anyone stay in business?"

"Pure cussedness. Though sometimes that's not enough. Last fall, the problems weren't over even when they'd finally harvested. If the crops had gone directly into the silo they'd have rotted—with double, nearly triple what the moisture content should be."

"There has to be a way—"

"There is. Grain dryers at the elevators. Soybeans it's not too bad—they blow air through them with no extra heat. But corn… Fuel's needed for heat, so it's not cheap. The corn was so wet it cut drying efficiency by eighty percent. With demand way up and efficiency way down, the elevators had to prioritize. They waited to charge their best customers until after they sold their corn, but since the elevators heard Chitmell wouldn't give Anne credit…"

"So the Hoopers came in with a much reduced crop, late in the season, with limited funds to pay for drying and—what else?"

"Transport. Maybe they could have caught up if they'd had an eighteen-wheeler to haul crops. As it was, Anne must have made a thousand trips with everything she could get in that truck. Well into December."

He rubbed the back of his neck. "The perfect storm. Doing its best to drown the Hoopers."

"But there's also how the county is changing with Zeke-Tech's arrival and—" She broke off, said under her breath, "She's here." Then louder, "Anne, come in."

Anne came through the door, already turning a glare toward him.

Jennifer stood. "Excuse me for a moment, you two. I have to check in with Jorge in the shop about parts." She was gone in a flash.

Anne went around the desk and took Jennifer's chair.

"What are you doing here, Quince?"

He raised his eyebrows. "Hmm. Why might I come to Stenner Autos?"

"Oh." Her shoulders lost their tension. "You're getting a car to replace the most impractical vehicle in the county?"

"Actually, I'm considering a truck."

"A truck? You?"

"Why not me?"

"I don't see you in a truck."

"You *have* seen me in a truck. One you were driving. Though I can't say I'd be sold on the same model."

She snorted. "I bet not. You'd probably go for leather seats and all the latest tech do-dads available in a pickup."

He rose and put his coat over his arm. "I would insist on all the latest tech do-dads and leather could be practical for wiping off the dirt. But I was not thinking of a pickup."

"You said a truck, so—"

At the door, he turned his head to look at her. "I'm considering an eighteen-wheeler. To haul crops."

CHAPTER TWENTY-THREE

H E WAS GONE and Jennifer was back before Anne had recovered.

"Oh, darn. Quince left. I was hoping—Anne? What's the matter?"

"That man is crazy. Do you know what he said?"

When she finished repeating the exchange, Jennifer was silent a beat, then started laughing. Laughing hard.

To her surprise, Anne joined in.

It felt good, even though she had the uneasy feeling she didn't know exactly what she was laughing at.

QUINCE ROLLED TO a stop in front of the bank.

Widely separated snowflakes drifted languidly onto the windshield.

Had it been Anne's antipathy toward Chitmell that had given him such an aversion to the man? Bob's own unappealing ways? Or something else?

Instinct honed from business dealings for Zeke-Tech, maybe?

And what about that thought he'd had connecting Chitmell and his father?

What was that instinct telling him about the man?

Out for himself.

Working an angle.

Trying to put one over.

Possibly a side issue, but worth a check. Now, who—

A soft *beep* came from behind him. Not a full-throated hostile blare like he'd get in most cities, but a gentle, questioning, *Are you aware you've been sitting there awhile?*

He waved apologetically at the driver behind him—Mrs. Mudge, the woman who babysat for Josh Kincannon's kids—and drove into the next block, where an angled parking space gave him a safe place to scroll through his contacts list.

There it was, one of his many former assistants.

But he didn't make the call.

He'd been trying so damned hard to look for ways to give the Hoopers what they wanted that he'd stopped operating as a problem-solving COO who dug for facts, faced them, and moved on from there.

Strip the wishful thinking away, and he could already see the outlines of reality. A reality that wasn't going to conform to their wishes no matter what he did.

The best he could hope for was that it would give them what they needed.

He hesitated, then hit a familiar number. "Brenda? I need help."

"I'm busy," Zeke's assistant said, predictably, "and you have a perfectly adequate assistant of your own, who—"

"I know. This isn't for Zeke-Tech."

Silence.

He dared to go on. "I need to have conversations with top farm consultants—crop farms, specifically. Preferably ones who know the area around Drago. Also real estate experts and an accountant or two. And I need them all fast."

"This isn't for Zeke-Tech?"

He knew what she was doing. And he'd pay the toll. "It's not. It's personal. I'm asking you for a personal favor."

After that call ended, he made the one to his former assistant.

"SNOW'S COMING DOWN hard now. Roads are bad," Everett said when Anne answered her phone. "I'm staying here in town. At Peggy's."

Anne could swear she heard a giggle in the background.

Yesterday's haphazard snow had organized into growing accumulation.

But the roads weren't *that* bad. Quince had made it home—to the *farm*—in his little car.

"Okay," she said. Because what else could she say?

"Don't want to ask anyone to go out in this," Everett added, as if he knew she wasn't really buying it. In fairness, that made sense. Anyone who brought him out to Hooper Farm would then have to drive back to town.

"I'll call you if I'm not going to make it back in the morning."

"Okay. Good night."

She stood with the phone in her hand. If she didn't tell Quince, he might not realize…

She needed to get a grip on herself.

She should have laughed at Peter Quincy III when he'd made that outrageous claim of looking to buy an eighteen-wheeler.

She should not have let her heart thud so hard when she'd recognized him in Jennifer's office.

She should treat him easy and breezy.

Or…

Maybe she should tell him the truth.

"Problem?"

She jumped, spinning around at Quince's voice behind her.

"Whoa. Didn't mean to scare you. Wondered if the call was Everett, if he's having trouble with the weather?"

"No—I mean, yes, it was him, but no trouble. He's staying with Mrs. Richards because of the roads."

"Makes sense."

"Yeah, uh, listen, dinner's going to be real simple. Soup and toasted cheese sandwiches. I'm, uh, I'm going to go up and take a shower first. Been out in the barn and, uh…"

"Okay."

"Won't take me long."

"Okay."

SHE CAME OUT of the bathroom in her zipped-up mid-calf robe, pulling the scrunchy out of her hair.

And stopped.

Quince was at the other end of the hall, just outside the door to his room, holding a folder.

Just standing and looking at her.

She burned.

Right there. Right then. *Whoosh.* Full cinder mode.

Her lungs pumped, her heart hammered, her legs shook as if she'd been running for miles.

If she turned and went into her room, that would be it. She knew that. He wouldn't follow.

Her hair had drifted down to her shoulders, but her hand was still raised.

She dropped the scrunchy, then slowly, deliberately lowered her hand to the robe's zipper.

She unzipped it to her waist.

The material didn't separate much, but she felt the cooler air seep in, tightening her nipples.

Then Quince was striding to her. The folder spun off toward the hall table, missing, and spilling on the floor.

He was to her, his hands sliding in the opening, around her, bringing her up against his hard body, his lips on her forehead, her chin—ah, her mouth. Their mouths open, seeking and meeting.

Then he pulled back.

"Anne—?"

"Don't ask. Don't let me be a chicken. Not now."

He chuckled a little, low and hot. Then he pushed back one side of her robe, bent and took her nipple in his mouth.

"Don't stop. Don't stop."

"Just for a minute," he promised.

Oh, he was carrying her. Into the bedroom. Door slammed shut behind them with one foot. The bed rising up as he lowered her down, coming with her.

She pulled at his clothes, his shirt, his belt, his zipper—hers had been so easy, why was his so hard.

Ahh, so hard. Him. All him.

And then hers wasn't easy anymore.

It didn't zip down all the way, it was one of those you stepped in to. Or out of. How was he going to…?

He pulled. Something ripped a little. Fine.

As long as he came back and… But he wasn't back. What was he doing? Oh.

"You're kidding? You had a condom in your pocket?"

"Condoms. Plural."

"That sure of yourself?"

"No." He was over her now, kissing her. "That determined not to be an idiot for your sake."

"I suppose I should say—*Oh*—Thank you."

"I think you just did."

He held his upper body up with his arms, bending to once again kiss her nipples.

"You're…" She swallowed. "You're inside me."

"I am."

She took his face between her hands and brought it up to hers. "Are you going to do something about that?"

"Yeah, I am."

"Now."

He complied.

HE RETURNED FROM the bathroom, and immediately brought her up against him.

She looked surprised when her body responded to the contact.

"Quince, that was… I haven't… Not since…"

Celibate since her husband died. And surprised that her body still experiences desire. And the complete and happy satisfaction of that desire.

"I know. It'll take me a while, but in the meantime…"

SHE WOKE TO the smell of corn chowder and toasted cheese.

Quince, wearing only jeans, held a tray with mugs and plates and glasses of water.

She sat up, pulling the covers with her. "You can cook."

"Toasted cheese and the microwave. That's it. I haven't been holding out on you. You just picked the right menu tonight. Hungry?"

"Starved."

He shed the jeans and they wedged pillows behind them and ate their dinner. Once he stopped to kiss a smudge of corn chowder from the corner of her mouth, which meant they ate the rest cold.

With the tray removed, they slid down under the covers, spooned into each other's warmth.

She talked about her family, as if introducing them to him, one by one.

"Now tell me about yours," she said.

"Mine's not worth talking about."

"But—

"Really."

"But," she said again, more slowly, "Fiona is worth talking about."

She felt a slight change in his breathing.

"Will you tell me about her?"

He told about their meeting outside the dorm the day he arrived, about the invitation to come to the party in her room with his roommate, about their conspiracy to get Zeke out, mingling with people. "We took those psych classes to learn ways to deal with him, took them together when she could."

"When she could?"

"She was already sick. When I got there as a freshman, she was returning after missing a year because of tests and treatments. She knew it was fatal. Told me so two weeks into our dating because she said it wouldn't be fair not to. But she was not done living. She taught me more about living in the five years with her than my parents ever did. Well, maybe that's not a fair comparison, since my mother wasn't around long. But you get the point.

"She also drew me into her family. Great people. A true family." He shook his head. "I hadn't known people existed like that. They're not perfect. They'd be the first to say that. But funny, generous, open, and they love each other like crazy. Her parents, her older brother, and her younger sister. They live in Palo Alto. She could have lived at home, especially … later. But she wanted the whole college experience. And they supported her."

She turned over to be able to see him.

"She made it, too. Graduated. Walked up and got her diploma."

He hadn't been smiling exactly but now the lines of his face shifted, leaving only the sorrow, devoid of the good memories.

"She wouldn't marry me," he said abruptly. "I must have asked hundreds of times the last month. She'd just say, *No, Peter.* Every time. *No, Peter.*"

Fiona had said no and now he said he never would marry.

"She said it was because of insurance. She was on her parents'. If we married, that would end, and I was right out of school, didn't have any. She'd laugh and say she couldn't afford to marry me."

"I'm so sorry, Quince. So very sorry for your terrible, terrible loss."

Slowly he brought his gaze to hers. "Do you know my father never once said those words to me?"

"Never? But…"

"He was too busy making plans. How I could *contribute* to his company after the *delay* of a year after graduation. That's all Fiona's last year was to him—a delay. The hell of it was, I was too numb to even fight him. I was a robot, going through the motions because I had nothing left." A flicker touched his lips. "Until Zeke came and kidnapped me."

"Not literally?"

"Yeah, pretty much. He doesn't talk about it, and I don't remember much until I was sitting in the passenger seat of this old beater of a car Zeke had. And a dim memory of my father shouting never to darken his door again or something like that. And Zeke saying, 'Wave good-bye, Quince.' And I did. Haven't seen him since."

"Oh, Quince, that's—Sorry." She'd put her hand on his chest, then snatched it back.

"What?"

"My hands. They're so rough. All the work. No matter how much lotion…"

He took her hand in both of his, kissed each fingertip, then returned it to his chest. "It feels perfect."

She laughed a little, hoping it didn't come out as giddy as it felt. The sensation of his lips on her fingertips … after all they'd done, how could that have her ready in an instant to do more?

"Perfect? A farmer's hands? I don't think so. My farmer's hands. My farmer's hands have the touch," he murmured.

He must be three-quarters asleep, lulled by the catharsis of what he'd told her, because his words weren't making a lot of sense.

That was fine with her. She drifted, too. Not thinking, not planning, not even worrying. Just existing in this soft cloud between desire sated and desire renewed. Wanting and being wanted.

Anyone looking at them from the outside might wonder at what a man like Quince saw in her. She smiled slowly. She suspected a few might wonder what she saw in him, complete non-farmer that he was.

But they were a match in wanting. A perfect match.

Awareness suddenly concentrated back in to the tips of her fingers. Because under them his heart had picked up a stronger, harder rhythm.

"What's this about?" She spread her hand over that heartbeat.

"I have an idea."

She kissed his chest and felt his heart jump under her lips. "Must be a good one."

"I think so." He wrapped his arms around her and drew her on top of him. "I think it's an excellent idea."

THAT *HAD* BEEN a great idea.

He could only hope that the one he hadn't told her about would turn out half as good.

It wasn't ready. There were still a lot of holes to fill.

But there was no choice. It wasn't something he could keep from her after tonight.

He had to tell her, Everett, and the others. Right away.

That's what had started his heart going faster … until her touch had done a much, much better job of that.

QUINCE WAS DOWNSTAIRS, but Anne was still in the shower upstairs when Everett came in the next morning, having gotten a ride with a plow driver he knew.

He was in a noticeably good mood, though he did cast one look up toward the ceiling in apparent recognition that the sound of running water emanated from the master bathroom.

Later, after Quince helped Anne clean up the breakfast dishes, he said, "I'd like you to come with me on a short drive. Both of you."

"I want to check my bids for—"

"It's important, Anne."

"How would we all fit in that car of yours?" Everett demanded.

Quince said, "We'll take the farm truck."

THEY HUMORED HIM. Including letting him drive.

They weren't even all that curious. Not until he turned off the highway, at a spot that was clearly familiar to both of them, judging by the look they exchanged.

He brought them to the rise he'd scoped out that gave a good view of the land stretching out to the northwest, with the flow of rich soil interrupted only by the house and buildings set against a protective windbreak of firs, and a ribbon of trees tracing the river's route.

"Let's get out and stretch our legs," Quince said.

They both eyed him, but didn't object despite the brisk wind and glowering sky.

They walked to the fence line, Everett stopping at the closest fence post, Quince and Anne moving past it a bit.

"Know anything about this farm?" he asked them.

Anne gave him a quick, searching look, but said nothing. Instead, turning to look out at the fields.

"Good-sized place," Everett said.

"I'm glad to have that confirmed. I wondered about that initially, since I didn't have much to compare it to. With all the talk at poker about farms, not one of those guys has ever said how big his farm is."

Everett grunted. "Those with more acres wouldn't want neighbors to think they were bragging and those with fewer don't want to let on."

"It's not just the land they own, it's what they work." Anne's squint-eyed focus was on the stubbled fields in front of them. "That's what's important about the size of a farm—how many acres you can work."

"In this case, it's the number of acres they own. You can't sell what you don't own."

"Sell?" Her word came out as dull as a bad note on an out-of-tune piano.

"By gum, the Macklins *are* selling?" Everett kicked at the frozen earth. Then he coughed and grabbed the fence post to keep his balance. "Oldest farm in the county. Prime soil, too."

Quince waited, letting them absorb that news.

Everett recovered first. "Real prime land," he said slowly. "They'd never so much as rent an acre before. But now maybe we—"

Anne interrupted him. "We can't afford it. As much as I'd like to…" She sighed. "Even if they rent it for less than the going rate while they sell, which shouldn't take long. Even if the new owner can be bamboozled into a bargain rate. Even if … well, even if anything. We can't afford to rent."

"You could if you liquidated your asset." Quince said.

Everett turned and looked at him, but Anne was the one who spoke, still gazing across the fields, now with some of that yearning he'd seen at the auction.

"Like we could get much for that junkyard of equipment we've got," she scoffed.

"He said asset." Everett's voice was a rasp. "Singular. The one thing that's worth anything, because it's the one thing people want to buy now."

As she turned, she sucked in on a gasp, then launched at him, "The land. The *land?* You want us to *sell* Hooper Farm? It's been in Everett's family for generations. It's where he was born. It's his home. He loves that place. He's put his whole life into it. You can't ask that of him."

"He's asking it of both of us."

At Everett's rough voice, she spun around to her great-uncle in-law.

Quince held still, watching her.

Everett limped closer. "It's your family, too, Anne. It's your home. You love it." He paused, cleared his throat, and added, "You're putting your life into it."

Tears glazed her eyes. She put a hand on Everett's arm, then faced Quince. "There you have it. We're not selling."

He dropped his head a moment, then slowly brought it up, looking straight into her eyes.

What he could do for her was give her the facts. No matter how much he wished they could be changed.

"If you don't sell, you'll go bankrupt and lose the farm anyway. Not this year. Maybe not next year. But the likelihood of losing it goes up each year. It's the hole you were handed, it's the hole that got deeper last year, it's the pressure of land values, it's all of it. But the projections—"

"Projections," Everett muttered.

Quince didn't look away from her. "Yes, projections. And numbers. And logic. But also your gut. You know it. You *both* know it. I've seen it in both of you day after day. For all your hard work and optimism and stubbornness, you know it."

The silence that followed was dense and deep.

He sucked in a breath and their silence came inside him, making his lungs work harder, his heart pump faster to ward it off.

"I'd change this for you if I could. I looked into putting money into Hooper Farm—"

"You will not."

"We don't need your—"

He spoke over Everett. "I'm not. Because it couldn't do enough to change the projections. You know that, Everett. That's why you haven't let Anne put the insurance money in. Because you know it wouldn't plug the leak, it would just flow out with the rest. With the need for housing because of Zeke-Tech, the tide's too far along. It's going to happen. Anne—" He made sure she was meeting his eyes before he repeated that, emphasizing each word. "—it's going to happen. You can't stop it, not the two of you together, not your neighbors, either. But you *can* take control. If you get ahead of it."

If he was hoping—or praying—for a *how?* He didn't get it.

He'd just have to do without.

"There's going to be a meeting tonight with the other landowners between Drago and the Zeke-Tech site and you two, of course. There's a way—"

"Why'd you bring us here?" Anne interrupted.

He hesitated. The rest had been solid ground, layers of facts. Now he'd venture into a murkier landscape.

"So you'd see you don't need to quit farming. Either of you. The idea would be to sell Hooper Farm and use the proceeds to buy another place. A fresh start where you're not under pressure from people wanting to build houses where you're trying to farm."

"Here?" Everett scoffed. "Even if we sold the farm, this'll be long gone by that time. This is prime land. That won't mean much to you, but I'm here to say it'll be snapped up before you can say boo. Bet there're bids in as we stand here."

"It's already been sold. To me."

The Hoopers gawked at him.

"What on earth are *you* going to do with a farm?" Everett finally asked.

It almost made Quince grin.

Almost.

"Have Anne and you farm it until—"

"Sharecroppers," Everett snapped.

"No. Owners. You buy it from me when you have the proceeds from Hooper Farm. I'd be a sort of bridge until you have money."

"Proceeds from Hooper Farm? You mean selling Hooper Farm."

He didn't like the way Anne said that. On the other hand, what did he expect?

"Yes. Selling it in a very specific way. That's what the meeting's about tonight."

CHAPTER TWENTY-FOUR

THE CHURCH BASEMENT was relaxed and comfortable. He wished the same could be said for the people gathered here.

These families represented the farms between Drago and the Zeke-Tech site, plus one the other side of it.

Ned and Candy Benzil, with two of their sons, one he recognized from town and one in a business suit with his tie loosened. Tammy and Todd Van Winkle. Will Larkin and his son. And the others he'd just met tonight.

They weren't any more talkative than Anne and Everett had been. Which was not at all. Not in the drive back to Hooper Farm. Not during supper. Not in the drive here.

He supposed he should be happy they'd come at all.

Darcie had said they would, that they all would, when he'd asked about a place to hold this meeting.

What he hadn't expected was that Darcie and Zeke would come, too, sitting quietly in the background. The only thing they'd said when they arrived was Darcie's, "Thought you could use moral support."

He'd been treading as carefully as he knew how.

He had to state the facts, but he wasn't going to rub in what they already knew about the financial state of their farms.

"This is unorthodox," he said. "Lots of precedents of landowners banding together to try to fight a development or save a particular piece of land. Not so much with the landowners coming together to form a cooperative like I'm proposing."

"Why should we try something unorthodox?" demanded Tammy.

"If no one was ever willing to be the beta—"

Anne snorted.

"Okay, take it out of tech." Quince looked around at all of them. "If no one's willing to be a guinea pig—"

Now Everett snorted. "My old dad used to say pioneers get the arrows, settlers get the land. That means you don't want to be the first one out there."

"Somebody's got to try new things or nothing ever changes. Especially when the status quo isn't going to keep working. And you all know it isn't."

No one met his gaze. As far as he could tell none of them looked at each other, either.

"So…" Ned cleared his throat and started again. "So you're saying to sell out to developers?"

"No." He said it vehemently enough that several heads came up, including Ned's business-suited son. "I'm saying to become the developers yourselves."

More heads came up, all looking puzzled. Except for Ned Benzil Jr.

"Developers take a big share of the money. And they take all the control. So you band together and act as your own developers, selling directly to the people who're building houses, keeping control of what happens, keeping more of the money. A lot more of the money."

"But not farming the land," Anne said.

Every head turned toward her, then back to him.

"No, not farming that land. But you'd have capital to get another farm. Perhaps, even—"

"Oh, yeah, just start over on another farm. A farm doesn't just spring from a box. You can't order it on the Internet."

"No, but you can buy an existing farm."

"Leaving the farm—our farms to be carved into pieces."

"Yes."

He wouldn't rush past that, play it down. It was a fact and demanded to be recognized.

Into the long silence that followed, Ned finally spoke. "We're no developers. We're farmers."

"I know. You'd need help. I've looked into people who could handle the details for you. You could combine that with local help." He nodded toward Ned's businessman son.

That brightened a few faces, at the prospect of someone they knew so well being involved.

Quince went on with a rough outline of how it might work, filling them in on the research he'd done, the resources he'd found. He also brought up the timeline, which pretty much defined the term delayed gratification.

"If we can't farm our land, we're going to need something to live off of, not to mention these people handling the details wouldn't work for nothing," Kevin Benzil said.

"You're right. You'd need bridge financing for—"

"Oh, right, like Bob Chitmell's going to fork over—"

"Not Chitmell." Again, Quince had been more forceful than he intended. "It would be wiser to look for financing from an entity without potentially conflicting priorities."

"Like one not in bed with a developer," someone muttered, low enough that Quince didn't recognize the speaker.

Figured that these folks were already aware of that. His research had given Quince good reason to think the banker was in cahoots with a developer with a reputation for pushing the limits of shady. Good reason, but not enough proof. Not yet, anyway.

"I have leads on potential financing in state, but not right here in the county, that I'd be happy to turn over to you once you've organized—if you decide to go this route."

"Would you be part of that organization?" Ned Junior asked.

"Don't worry, I'm not setting myself up to be part of what's your—"

"*Could* you be part of it?" he amended. "At least as a consultant."

Quince couldn't stop himself from looking at Anne. She still had her head down.

"There would be a lot of decisions to make before that possibility would come up. An impartial expert might be concerned about possible conflicts of interest because of my Zeke-Tech role."

"A lot of decisions to be made...." Ned shook his head.

"Where would we even start?" added his younger son.

It was the opening Quince needed, but not from the person he'd wanted.

He shot another look at Anne, with no response.

Consciously shifting to business mode, he began to lay out the possible paths.

OUTSIDE THE CHURCH, with people still milling around, she watched Ned clap Quince's arm. "Noticed you didn't say absolutely no to my boy's proposal about being a consultant."

"Ned—"

"I know, I know. Down the road."

The Benzils left, apparently in relatively good humor.

Anne said to Everett, "I'm getting a ride with the Larkins."

Quince reached for her. "Anne—"

She jerked her arm away.

"You said you always wanted to grow things," he said. "This way you still can. And you can do it the way you want to. You'll have the resources from your share of Hooper Farm to give you a cushion, a stake. Instead of always scrambling."

"Don't. Just don't."

"You're not going to stop this."

"This what? Progress? You're going to tell us we can't stand in the way of *progress*? Well, progress can't run us over, either. It can't push us out of our homes."

"You can stay in the house, all of you can stay in your houses, once you sell off the land, or—"

"With all those *people* around us?" Everett started. "Wh—"

"Or," Quince interrupted firmly, "you can sell the house and land to buy somewhere else. Or you can continue going the way you're going until you're bankrupt and get a lot less for the land or house. You have choices. They don't include the one you want. But if you're not brave enough to make the choice, it will be made for you."

"I won't. I won't give it up—I won't give up."

"Anne, I want to help. I'm trying to help. It's what I do at Zeke-Tech and I'm good at it, if you'll—"

"He is," Zeke said.

"I'm—the farm isn't a problem to solve then move on from."

"Well, once a problem's solved, why would he—"

"Shut up, Zeke," Quince snapped.

"No, he's right. And he's telling the truth. I appreciate that. Thank you, Zeke."

"You're welcome." The owner of Zeke-Tech sounded confused.

"C'mon, Zeke, let's go," Darcie said.

Everyone was melting away, leaving her and Quince facing each other in the cold dimness.

"It's what you don't understand, Quince. A farm is a never-ending series of problems to solve, to resolve, to improve, to reconcile yourself to not solving. You can't do that. That's not who you are. I see that after this meeting. You need to solve it. I understand after—I understand. I do. But this isn't going to work. Us. It was a bad idea. A very bad idea."

"Anne—"

As she backed away her fingers trailed across his cheek as if reluctant to leave his skin. "Thank you for trying, but no. I can't let the farm go. I can't do that to him."

"To Everett? But—"

"Chris.

She was calm. Too calm.

"It's the one thing I can do for him now. Save the farm. I couldn't save him. He was gone when I found him. Hanging from the hayloft pulley. I got him into the hayloft, but I couldn't get him free. I couldn't..." She sucked in a breath. "I broke the pulley. That's why it doesn't work. I broke it."

SUICIDE.

Quince fought to keep his breathing even.

Her husband had committed suicide and no one had ever told him.

What the—

Later. Deal with that later.

Right now there was Anne. Those bruised eyes, and the blow she'd sustained.

"Was there a note?"

"Yes."

If Chris Hooper had blamed her…

Well, the man was already dead, so he couldn't kill him. Besides, what mattered was Anne.

She was too contained. Too withdrawn.

Even if the answer was the worst possible one, she needed to let it out.

"What did it say?" He didn't let himself touch her. Just waited.

Tight, raw, determined, her voice came slowly. "He was sorry to let us down—Everett and me. He loved us. He couldn't take the failure anymore. We'd all be better off without him, including the farm."

No recriminations against his wife. Quince breathed out, then in. "That was all?"

"Wasn't that enough? I'd made him feel like a failure. I'd made him feel like he couldn't make a success of the farm."

"You can't blame yourself for how he felt. He was a farmer. He formed his own conclusions."

She pushed her hair behind her ears, then kept the movement going to meet at the back of her neck, as if to rub a knot there. "I wasn't paying close enough attention. Like you said about the suicide rate among farmers, he wasn't getting help. He was putting it all on himself. And I was so caught up in the farm and my fantasy of living on a farm…"

"So now you're doing the same thing, putting it all on yourself?

That's wrong, Anne. Besides, every word I've heard is how good you were for him. How much better he was with you. How he adored you."

"If he hadn't adored me would he still be alive? Because he adored me he couldn't stand living with what was happening. Loving me made it harder for him to face—impossible for him to face. That's what loving me did to Chris Hooper."

"Anne, you aren't the reason he killed himself."

"How could you know? How could you possibly know?"

She came toward him and for an instant he thought it would be okay. Because her expression was so soft. Softer than he'd ever seen it. Even after they'd made love. It was … yes, almost yearning.

Then she reached up one hand to his cheek and kissed him on the other one, and his heart dropped to the bottom of his gut like a rock.

"Anne—"

"I can't ask you to move out—" The sound wasn't a laugh. It had far too many edges. "We need your money too much. But a few days. I need a few days with you not there. Not at Hooper Farm. I need that."

HE STOOD ALONE until the departing trucks left no echo.

Then Darcie and Zeke reappeared as quietly as they had disappeared.

"I didn't mean to say the wrong thing," Zeke said. "Maybe if I went after her and told her—"

"No," Darcie said in unison with Quince.

"No," Quince repeated. "There's a time to admit defeat."

Zeke looked at him with such disbelief he almost thought he could laugh. Almost.

To Zeke there was no such thing as defeat. There was simply working harder, smarter, longer until you defeated the problem.

But Zeke didn't work with people.

"I, uh, better go now." Quince said.

"Where?"

As usual, Zeke had zeroed in on the core issue.

Where the hell did he go now? If his being there hurt Anne so much—

"You're staying with us," Darcie said.

Oh. Right. They were talking about where he'd sleep—at least lie down—tonight.

"I can't intrude—"

"You're not intruding. You're staying. That's final."

"It's not neces—"

"Don't make Darcie arrest you," Zeke said. "She says it's final, so it's final."

"HERE'S YOUR TEA, dear. Much better for an afternoon break than coffee. Come join me," Mrs. R patted the kitchen table at Hooper Farm in invitation. Or was that an order.

Everett had been in bed yesterday and today with a bad cold, or possibly the flu that had been making the rounds of the poker group.

Mrs. Richards had gotten a ride out to visit him.

Then he fell asleep.

Well, sleep was the best thing for him.

But Everett sleeping was not that good for Anne, because Mrs. R settled in at the table in a way that made it clear she expected to have a nice, cozy chat.

Suppressing a sigh, Anne closed the computer tax program and joined her at the table.

Mrs. R nudged a mug toward her. "You know I'm a widow, too."

She blinked. "I, uh… Yes, I did know that."

The older woman nodded. "Trouble with that term is it's all about what you aren't. You aren't married anymore. You aren't sharing your bed and your life with the man you chose to pledge yourself to. You aren't single exactly but you're single enough to not fit in with married couples, either."

"I suppose so." Where on earth had this conversation come from?

"You know what Vanessa gave me for Christmas?"

And now they were off in another direction—equally unfathomable.

"No, I don't."

"My own computer. I told her it was too much, told her I like going to the computer lab, because I get to see my friends in Drago along with those online folks. But she wasn't taking no for an answer. And Josh weighed in, saying when the weather's bad, we couldn't have Vanessa fretting about me getting back and forth to the computer lab on foot, especially if it was when she had to be in Virginia or somewhere else for work. As it is, she's checking up on me two, three times a day. So I had to agree that Josh had a point. So I've been using that little computer and I've discovered something."

Still lost, Anne dutifully asked, "What did you discover?"

"That other people have been feeling some of the same things I've been feeling. All this time I thought I was alone. But typing on that thing at home, with nobody around me who might just be trying to look over my shoulder has opened me up. Saying things I'd only thought until now. You know, what I mean?"

No.

She was trying to come up with a way to convey that without being rude when the older woman continued.

"And what some of us have been talking about is being a widow. Or a widower. They got their problems, too."

Ah. The winding path of the woman's words had come back around to where she'd started. Though that didn't help all that much.

"We've been talking about how at the start of being a widow—or a widower—all you see are the things you aren't. And how it takes a while to see that there are other things that you still *are*. You're still a woman, for one—or a man, if you're a widower. And you're still a person. You still have a heart and a body and a soul and a brain. And you've got to keep using those things. Some say that's because that's what their dead spouse would want. They'd want them happy.

"Well, I wasn't so sure about my Ron. I don't think he would, not if he were honest. On the other hand, maybe being dead's made him less self-centered, because it would make sense if the afterlife improves a person's character, don't you think?"

"Um. I can see the logic, I guess."

Mrs. Richards said emphatically. "Me, too. So I believe my Ron does want me to be happy. He might even be sad that I've waited so long to get back to focusing on what I am instead of what I'm not." She considered that a moment, then added with decision, "And if he doesn't want me to be happy, shame on him, because I was always a good wife to him and he should appreciate that enough to want me to be happy."

The best Anne could produce was a nod.

"But there's no question with your Chris. He was a fine man. Oh, I know he had his problems, poor soul. But how he looked at you… And you brought out the best in him. Got him involved, part of the community again. Then when he died you drew in worse than he ever did. Nobody's saying how long you should grieve, but here's something I've learned—being alone and sad doesn't help the grief any, being with other people and having a good time doesn't make it go away, either. It's going to be there no matter what you do. Going to be there and be there and be there, until you notice one day that it's not as bad as it was. And then a while longer you realize it's gotten better than not-quite-as-bad-as. And it goes on like that. Never away completely, but sort of worked in to how you're living, including being happy."

Quince had grieved. Grieved so strong for Fiona.

But he hadn't died from it. He'd gone on.

"You understand what I'm saying?"

"I… I think I do."

And maybe he'd also taught her baby steps in going on. The problem was she was so far behind him on that path. So very far.

"Good. So you might as well try your best to be with other people and have a good time, especially if there's one special person." Mrs. Richards took her hand between both of hers. "I made a mistake I don't want you making. I stopped living. Did that for far, far too long. Didn't help a thing. It just hurt. And I don't want you doing that. So, you talk to that boy."

ANNE THOUGHT EVERETT was asleep, but when she put down a pitcher of water and fresh glass on the bedside table, his eyes opened.

"Been thinking." His voice was crackly and thin. "Maybe it's time."

"Time?"

"Give up this old farm. Try something new."

"Everett—"

"What's the point of staying on if it's just because we've always been here? Farmin's farmin'. Doesn't have to be this same piece of land. Was always happy enough to farm the extra rented acres. Besides, you're a young woman. You should—"

"No." She swallowed against the swell in her throat. "No. it's not time for that."

CHAPTER TWENTY-FIVE

EVERETT LOOKED BETTER the next morning and loudly insisted he was. They were low on fresh produce and she was overdue for a stop at the dealership, so Anne headed to town.

She caught herself looking for Quince or his car as she passed the café, the computer lab, the Zeke-Tech temporary offices.

She told herself to knock it off.

She'd gone off the rails, but she'd get back on them now. Doing what she'd been doing these past years, fighting tooth and nail for Hooper Farm.

The first small step was seeing to her duties at the dealership. In and out. Clean and simple.

Jennifer had other ideas.

She relinquished the computer and chair to Anne as always, but then she went to the door, closed it, and returned to take a chair on the other side of the desk.

"I have something to say. I know about wanting to do things yourself. I know about the importance of it. The…" Jennifer's gaze drilled into Anne. "The apparent necessity of it."

She leaned forward, propping her arms on the desk, pointing her clasped hands at Anne. "But it's just as important, it's just as much of a necessity to learn how to work with people. Sometimes to accept help from people. From friends."

Jennifer's intensity wouldn't let her look away.

"I appreciate what you've done for me by giving me this job, and—"

"Don't confuse things, Anne. The job is a job. And you earn your pay and probably more with the work you do. That's not what we're talking about."

"Okay." She released a breath. "Okay. You mean the farm. I know that. It's just—"

"Right. The farm, and all that Quince has tried to do for you, and now this opportunity."

"*Opportunity?* Opportunity to give up. Whatever his intentions, this is wrong. Wrong, wrong, wrong. I will not be the person responsible for the farm going out of the Hooper family. I will not be. I can't—" She stopped, because the next sound out of her throat would not have been anything as controlled as a word.

"You aren't."

"Of course I—"

"No, you're not. Everett's name is on the deed, and it's his decision. And it should be, because he ran that farm for how many decades? Maybe nobody could have avoided the financial trouble Hooper Farm is in now, with prices and weather and the pressure from the town growing. But Everett made his share of mistakes. And so did Chris. And one of the biggest for both of them was being too damned stubborn to accept help."

"That's not—"

"Oh, yes it is. You don't believe me? You ask other farmers around. Will Larkin had his truck in for repairs and I heard him telling about the year Everett reinjured his leg the last time and Chris was out every night, all night trying to get the harvest in. And when people came round offering to help he told them no—and not all that politely—because he hadn't helped them in the past year and he wasn't going to take *charity.* Let me tell you, that put backs up. Because it said anybody who'd accepted help in the past was taking charity, and you know people around here don't like that at all.

"And Everett was just as bad if not worse from what I hear. The old-timers all talk about how much he's softened up since you came. When he got them to give Zeke-Tech data for that truck farming program, most of them were too stunned that Everett Hooper was cooperating to consider refusing themselves."

Anne's thoughts whirled, but one caught hold. "Softened?"

"Yeah, so you can just imagine what he was like before."

"I... I..." She wasn't sure what words she was trying to form, except that they absolutely weren't the ones that came out. "How did you ever get past what your ex did? How could you ever trust any guy again, much less his *brother*? I mean, *how*?" Immediately, she clapped one hand over her mouth and half stood. "Oh, Jennifer, I—"

"I—"

"No, no. Don't say anything. I'm sorry. I never should have— Please, please forget I ever—"

"It's okay, Anne." Reaching across the desk, Jennifer gripped her arm. "Really it's okay. Sit down. Please?"

Anne sat.

Jennifer stared toward the closed door for a long moment.

"I didn't think I could." She spoke slowly. "In fact, I was sure I couldn't. I didn't even try, really. Maybe that's why it happened. It sneaked up on me. Because I was sure it wasn't possible. But then I started seeing how other people responded to him. So different from Eric. And from seeing how other people responded to Trent, it was natural to turn and really look at *him*. How he treats people. How he handles responsibilities. How he honors commitments. How he is with me and with Ashley. That was when I was able to divorce him from his family."

Anne sat there, knowing she should respond, but finding nothing remotely reasonable to say except "Thank you." It came out a croak. She cleared her throat. "It's so generous of you to share... To..."

"You don't have to forget Chris to move on, Anne. You don't have to forgive him, either. Not yet. I know you will eventually, but you don't have to do it yet. Not in order to let yourself love Quince. To let yourself admit you love Quince. You just need to accept all the way down to your soul that they're different people." A faint smile touched her lips. "Even if they were brothers, they would be different people."

There was a drought on coherent thought. Bone dry. No hope of a drop. "I don't know what to say."

"No need to say anything, Anne. And I'll stop talking at you and leave you to do your work now."

WITH THE LAST thumb drive nearly finished, Anne's heart gave a painful lurch at a tall shadow in the office doorway.

She was breathless when she looked up to an entirely unexpected sight.

"Zeke?"

"Hi, Anne. May I come in?"

She gathered her breath and her wits enough to say, "Of course. It's Jennifer's office, so—"

"I know. Jennifer told Darcie you were here. That's how I knew." When he stepped inside, he swung the door closed behind him.

Two closed-door conversations in one day? Uh-oh.

"Can I get you something to drink? Water or coffee? Or—"

"No. I should probably get right to what I came to say. Darcie doesn't know I'm here." He sounded half like a guilty child, half worried. "Quince, either. They said not to talk to you. I guess they figured I did enough harm already."

"You didn't do any harm." She looked at her hands. Rather surprised that they were just resting there on the desk. No tremor, no shake. "You—"

"Yes, I did. And you're going to say I told the truth, but it wasn't—"

"Zeke, it's very sweet of you to—"

"Nothing to do with sweet. I'm not sweet. Anybody'll tell you that. But I'm as honest as I know how to be. And what I told you earlier wasn't the full truth. Yeah, Quince does like the challenge of fixing a problem. Me, too. Though not the same kind of challenges. But here's where I was wrong. All wrong. Quince doesn't walk away. I know, because I've seen first-hand how he is on a really tough, long-term problem."

He paused so long she looked up.

"Me."

Before she'd fully absorbed that, he asked. "You know we were roommates in college? Randomized matching, but it couldn't have turned out better for me if I'd designed it myself. It wasn't as good for Quince."

"Of course it was," she protested. "He gained a best friend, a career, and—"

"Only after he made me somebody who could be a friend and build a company." He said it with such conviction. "I'm not saying my parents weren't great. And if it hadn't been for getting to know Darcie during high school I don't think Quince could have gotten through to me at all. As it was, he had a tough time with me. Still does. I tried to ignore him. I really tried. He says I didn't say a word for the first week. But he kept talking. He wouldn't let me be."

That last sentence held conflicting currents. A lingering irritation. And gratitude.

"He'd drag me out to be with other people. It was awful. I just wanted to stay in my room or the labs, dealing with what I understood. But Quince wouldn't give up. He'd give me sentences to say when certain circumstances came up. Like when I stop listening to somebody, because my mind's off on other things and they realize it and say 'Did you hear me?' and I say 'Hearing you is not the same as agreeing.' It—"

"I've heard you say that."

He nodded as he continued. "—almost always starts them repeating whatever they've said because they're rearguing their case. They don't know I wasn't listening and they don't get pissed at me. And with the business... well, there wouldn't be a business without Quince, because he's the one who deals with people. I'm better—a lot better—than I was, thanks to Darcie, but there's no way I could do it even now without Quince."

"Quince said you took care of him after Fiona died."

He ducked his head. "If I did, it was Fiona's doing. She asked me to visit her, about a month before she died. Made sure Quince wouldn't be there. She said she was counting on me to get Quince looking to the future again. That I needed to make him see he was needed. I said how would I know what would make him feel needed? And she said not *feel* needed, *be* needed, and talked about how there was a big difference for someone like Quince.

"I'll tell you, that was one of the hardest conversations I've ever had. And it wasn't even because she was dying. It was because she wouldn't take no for an answer."

"She sounds like an extraordinary woman."

"I thought so. More important, she sure was right about Quince. I started talking to him about my idea for Zeke-Tech. He didn't listen, not at first, because that was right after Fiona died. After about four months he was sinking deeper and deeper, and I started thinking what Fiona would say. So I went and got him. Took him right out of his father's house, to the room I'd rented."

He shook his head. "What scared me was he didn't notice what a dump the place was—not for months. The day he started griping about the place, I wanted to do a jig—that wasn't for nearly a year. About the time Vanessa joined us. But right from the start, he worked like crazy. He's the one who talked the landlord into letting us stay when we owed back rent. And he was out every day looking for backers—even when I was picky about who'd we take money from. The point is, if you think Quince solves an issue, then moves on to something new, I'm here to tell you he doesn't. Not when he's your friend." He held her gaze. "Not when he loves you. Then all he wants to do is make things better for you."

The one thing he hadn't been able to do for Fiona, as much as he'd loved her.

Her eyes filled with tears.

…You can't fix everything. Quit thinking you can.

I know I can't.

Oh, God. She'd been cruel. Unintentionally, but still cruel.

And now… She'd walked away from him because he hadn't fixed Hooper Farm.

Hadn't fixed facts and history and the future.

Hadn't fixed her guilt that she hadn't been able to save the farm her husband had loved so much.

Hadn't fixed her fear that she hadn't saved her husband because she hadn't loved him enough.

She let out a sound.

"Anne?"

"I—I've gotta go." She was throwing stuff in her bag, not focusing. Keys. That's what she needed. Her keys.

"To see Quince?"

"No. Not yet. I have to talk Everett. I have to get home and talk to Everett."

THE INSTANT ANNE opened the mudroom door the smell of burnt coffee cut through the numbness of her cold nose.

It was the first thing that had pulled her out of her own head since she'd left the dealership.

Her thoughts were like a tornado inside her skull, picking up random pieces, slamming them together in no semblance of order. Dropping a fragment of a memory, then swirling a look, a phrase, an action around and around and around until she had to close her eyes.

She automatically left her cell phone on the kitchen table and kept going to switch off the coffeemaker Everett had left on. But underneath the habitual action and trickle of annoyance, concern welled up. He'd never before left it so long.

Surely he smelled it, so…

"Everett?"

She pounded up the stairs, calling his name again. No answer. Her throat closed. His door stood two-thirds open at the far end of the hall. She pushed it open, forced herself to step inside.

The bed was empty. The covers thrown back, their disarray no more than usual. Nor did anything else in the room raise alarms.

She spun around and checked the bathroom door, but that, too was open. She stuck her head in, just in case. Empty.

"Everett!"

She headed for the stairs again. God, he couldn't have gone outside, could he?

Almost to the bottom of the stairs, she thought she heard something over her own steps. A rasping, gasping cough. She stopped. Listened for half a beat, then sprinted to the parlor, pushing the pocket doors wider.

Everett slumped on the sofa, both hands to his chest as a rattling cough wracked him. Beside him and on the floor at his feet, old photo albums assumed odd angles, like dead leaves deposited by a fitful wind.

He wore his robe and slippers, but the room was chilled. She barely slowed down to snag the aged quilt off the rack just inside the door. She wrapped it around his unresisting shoulders, already looking for something to warm his feet. Two pillows and a knitted throw had to do. She put one pillow under his feet to raise them from the cold floor, the other on top, and looped the throw around to keep them in place.

"Oh, Everett. What did you—?"

Her first look at his face evaporated the scold like snow on a hot griddle.

His skin was gray. His eyes unfocused. His mouth open as his breathing produced a rattling sound like a distant echo of the cough she'd heard.

"Everett, I'm calling 911."

He didn't react at all. She gasped out a brief, inarticulate plea, and ran for her cell phone.

A familiar voice answered as she hurried back to him. "Corine? Thank God. Something's wrong with Everett."

She answered Corine's professional questions with as much patience as she could muster, but when the dispatcher said to stay there until the ambulance arrived, Anne cut her off. "No. It'll be too long. Tell the ambulance I'll meet them. Look for the farm truck—rust over green—and I'll have the flashers on."

"Anne, how'll you get him in the truck? Is Quince—?"

"No. I'll get him in. I'm hanging up now. I'll call back when we're on the road."

She pushed the parlor doors the rest of the way open and jacked up the thermostat before she ran outside again, pulling on her coat as she went. The truck started right away. She brought it around to the front porch—a shorter exit from the parlor than down the hall and through the kitchen. Back inside, she tried to lift Everett. It wasn't going to work. Not to carry him any distance, not without the likelihood of dropping him.

Think, Anne. Think!

She ran back to the kitchen, grabbed Everett's warmest jacket, his farm coat, a number of scarves, loaded them onto a kitchen chair, and ran back with it to the parlor. As she removed the quilt to put the jacket on him, another shuddering cough shook him so hard, she couldn't even guide his arm into the sleeve until it passed. He still didn't respond to her, even as she talked to him, constantly telling him what she was doing, and why.

With the jacket on and the quilt wrapped around his legs and feet, she heaved him into the chair, panting with the effort. She added the coat, then used scarves to tie him into the chair. Then, holding onto the chair back, she tipped it back and dragged it across the resistant rug, moving backward one hard-fought step at a time.

At the threshold to the hall's wood floor at last, she took only enough time to check that Everett, still unresponsive, was secured in the chair, ran back to the kitchen for a cotton rug, and maneuvered the chair onto it. Using the rug as a skid, she pulled the chair to the front door. The uneven front threshold held dangers, but she managed to maneuver the chair out by using her body and legs to cushion it.

The three steps down from the porch to the drive were much worse.

The first was mere torture. The second, the chair slipped on an icy patch, and pivoted, nearly tipping all the way over. Anne caught it—

barely—taking the full weight on her right shoulder and breast. She didn't even gasp at the pain. She had no breath left for that. And no time.

She saw Everett's face for the first time since she'd tied him into the chair, and he looked worse.

No time for finesse, she yanked the chair down the third step, cushioning some of the jarring with her body. She had to get him in the truck—out of this cold and on the way to the hospital. Fast.

She swung open the truck door, and refused to think how impossible it was to get him up to that high seat. She untied the scarves, trying to tell Everett what she was going to do, but not sure that even if he'd been capable of listening that he could have understood her panted words.

She got him over her shoulder in a fireman's carry. Her first try to swing him up onto the seat was pitifully short. She backed up, tried again, with a couple steps' momentum. Closer. A third try was closer still. The fourth time, she got him partway on the seat. He started to slide back toward her. She shoved with all her might, closing the truck door. A corner of the quilt stuck out the door, she just prayed she hadn't caught any of Everett. She left the chair where it was, didn't bother to close the front door, just ran around the truck and got in.

The old beauty was in one of its rare fits of spewing out heat like a furnace. She half sobbed, half gasped, trying to pull in oxygen. She levered Everett to a half-sitting position, but there was no way she could get his seatbelt hooked.

She had to go.

She had to go *now*.

Her hands shook so hard she had to wrap one hand around the other to release the emergency brake. But they were on their way.

Each motion of driving seemed foreign. To keep her concentration on the road so she didn't have a wreck, she muttered reminders to herself—avoid the pothole at the third fence post, ease into that icy patch, look both ways, keep speed steady for the turn into the highway—like a teenager with her first permit.

On the highway, she turned on the emergency blinkers to catch the attention of an oncoming ambulance, forced herself to pull in long, slow breaths, then fished out her cell phone, and hit redial.

"They're on their way," Corine said.

"We're on the highway. A mile from the farm."

"Okay. How's he doing?"

"Not good. The truck's warmer than that parlor, but his breathing's still bad. And his color … he's so gray."

"Talking to you?"

"No, but—I might be imagining it, but I think he's heard me when I talked to him."

"That's good. That's good, honey. Now, you just keep talking to me until you see the ambulance."

Talk? Breathing was still a chore. "You talk. I'll listen."

That's what they did—Corine talking, Anne grunting breath-saving responses—for the eighteen minutes until she heard the wail of the siren and caught the first strobe of the flashing lights.

CHAPTER TWENTY-SIX

THE HOSPITAL ROOM was quiet and dim. The doctors and nurses gone. Everett sleeping, his breathing easier.

A sound, an awareness. She raised her head.

The door opened slowly and Quince entered.

Well past visiting hours. He wasn't a relative, but of course he'd gotten in.

He remained by the door. Waiting for his eyes to adjust to the dimness? Or assessing?

"How is he?" he asked quietly.

"It's pneumonia." Her voice broke.

He was to her in two strides. Picked her up, held her against his chest—a pang of envy struck her that she couldn't have picked up Everett with such ease. Sometimes life just wasn't fair—but also relief to be held that way.

He sat in the chair with her in his lap, her head on his shoulder.

Stumbled words, telling him what the doctor had said.

"…think he'll be better in a few days. But … he's got bruises." A sob tore the words. "From me. It was the only way—"

"You did great, Anne. You did amazing. You saved his life. You know you did. You think he's going to complain about bruises?"

A small, hiccupping laugh. "He's going to complain about the heating bill. I left the thermostat up and the front door wide open."

"Don't worry about that. Corine let Darcie know and she and Zeke have gone out to take care of things at the farm. They'll even checking on Grandy."

"That's how you knew, from Darcie?"

"Yup."

She started to sit up, but he held her tight. "I have to let Mrs. R know," she protested.

"All taken care of. Darcie called Josh. He and Vanessa are going over there to tell her in person. You just rest now. I'll wake you up when he stirs."

She stroked his cheek, absorbing the comfort of his body around her.

"There's something else, Quince. Everett wanted to—before this. He said we should sell. Do the co-op. That's what we're going to do."

"We can talk about that later."

"No. No need. It's settled." She looked toward the bed. "It's all settled."

She rested her head on Quince's shoulder and slept.

SHE WOKE WHEN a nurse came in to check on Everett.

"Stable," she said with a neutral smile. "Want some coffee?"

"Please," Quince said.

An aide came in with two paper cups on a little tray.

She took a sip and put it down. Quince kept drinking. "Wish they'd repeal the law that hospital coffee has to be crappy," he said.

He must have spent many nights with Fiona in hospitals— probably nights like this when what the morning would bring hung in the balance.

Nights when he'd felt as helpless and uncertain as she did now. When he would give anything if he could make things right for the person in that bed. A person you loved.

If only you could … fix everything for them.

"I'm sorry, Quince."

"You? What are you sorry about?"

"What I said about you thinking you could fix everything."

He made a harsh sound. "You were right. That's what I tried to do. And failed." He rested his forehead against hers. "I can't stop you from losing Hooper Farm, Anne. I know what having your roots there means to you. But all I can do is offer an alternative that lets you and Everett come away with something."

"That's a lot, Quince. That's everything. Just as truly loving someone is everything. I'm not sure I did."

It took him an extra beat. "Chris?"

"I loved the farm—that was love at first sight. I loved farming. I loved the idea of being his partner. I'm not sure, I'll never be sure, I really loved *him*." She turned partway to him. "And I'll always wonder if that's why he killed himself."

"Anne Hooper, you listen. All I've heard from Everett and everyone else is how good you were for and to Chris. How he became part of the community again when you came into his life. And how he loved how you look out for Everett. You have not one solitary reason to feel remorse or guilt. And you damned well better start believing that."

"I…" She swallowed the protest, instead letting the certainty in his eyes cushion and warm the jagged piece of ice that cut at her. It wasn't gone. Maybe it would be someday, with Quince melting it away, bit by bit. "I'll try."

"Good." He tightened his hold on her, rubbing his cheek against the top of her head. Then he eased her away, still supporting her back, but leaving enough room between them so she could see his face. "Besides, it doesn't matter whether or not you married him for the farm when you would have given it up to save him. Just as you're doing for Everett."

CHAPTER TWENTY-SEVEN

THE FIRST WEEK, Quince figured it was because of Everett's recovery.

The man was not a good patient, to no one's surprise. He was more cheerful when he was released from—or kicked out of, depending on who was telling the story—the hospital, but no less demanding.

Mrs. Richards helped with his care, but that meant even less privacy for Quince and Anne, as well as another person for Anne to feed.

All that tired Anne out, plus the work she was putting in as she and the others moved forward on the co-op plan.

The bank chewed up more time, interviewing her about her dealings with Chitmell, who was no longer manager.

Somehow the bank board had gotten wind that it should look into Chitmell's activities. Lo and behold, he was in cahoots with a developer who'd been trying to scoop up farms near the Zeke-Tech site for less than the going rate.

Quince's name didn't come into that anywhere. Not even when a suggestion came to the bank's attention that a possible good-will gesture to ease bad feelings over Chitmell's machinations would be to fund repairs—and updates—to the high school's Chem Lab.

Heck, the Hoopers had even agreed to buy Macklin farm from him when the proceeds from the co-op sale of Hooper Farm came through.

Everything was going better than he could have imagined.

So what the hell was the problem with Anne?

She was never around. At least not when he was, except for brief updates that felt more like a board meeting than a conversation.

He'd kissed her precisely twice since Everett came home. As for sleeping together—

"Right, Quince?"

He heard Zeke's question. It was the words before it he'd missed—the words he was supposed to be agreeing with.

"Sorry. I wasn't listening."

He and Zeke and Vanessa were meeting at the temporary Zeke-Tech headquarters. He should have been listening.

Zeke opened his mouth, probably to repeat what he'd said, but Vanessa forestalled him. "What's wrong, Quince? Is it Anne?"

Another time he might have smiled—Vanessa Irish asking about his private life. His *emotions* for crying out loud. My, how things had changed.

But maybe they hadn't changed enough. Not between him and Anne.

Was that why she was so distant?

"Or Everett? The new farm? The deal?" Vanessa was trying to draw him out.

He shook his head.

"Everett's making good progress. The rest is on track."

"Anne," Vanessa said, and it wasn't a question.

He shook his head again, but not in denial this time. "Something's going on. There's something she's not telling me."

Vanessa looked down at her hands. Zeke discovered a sudden interest in the ceiling.

"She's pulling away, withdrawing."

"Maybe you're imagining it," Zeke offered, still looking at the ceiling. "Or … or it's a mood. Women have hormones, you know."

"It's not my imagination or a mood or hormones," Quince said shortly. "I'm the people person, remember?"

"But Zeke is married now," Vanessa said. "So he knows—"

"Darcie. I'll grant that. Not women in general, and *not* Anne." That brought both of their gazes to him. "Sorry. I shouldn't have snapped. I know you're trying to help."

Zeke and Vanessa looked at each other, then their gazes ricocheted away.

"Why don't you give it a couple more weeks," Vanessa said. "You're all so busy, and with all the changes. Give yourselves time."

Changes…

He kept thinking it was Anne, but what about him?

He needed to find out.

QUINCE SOUNDED STRANGE when he called her from the airport.

The *airport.*

Had she seen his note? A sudden trip came up. Wouldn't be gone long. No, didn't know exactly how long. She could always get him on his cell if she needed him.

I need you. Now. Here.

"I hear there's a warm front coming in," he said. "Don't work yourself too hard, Anne."

A warm front.

What he'd been in her life. Warming and thawing and loving.

Maybe if she told him…

No.

Telling him wouldn't do it.

"Have a good trip, Quince."

HE PARKED THE rental car outside the Dutch Colonial house with two big trees in front, separated by a walkway to the bright blue front door.

Fiona's favorite color.

The door had been subdued when he first came here. Her dad had painted it this color before she came home the last time.

And clearly had kept it this color in memory of her.

He hesitated a couple yards short of that door.

How would they feel having memories stirred by seeing him?

They'd said it was okay when he'd emailed. But they might have felt obligated. And what the hell did he hope to accomplish?

Like they could unravel Anne for him.

Or unravel him.

Someone flung the door open with a shout of "Quince!"

His head knew it wasn't Fiona. That it had to be her little sister Mandy, now college age herself.

His heart stopped.

For what had been.

For what could never be.

And then Mandy was pulling him inside to where they all waited.

Her parents hugged him. Her brother and his wife, now parents of three rambunctious kids, pumped his hand. Even her formidable aunt, Justine, smiled at him.

Welcoming him.

"JENNIFER? QUINCE IS gone. He took his coat—his good coat. But he left his jackets."

"Uh-huh." Jennifer didn't sound impressed. Maybe she didn't get the implications—he'd left his farm jackets, taken his beautiful city coat.

"What if… What if…"

"Was there a note?"

"It just said he'd be gone a few days. Then he called from the airport and that's what he said, too."

"There's your answer. Quit juggling what ifs—*useless* what ifs."

"What do we do if he doesn't come back? In time, I mean."

A lie. A total lie, because what she really meant was what if he didn't come back at all.

"We'll adjust." Then, as if answering the deeper question, Jennifer added, "And go on."

THE AFTERNOON WITH Fiona's family lingered into dinner.

There had been a few tears, but far more laughter.

Memories had been leavened with much discussion of what each of them was doing now.

Fiona would be so happy to know—if she didn't already—they had joy in their lives, that their mutual missing of her drew them even closer.

Finally, he said goodnight and started back to the car.

"Quince."

It was Aunt Justine. The front door hadn't reopened, so she must have come around from the back.

She stood at the end of the driveway, where a camellia hedge blocked the view if anyone happened to look out the living room window. He joined her there.

"It was good that you came. Good for them." Before he could say he was glad she thought so, she added, "And good for you. I've been waiting for this visit."

"You have?" He might as well have said, "Huh?"

"Yes. You've fallen in love."

She didn't make it a question. She left him no room to hem or haw.

"Yes."

She nodded curtly. "Fiona hoped you would. You took your time about it."

He almost smiled at that. "Wasn't intending to do it now."

Her eyes narrowed and he had the uncomfortable feeling she saw more than anyone should be able to in these shadows.

"Is she dying?" she asked abruptly.

"What? No."

"But she's in trouble."

"Yes, but—"

"Let me ask—No, it's not me. It's really Fiona. Because she talked to me about this before she died. She's the reason I'm out here. She gave me instructions—a message. So consider this Fiona asking if you would have loved her if she'd sat back, waiting to die, and said woe is me?"

At another time he might have laughed at the idea of Fiona responding like that. "She never would have done that. Just wasn't her."

"So, you loved a woman who *wouldn't* sit back, wait to die, and say woe is me. Yet you're worried that you loved her *because* she was dying—"

"I didn't—I never—" He broke off the protests in the face of Justine's implacable calm. Then another angle pierced him. "Fiona?"

Slowly, she nodded. "She knew you worried about that. She also knew you were wrong." A smile lifted her stern mouth. "She was a remarkable girl—woman—to never doubt your love when most females would have been fretting about their looks and their physical abilities being taken away. She never did. She would have said that was because of you, Quince." Her eyes gleamed in the dark with unshed tears. "We'll always be grateful to you for that."

Pressure built behind his eyes. "But she wouldn't marry me."

"You know why."

"Insurance."

She nodded. "Yes, the insurance. She didn't want you to start the rest of your life with the burden of debt. Or with being a widower."

"She said that, but—"

"But you thought it was because she worried that you loved her because she was sick. She knew better, Quince. She knew you loved her for her. And because of the way she lived. You have to know that, too, now that you love again. Love someone because of the way she lives."

He was back.

First, Anne thought she'd imagined the familiar growl of his car as she twisted under the covers in useless pursuit of the sleep she needed.

She stilled. It *was* his car.

She listened for him opening the back door, entering, quietly come up the stairs. Stopped breathing when he paused at the top of the stairs. Resumed on a sigh when he turned toward his room, not hers.

That's when she looked at the clock.

Four Sunday morning.

She stared at the ceiling, drifting until it was time to get up. Still dark, she sent three texts saying Quince was back, then got into her work clothes.

Quince was still in his room, presumably asleep.

"He's back?" Everett asked from the kitchen doorway.

"Yes."

That was it for conversation.

He sent several sharp looks her way over breakfast. She didn't return them.

When Peggy Richards and Beverly Mudge arrived to give him a ride, he paused a long moment, then said to her, "It's up to you now."

"I know."

He grunted. "See you later then."

"See you later," she echoed.

Before she went to the barn, she took the precaution of taking Quince's car keys from his coat pocket so he couldn't leave.

Still not a peep from him when she came back in not long before noon. But as she hung up the last of her outer clothes, she heard the shower turn on upstairs.

"Quince?" she said, at the same time she tapped on the door.

"Hi, Anne. I'm in the shower."

"I, uh, I know. May I come in?"

"Sure."

She stepped in to the warmth of the small room. Not quite steamy, but getting there.

He pulled back the shower curtain a slice and smiled at her.

She hurried to speak before she lost her nerve. "I thought—if you don't mind… I've, uh, I've been working and I could use a shower, too, so maybe—"

"Hell, no, I don't mind. But you're way overdressed."

Aware of him watching her, she shed her clothes with more economy than grace.

He welcomed her by widening the opening of the shower curtain.

As she stepped over the side of the tub, she reached out to steady herself with a hand to his chest, then snatched it back, nearly pitching herself headfirst into the bathtub.

He grasped her arms and half hauled her in.

"Sorry, sorry," she said, not looking at him.

"Anne."

"I forgot how cold—"

"Anne."

"—my hands are."

"Anne."

Finally, she looked up at him.

"It's good to see you."

She found a smile to reply to the bit of wryness in that, since she already had evidence he was glad to see her. "It's good to see you, too."

He slid his hold down her arms to take her decidedly cold hands in his, then brought them up to his chest, warming them between his hands and his heart.

"As for the cold hands, we'll take care of that."

He shifted both her hands into one of his while his free hand stroked down her side, over her hip, then reached behind her thigh. With that encouragement, she raised her leg, supported by his hold. He came up against her.

He kissed where her neck angled into her shoulder. Then sucked there.

Against her skin, wet and now well-heated, he murmured, "We'll take care of that and more."

And they did.

SOME TIME LATER, she looked over her shoulder at him, as his soap-slick hands slid over her. "I don't know how much longer the hot water's going to last."

"I think we're heating the water instead of the other way around. Ahhh. Especially when you do that."

She'd reached behind her and was reciprocating the soapy hands-sliding.

"Just be ready to jump out when the hot water goes so we don't become icicles. There are beds, after all."

"How long is Everett gone?"

"For a while. But I want you to come with me someplace—Ah. What are you…? *Oh*. Yes. That's so good…"

"I'll go anywhere with you." He grasped her hips and slid deeper. "Anywhere."

THE HOT WATER ran out.

That wouldn't have bothered him—after all there was a bed only a few yards away—but it seemed to chill Anne in other ways.

She was holding him off again.

He wanted to tell her about the trip. But Anne evaded his efforts to open discussion.

Instead, what he got from her was that they needed to get dressed. They needed to get downstairs. They needed to go somewhere—where, she wouldn't say—without even delaying for some food.

Behind the wheel of the truck, on the way to a destination she wouldn't disclose, but was in the opposite direction from town, she fell back into the tormenting silence and distance of the past weeks.

"You're doing it again."

Anne jumped. Maybe at his accusation. Maybe from the truck hitting a rut.

Unlike the arrow-straight county roads, this unfamiliar back road wound along a river. Had to be an extension of the Drago River, he supposed.

He didn't much care.

"Okay, you're not going to talk—" She shot him a look at his stark tone. "—then you will listen. I went to see Fiona's family. That's where I was."

"Oh."

Now what on earth were her feelings behind that syllable? Glad? Worried? Unsettled? Relieved?

The hell if he knew.

"It was good." He considered that. "Really good. Especially talking to her aunt. That woman used to scare the, uh, manure out of me. Still does."

"More than Darcie?" She produced a little smile with that.

"Darcie times two and several more decades of experience. That's Aunt Justine."

"Whoa. That's impressive." She turned the truck into an open gate and a rough track that led up an incline. "So what did she say to you?"

"She said I'm an idiot."

"She didn't." That sounded more amused than indignant on his behalf.

"She did. And she's right. I am an idiot. I *was* an idiot. An idiot who didn't do you or Fiona justice. At some level I wondered if I was drawn to your needs, to your vulnerabilities, to—" He met her eyes, knowing he was taking a risk. "—your weaknesses. Wait. Don't start denying you have needs or vulnerabilities or weaknesses. We all do. The question is how we deal with them. And, I suppose, how other people react to them." This might be the hardest part. "I thought—I feared—I'd loved Fiona *because* she was dying. And—"

"Oh, Quince. How could you think that? If you held back from women you could have loved—"

"No. It's safe to say I didn't love anyone in between Fiona and you—because God knows I didn't have any trouble falling for you."

Eyes wide, she looked at him. Until a hole nearly wrenched the wheel out her hands and she focused again on driving. Damned road.

"I was in trouble from the start, especially when you said I was no farmer, because I suddenly wanted to be a farmer more than anything. No, no, don't worry, I've gotten past that. No illusions about my farming ability."

Though a soft bell rang in his head, because Anne was driving through an open gateway and didn't stop to close it behind them.

He started to ask about that, then forgot it when she said, "You're trying."

"I know. *Very* trying." That drew a smile from her. "The episode with Grandy was when I fell in love with you, but—"

"Which one?"

"The first one. But, as I was saying before I was interrupted," he said sternly, "something held me back."

"You felt guilty about deserting Fiona."

"Maybe," he acknowledged. Glancing back, he realized they'd climbed more than he'd thought from the river level. Ahead was a stand of fir trees. "Probably."

"Strange how I can see so clearly that *you* have nothing to feel guilty about."

"Yeah. And I see it so clearly for you with Chris." She continued to look straight ahead. "Anyway, I went to see Fiona's family. Learned what I've told you I learned, and came back to you, hoping the time I was away—"

"Fifty-four hours."

"—would have let you learn some things, too. Only to find you doing exactly what you were doing when I left."

"What?"

He knew the question was a time-buyer, but that didn't mean he had to treat it that way. "You're clamming up, shutting me out, acting like you alone can carry the weight of the world on your shoulders."

They passed through a line of windbreak firs to a farmhouse. It looked familiar. But then many of the older farmhouses around Drago were similar.

"Quince—"

"Damn it, I thought we were past this. I thought you were done holding back."

She chuckled—nervous, but still a chuckle—as she finally ended the assault on his bones by braking the truck to a stop at the farmhouse's front porch. "Come on, Quince, you can't accuse me of holding back this morning in the shower."

He refused to be sidetracked.

He refused to be subtle or understanding.

He refused to talk around this.

He got out of the truck, waiting for her to do the same before saying, "I'm not talking about sex, and you know it." He slammed his truck door for emphasis. "If you don't want a future together, you're going to have to say it."

"*Shh.* You don't have to shout."

"Apparently, I do have to shout, to make you hear me."

She kept walking, staying ahead of him, and taking the front porch steps at double-time, with every appearance of wanting to get away from him. "Quince, can we talk about this later? I don't want to talk right now."

"Too bad, because I do." She had the front door open, holding it wide. And now he did shout. "I want to talk about it now. Because I love you and I want to marry you, Anne Hooper."

He had a split-second vision of Anne holding onto the edge of the open door for all she was worth, her eyes and mouth wide.

And then all hell broke loose.

CHAPTER TWENTY-EIGHT

"S URPRISE!"

"Surprise, Quince!"

"Surprise!"

"Surprise!"

People came at him from every direction, shaking his hand, pounding him on the back, patting his arm, kissing his cheek, saying things he couldn't make sense of.

Automatically, he returned hellos, handshakes, and cheek kisses—all the while, looking at Anne for an explanation.

Or at least the reassurance that this was all real.

She smiled. He thought the smile was meant to be reassuring, but the way it wobbled did little to reassure.

And when Zeke spoke into one of those sudden silences that can strike a gathering, the smile fled.

"One hell of a way to propose, Quince," he said.

Anne sucked in air and froze.

Jennifer came to the rescue. "Quince, Anne organized this surprise open house here so we could all—"

She gestured to the group, and he saw not only his personal friends and their significant others, not only the poker-playing group, but a broader range of farmers, Drago residents, and Zeke-Techers.

And then another recognition clicked into place. He knew where they were.

The farm he'd bought.

The farm she and Everett were taking over.

New Hooper Farm.

Anne had brought him by an unfamiliar route, which meant they'd approached from a different angle, and the house had been painted inside and out, all combining to delay recognition.

The open gate.

Ah. Left open for them purposely.

"—celebrate this new venture and thank you for helping bring us together to make our town and our county better and stronger."

Someone started "For He's a Jolly Good Fellow," quickly joined by many voices. As it tailed off at the end, he heard Zeke saying to Darcie, "All I said was it's one hell of a way to propose. And he's supposed to be so good with people."

This time general conversation covered Zeke's words, and Anne seized the moment, calling out, "Let's cut the cake."

In the general surge toward the kitchen, Vanessa ended up beside him. "I *told* you to give it a little time."

He stopped, drawing protests from eager would-be-cake-eaters behind them. "Good Lord—*that's* what those looks between you and Zeke were about the other day? How the hell did I miss that? Either you two have gotten a whole lot more devious, or I've become a total idiot."

"It's not devious to keep a secret for a surprise party. As for you being an idiot, you have a lot on your mind." She smiled up at him. "And in your heart."

Mrs. R tugged at his arm, drawing him down so she could kiss his cheek. "You've done a wonderful thing here, Quince. Wonderful."

"Don't be sure until we start selling lots and we see how it goes."

"There are already reserves on lots," Vanessa said.

"No matter what," Mrs. Richards picked up, "you've done a wonderful thing, because you gave all these people a chance to take back control, when they felt like they were being swamped by a tsunami. Including this crotchety old fellow."

She accompanied the final words by tucking a hand in Everett's arm and beaming at him.

He smiled back at her, but then turned a frown toward Quince.

"Took you long enough to get back here after disappearing like a thief in the night. And her—"

"Like a thief in the night?" He wanted to laugh and be outraged simultaneously.

"—wearing herself down getting the place painted and all. And these past days, hopping from this foot to that. Should she get everybody to try another date or call the whole thing off or what? Thought her head would spin right off her shoulders."

He ignored Everett and looked down at Mrs. R. "How long has she been working on this?"

"Well, let me see. It wasn't long after Everett got out of the hospital—"

"C'mon, Quince, get in here and get cake so the rest of us can have some," ordered Darcie.

THE HUGS AND handshakes and kisses didn't stop.

Ned and Candy Benzil, their sons, Will Larkin and his son, Jennifer, Trent, Mrs. Zeekowsky, Darcie's mother and the chief of police, two more farmers he'd played poker with and their wives. He even got a triple-decker, with Josh's youngest wrapping him around the knees, his son Topher shaking his hand, and his oldest giving him a quick hug. Vanessa added a kiss on the cheek and Josh topped it off with another handshake.

"You look shellshocked," Jennifer said quietly, handing him a second cake plate, because the first one had fallen on the floor thanks to an over-enthusiastic hugger.

"I am. And touched and I'll never forget this. But I haven't had a single word with Anne since we walked in, much less talk to her alone about, uh, what happened at the door."

Jennifer and Darcie exchanged a look, then a couple words too quiet for him to hear.

"Leave it to us," Darcie said.

Jennifer grabbed his arm and steered him through the crowd.

"Here," she said, opening a door. "Wait in here."

He looked around. "The pantry?"

"Yup."

He heard Zeke say before the door shut, "He griped about going in our pantry, so why—?"

This wasn't as large as Darcie and Zeke's pantry and the light wasn't automatic. But he'd seen a cord before Jennifer closed the door.

He'd just turned the light on when the door opened again and Anne came shooting in, apparently propelled by a push.

Quince took half a second to admire Darcie's technique, and reminded himself never to get on her bad side.

But only half a second. He took her into his arms.

"Anne—"

"Quince, I'm sorry. I didn't know you felt I'd pulled back. I was trying so hard to keep this a surprise."

"It's a surprise all right—a wonderful surprise. But the lead-up was misery."

"With the way I feel about you, I knew I'd spill it all if we spent time or … uh, time together."

"The way you feel about me? How about sharing?"

She smiled, starting slow, but spreading with certainty. "I love you, Peter Quincy. I truly love you."

He drew in a deep breath. "I love you, too."

They looked at each other for a long, long time.

"Are you going to kiss me or something?" she asked with a smile.

"Both." He kissed her. "I'm going to kiss you now and or something later."

They kept on kissing.

Not until oxygen depletion hit did they pause long enough for her to say, "It's nice to hear the words *I love you* when you're not shouting at me."

He huffed out a half laugh. "Sorry about that. I have something else to say, not shouting. Will you marry me?"

"Yes."

"For better for worse, but always with a farm?"

"I'll marry you *without* a farm, Quince." She kissed him quickly, then added. "Since Everett and I will own it. Oh, we have so many things to decide and plan. I have to learn this farm practically from scratch and planting will start soon, though we need more seed, and we could get livestock and—"

"And I want to hear about every farming choice. But if we start now, in here, there might be a riot by the people waiting outside. That would be a shame since I hear you repainted the place."

She smiled at him. "Good point."

Hands clasped, they exited the pantry to a packed audience zeroed in on them.

"Anne and I would like you all to be the first to know that she's accepted my proposal of marriage."

Among cheers, exclamations, and well-wishing, two voices stood out.

"He must have done a better job of proposing the second time," Zeke said.

"Knew this'd happen from the first day I brought him out to the farm," Everett said. "Saw it all along."

EPILOGUE

"Where's my nail polish?"

Quince paused in the act of pulling on his underwear to answer. "The box labeled *Anne – Bathroom* maybe?"

They'd moved in two weeks ago during a rainy spell, but the weather had been too good since then to waste any on unpacking boxes.

She'd gotten a lot done on the Hooper-Macklin Farm—Everett had been the one to suggest including the original owners' name—and didn't regret her choices of how to spend her time. It was just that still having things in boxes made it hard getting ready for Jennifer and Trent's wedding, being held this evening in Darcie and Zeke's backyard.

And perhaps she and Quince shouldn't have made love after their first round of showers, requiring a second round, and putting them way behind schedule.

Nope.

Didn't regret that choice, either.

"Got it." She pulled the bottle triumphantly out of a box and set to work.

Her task wasn't made any easier by frequently looking up to watch Quince dress. Not quite as much fun as watching him undress—or helping him undress—but still very good watching.

"Did you hear two more lots sold?" After her "uh-huh," he added, "That's more than half, and that's not counting the extra ones Trent and Jennifer are getting around the house."

Trent and Jennifer had bought Hooper Farm's house and barn,

and now were talking about adding a ring of lots around them for more space. They had brought the plans out to show Everett and Anne. Updates in the house would be in keeping with its heritage. The barn was going to be completely renovated with a family room, a workout area, and offices.

Anne was thrilled for them. And even more thrilled that the limited renovations to this house—*their* house—were finished. They'd spruced up the first-floor bedroom suite, perfect for Everett and Mrs. R when they stayed at the farm.

The older couple spent more time in town, however, because Mrs. R was teaching a course called Computers for Farmers at the lab. Its sessions were on an erratic schedule—waiting for bad weather days.

"Of course Everett only stays with me when Vanessa's not in town," Mrs. R had explained to Anne while helping her cook breakfast last weekend. "Don't want to set a bad example for the girl."

"Hah," Everett had said. "She and Josh'll both thank us if we spend all our time here on the farm when she's in town so they can have your house, since he's got three nosy kids at home."

"Everett Hooper," scolded Mrs. R, wagging a spatula. But then she'd smiled and hugged him.

There'd been hints that she might not be Mrs. R much longer.

Anne and Quince were talking about a December wedding. With a good cushion after harvest but with enough time before Christmas that they could go on a real honeymoon.

Quince passed by where she was sitting on the corner of the bed, holding her fingers wide to let the polish dry. He kissed her on the top of the head.

Then he bent and kissed her mouth, demanding all her discipline to keep from grabbing on to him, which would have required another round of nail polish ... not to mention a fresh shirt for him.

"About ready?" he asked as he put on his tie. He looked almost as good in his clothes as he did out of them.

"Not quite. This nail polish needs to dry a bit more."

"Always liked that red nail polish on you. Noticed it at the New

Years Eve party at the computer lab."

She giggled. A genuine, mischievous giggle.

"What?" he asked.

"You know why farm women wear red nail polish?"

"No."

"Because you scrub and scrub and still it can look like you have dirt under your nails. So this is insurance. Covers all sins."

He smiled slow and hot. "Don't want to cover *all* your sins ... at least not when we get back here tonight."

She laughed. He looked at her, and that look brought tears to her eyes even as she continued to laugh.

He held out his hand to her. "I want to listen to that sound forever."

Thank you for reading Anne and Quince's story. I hope you enjoyed all the new beginnings for the good people of Drago, Illinois, in this series!

If you like small-town romance, also try my Marry Me series. Second chances at love abound in Tobias, Wisconsin … nudged along by an eccentric matchmaker.

To explore more romance set in Illinois, get the seven-book (with two prequels) The Wedding Series. A group of college friends embark on the greatest education of all—falling in love. The series starts in Chicago, but ranges to Wyoming and then overseas to a mountainous European kingdom.

Marry Me Series
The Wedding Series

Darcie, Jennifer, Zeke, Josh, Quince and friends ask if you'll help spread the word about them and the Seasons in the Small Town series. You have the power to do that in two quick ways:

Recommend the book and the series to your friends and/or the whole wide world on social media. Shouting from rooftops is particularly appreciated.

Review the book. Take a few minutes to write an honest review and it can make a huge difference. As you likely know, it's the single best way for your fellow readers to find books they'll enjoy, too.

To me—as an author and a reader—the goal is always to find a good author-reader match. By sharing your reading experience through recommendations and reviews, you become a vital matchmaker. ☺

For news about upcoming books, as well as other titles and news, join Patricia McLinn's Readers List and receive her twice-monthly free newsletter.
www.patriciamclinn.com/readers-list

The Seasons in a Small Town Series

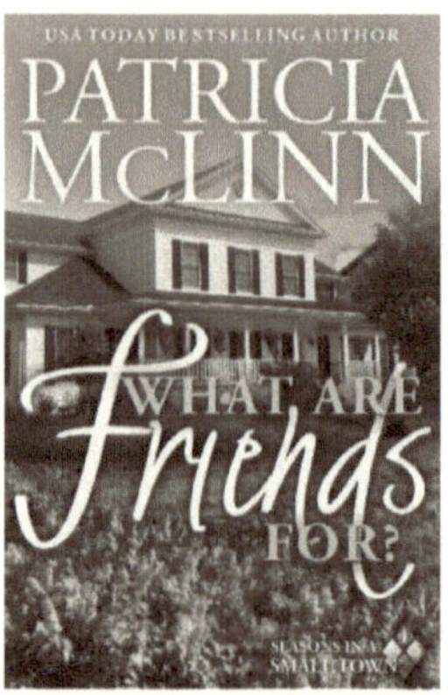

What Are Friends For? (Spring)

Billionaire tech guru Zeke the Geek reluctantly returns to his Illinois hometown as a favor to beauty queen Jennifer and Darcie—the only girl who "got" him.

The Right Brother (Summer)

Pretty, popular Jennifer had it made—until her ex-husband left her deep in debt with a child to raise. Enter Trent, who just might right his brother's wrongs.

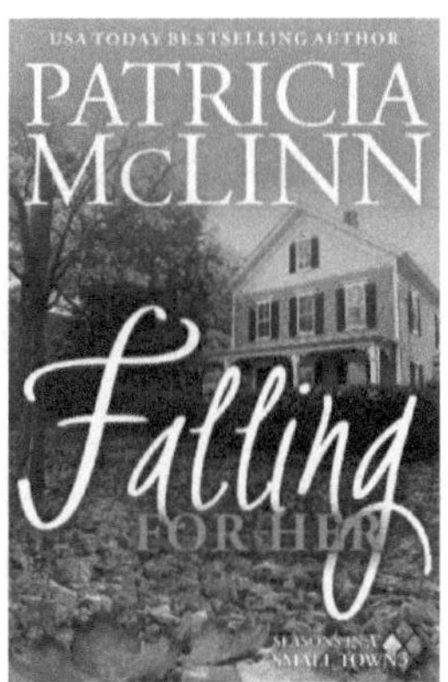

Falling for Her (Autumn)

Vanessa is comfortable with numbers, not with people, especially that high school principal. Josh Kincannon not only looks at her, but *sees* her, when that's the last thing she wants.

What people are saying about the
SEASONS IN A SMALL TOWN series

"You laugh, you angst, you maybe shed a couple tears or two, and at the end of it you move immediately onto the next book because—unlike teenage Zeke—you don't want to get away, all you want to do is go back."

"The town of Drago has insinuated itself into my heart and I can only hope there is another installment with this small town as its setting."

"Strong characters with enough faults to make them human and real" yet "The other characters in Drago all add to the story rather than taking attention from the main action."

"McLinn delivers a fun, engaging, and emotionally complicated romance."

"Poignant, heart-warming" ... "Funny and heart-wrenching at the same time"... Passionate and sensual without being distasteful or vulgar."

The Right Brother "is excellent in looking at [being female in a world run by men] from both a young teen's actions and her single-parent mom trying to help her daughter not make the same mistakes she had. The romance between the two main characters gradually builds in spite of family problems, outside pressures, and financial decisions. This was a thought-provoking book as well as a good story."

Also by Patricia McLinn

Marry Me Series

Wedding of the Century

The Unexpected Wedding Guest

A Most Unlikely Wedding

Baby Blues and Wedding Bells

The Wedding Series

Prelude to a Wedding

Wedding Party

Grady's Wedding

The Runaway Bride

The Christmas Princess

Hoops (prequel to The Surprise Princess)

The Surprise Princess

Not a Family Man (prequel to The Forgotten Prince)

The Forgotten Prince

Wyoming Wildflowers Series

Bardville, Wyoming Series

A Place Called Home series

Explore a complete list of all Patricia's books
patriciamclinn.com/patricias-books

Or get a printable booklist
patriciamclinn.com/patricias-books/printable-booklist

Patricia's eBookstore (buy digital books online directly from Patricia)
patriciamclinn.com/patricias-books/ebookstore

About the Author

USA Today bestselling author Patricia McLinn spent more than 20 years as an editor at the Washington Post after stints as a sports writer (Rockford, Ill.) and assistant sports editor (Charlotte, N.C.). She received BA and MSJ degrees from Northwestern University.

McLinn is the author of more than 50 published novels, which are cited by readers and reviewers for wit and vivid characterization. Her books include mysteries, romantic suspense, contemporary romance, historical romance and women's fiction. They have topped bestseller lists and won numerous awards.

She has spoken about writing from Melbourne, Australia, to Washington, D.C., including being a guest speaker at the Smithsonian Institution.

Now living in northern Kentucky, McLinn loves to hear from readers through her website, Facebook and Twitter.

Visit with Patricia:

Website: patriciamclinn.com

Facebook: facebook.com/PatriciaMcLinn

Twitter: @PatriciaMcLinn

Pinterest: pinterest.com/patriciamclinn

Instagram: instagram.com/patriciamclinnauthor

ISBN: 978-1-944126-51-3